The Writing Mind

Creative Writing Responses to Images of the Living Brain

edited by
Julia Prendergast
Eileen Herbert-Goodall
& Jen Webb

RECENT
WORK
PRESS

The Writing Mind: Creative Writing Responses to Images of the Living Brain
Recent Work Press
Canberra, Australia

Copyright © the authors, 2023

ISBN: 9780645651393 (paperback)

A catalogue record for this book is available from the National Library of Australia

Cover image: 'Image 60' © Paris Lyon/ Annalaise Takla
Cover design: Recent Work Press
Set by Recent Work Press

recentworkpress.com

Produced with the support of the Australasian Association of Writing Programs (AAWP) and the Science Art Network (ScAN)

Contents

Introduction   1

Julia Prendergast (on behalf of the editorial team)

Image 1: Movie   5

Still Living in My Head *Katharine Coles*
Smile *Paul Hetherington*

Image 2   9

The Canals of Venice *Sudesh Mishra*
Planetary Nebula *Cassandra Atherton*

Image 3   12

Untitled *Shane Strange*
Fireworks *Katrina Finlayson*

Image 4: Movie   16

Untitled *Julienne van Loon*
turning *Quinn Eades*

Image 5: Movie   20

This is a Photograph of You (for JP) *Jen Webb*
When I was Joan of Arc *Katharine Coles*

Image 6   23

Orange *Julia Prendergast*
For a Long Time Now I've Been Burning *Sam Meekings*

Image 7: Movie   26

Disney to Acquire The Bible Ltd *Luke Johnson*
Pike *Shane Strange*

Image 8: Movie   30

The Flights of Bats *Paul Hetherington*
Jangle *Cassandra Atherton*

Image 9: Movie   33

Avocado *Cassandra Atherton*
Turning *Willo Drummond*

Image 10   36

The Greening of Neuro-Humanities *Gay Lynch*
Chernobyl 35 Years on *Jeri Kroll*

Image 11: Movie   40

  Who is This Strange Being? *Nigel Krauth*
  Passerelle *Paul Hetherington*

Image 12: Movie   44

  Transmission *Nicola Redhouse*
  The Third Kind *Tom Evershed*

Image 13: Movie   49

  Body, Not-Body: A Brain Scan Response in
  Three Case Studies *Shady Cosgrove*
  Breathless *Catherine McKinnon*

Image 14: Movie   54

  Body Mapping Inside the Arachnoid Disco *Willo Drummond*
  Dreaming in Colour *Deedle Rodriguez-Tomlinson*

Image 15   59

  Brain Clock Face Scan *Katrina Finlayson*
  Rhodes *Julia Prendergast*

Image 16   63

  What's in a Name? *Eileen Herbert-Goodall*
  Topography *Jessie Seymour*

Image 17   67

  Purpling *Daniel Juckes*
  Matryoshka: In Utero *Sue Joseph*

Image 18: Movie   71

  Freefalling *Julia Prendergast*
  Champagne Supernova *Dominique Hecq*

Image 19: Movie   74

  Brainwork *Joshua Lobb*
  The Rabbit *Christine Howe*

Image 20   78

  Neurowomb *Kay Are*
  Still Life *Stephanie Green*

Image 21   81

  Untitled *Patrick Allington*
  Twelve or More Brain Facts in John Cage's
  Thirteen Harmonies *Tim Tomlinson*

Image 22   85

Imaging the Future *Jeri Kroll*
Kim *Donna Lee Brien*

Image 23   89

Sense/Making *Amelia Walker*
Untitled *Jen Webb*

Image 24   93

Sucked Into my Floral Veins Like Fresh Data *Antonia Pont*
Somewhat of a Loss, After 'The Broken Fountain'
Autumn Royal

Image 25: Movie   97

Red Tree *Nathan Langston*
Red Brain: Red Games *Gay Lynch*

Image 26   100

Boundary Lines *Rebekah Clarkson*
Not Easy to Die *Julia Prendergast*

Image 27   103

Untitled *Graeme Harper*
Brain *Frank T. Simes*

Image 28   106

Where the Tree Begins *Rose Lucas*
Twinklewinkalling/Aseptic Perception *Dominique Hecq*

Image 29   110

The Weight of Thought *Ravi Shankar*
The Fire Inside Your Head *Michael Salcman*

Image 30   114

Blue *Deedle Rodriguez-Tomlinson*
For the (Fossil) Record *Deb Wain*

Image 31   117

Opus 23 *Tim Tomlinson*
Pagudpud *Deedle Rodriguez-Tomlinson*

Image 32   121

Sea-Song *Julia Prendergast*
Castle *Paul Hetherington*

Image 33   124

    Punishment *Shady Cosgrove*
    Taken/Not Taken *Alan McMonagle*

Image 34   127

    Untitled *Barrie Sherwood*
    Carol Burnett *Nicola Redhouse*

Image 35   131

    Aqua Profonda (after Milton) *Dominique Hecq*
    Ghost Ship *Katrina Finlayson*

Image 36   136

    tunnelling *Quinn Eades*
    Overthinking *Dominic Symes*

Image 37   139

    Slow Burn *Deb Wain*
    BBQ *Julia Prendergast*

Image 38   143

    Time *Julia Prendergast*
    Quantify *Nicola Redhouse*

Image 39   147

    Firesky *Julia Prendergast*
    I Don't Know What I'm Looking at *Patrick Allington*

Image 40   152

    Conclusion of Phase 4 Study Meeting all Primary Efficacy
    Endpoints Demonstrating that Purple Vaccine BLT1984 is
    95% Effective Against 'Belief that the Universe is Made of
    Stories' (BUMOS)
    Roanna Gonsalves

    …, screaming *Daniel Juckes*

Image 41   156

    The Stranger *Maria Takolander*
    From Mars the Earth Looks Red *Ravi Shankar*

Image 42   161

    Synaesthetic Submersion *Sue Joseph*
    Head Study *Dominique Hecq*

Image 43   166

    Untitled *Debra Adelaide*
    Mourning *Deb Wain*

Image 44   169

The Green Light *Sam Meekings*
Nature Abhors a Vacuum *Roanna Gonsalves*

Image 45   172

Blue Smoke Inside My Head *Michael Salcman*
Blue Hour *Paul Hetherington*

Image 46   175

Alas, Poor Yorick *Christine Howe*
Logos *Spiri Tsintziras*

Image 47   180

Full On Mind *Elisabeth Wentworth*
Chronics *Amelia Walker*

Image 48   184

Untitled *Jessie Seymour*
B-Sides; Memories *Daniel Juckes*

Image 49   188

Meta-Musical Field *Frank T. Simes*
Untitled *Graeme Harper*

Image 50   192

Prince and Dr John *Dan O'Carroll*
Purple Haze *Barrie Sherwood*

Image 51   195

Pigments and Paints *Donna Lee Brien*
Red Brain Fog *Gay Lynch*

Image 52   200

Blacking Out *Lynda Hawryluk*
The Seasons of Ambivalence *Jacqueline Ross*

Image 53   203

Covid Dreaming *Shady Cosgrove*
The Forest *Sarah Giles*

Image 54   206

Pomegranate *Paul Hetherington*
Intergenerational Trauma in Five Parts *Helen Thomas*

Image 55   210

Endings *Catherine McKinnon*
Brain Coral *Shady Cosgrove*

Image 56   213

Every Gesture Like Thought *Stephanie Green*
Bloodheat *Rose Lucas*

Image 57   216

Raising a Subject *Autumn Royal*
Gotcha *Nicolas Brasch*

Image 58   219

Mind's Eye *Julian Novitz*
The Entombment *Dominique Hecq*

Image 59   222

Clueless *Dominic Symes*
Mandragora/The Hand of Glory *Tom Evershed*

Image 60   226

Crossed Wires *Julia Prendergast*
My Two Sons, for Winifred *Rebekah Clarkson*

Image 61:   230

Coda *Tom Evershed*
The Wind in My Open Mouth *Julia Prendergast*

Author Biographies   234

Introduction

Julia Prendergast (on behalf of the editorial team)

This book began, in 2019, as a passion project. It arose as the result of a broader research initiative, a partnership with Swinburne Neuroimaging (SNI). Through this research, I was exposed to what I've come to call the secret underground world of neuroimaging. In the basement facility, at Swinburne University in Melbourne, there are various colour images of the living brain, some of which appear in this book. The images are Magnetic Resonance Imaging (MRI) pictures of Paris Lyons' brain, collected by radiographer Annalaise Takla. The images were creatively enhanced by Paris, updated to colour images, moving and still representations of the living brain. Upon encountering these pictures, I was captivated by their beauty and overcome by a desire to write in response to them. As I wrote, and considered my ekphrastic immersion, I felt compelled to invite others to join me. The result is 122 creative writing responses to 61 images of the living brain.

This project was conceived through a partnership between Science Art Network (ScAN), affiliated with the neuroimaging department at Swinburne University, and the Australasian Association of Writing Programs (AAWP), the peak academic body representing the discipline of Creative Writing in Australasia. I was asked to work alongside Paris to co-lead the art aspect of ScAN. Our first initiative was to establish a partnership between ScAN and AAWP, and to commission the contributions that appear in this book, produced by members and friends of the AAWP. We invited 61 authors to respond in Stage One and 61 authors to respond in Stage Two. Authors in the second stage responded to the images without access to the responses generated in Stage One.

The broader context for the ScAN|AAWP partnership is a Creative Writing | Neuroimaging Research Study. I am leading this project in partnership with colleagues in the neuroimaging department at Swinburne University. The study investigates the activity in participants' brains while undertaking a creative writing workshop. Participants write imaginatively from short-term and long-term memory, undertaking tasks focusing on processes of deep, sensory imagining. We use Magnetoencephalography (MEG), neuroimaging technology, to determine where and how the brain is processing information, at distinct stages of the workshop. Following the workshop, participants undergo a structural MRI scan, assisting researchers in identifying the brain regions activated during the workshop.

This book, *The Writing Mind: Creative Writing Responses to Images of the Living Brain,* is a sister project to the research study. It illustrates my abiding obsession with something Gordon Weaver refers to as felt presences. Weaver asks, 'In how small a space can [we] create the *felt presences* that animate successful stories?' (1983, p. 228, my emphasis). My personal response to these images was a reaction to Paris' art-making, to the felt presences within each image. As I invited other authors to take part, I bore witness to connected acts of making—to felt presences as a facilitative pathway, to the way art generates art in iterative acts of making.

One contributor, a poet pal, whose work appears many times in this collection, responded to the issue of felt presences. When sending one of their contributions, they wrote: *I don't know what these images do but they DO SOMETHING* (personal email correspondence). Upon reviewing proofs of the collection, another dear writing pal, a life writer with a propensity towards the braided essay, wrote via email:

I love-love-love how the other pieces of writing on the same images so perfectly pair with my work. Perhaps that's the nature of two writers working from one image but, geez, what a great effect. This is only now revealed to me by the grouping under images in the book [...] I didn't realise this symmetry on the website. It's beautiful and so brain-like.

This email led to further correspondence or, more aptly, to an exchange of love letters in homage to the uncanny. My impetus for inviting authors to gather as a Community of Practitioners is underpinned by my obsession with collaborative acts of making—a collective means of responding to felt presences within, and between, works of art. This encounter is consistent with Freud's definition of the uncanny—the mystifying process Freud outlines where 'the word *heimlich* [...] develops in the direction of ambivalence until it finally coincides with its opposite, *unheimlich*' (Freud, 1919, p. 421). Through this definition, Freud recognises the spirit of Aristotle's concept of metaphor as an appreciation of the 'similarity [to homoion theorein] in dissimilars' (Ricoeur, 1978, p. 23). We see the similiarity-in-dissimilars across the collection, not only in the ghostly playoff between Stage One and Stage Two contributions but in the repetitions and inversions—felt presences in translation—throughout the collection.

Across the creative writing responses in this book, I read a metaphorical constellation of 'feeling-thinking'—sensing the concepts that underpin individual contributions, and the intersections between them, weaving connections. In so doing, I'm prompted to think about the relationship between sensory data and ideas, as well as the manner in which ways-of-saying and ways-of-feeling (and thinking) rub up against each other. This 'stitching together' relates to my abiding interest in Danko Nikolić's theory of ideasthesia. The concept arises from the 'Ancient Greek words *idea* (for concept) and *aesthesis* (for sensation). Hence, the term ideasthesia [or] *sensing concepts*' (Nikolić, 2016, p. 2, emphasis in original). I formulated the concept of ideasthetic imagining, to describe the way that writers sense concepts, translating ideas into concrete and specific narrative detail. What a joy it is to see processes of ideasthetic imagining in play, in the cross-weave of this collection.

Our reflection upon practice is fundamentally driven by questions about modes of poiesis. I wonder about the relationship between the ideas that underlie works of art and the medium used to convey those ideas. What are the dynamics of the conversion process? These ruminations underpin my entangled engagement with the contributions in this book—my fascination with our combined quest to utilise embodied (sensory-like) experiences to engage with a work of art, and to respond as makers, despite the wild circumstances—i.e., without any context markers other than the creatively-enhanced brain itself. *Glorious* …

I would like to thank many people for their labour in bringing this project to fruition, initially as a showcase via the ScAN website and now as a published book. First and foremost, thank you, Paris, for your deft creative vision in producing these images. Thank you for your willingness to run with my idea in commissioning responses in prose and poetry, for your skills in project management and, finally but *not least*, for ruminative and provocative discussion about the intersections between art and science. I am deeply grateful to have worked with you on this project and in an ongoing capacity, as we continue to work on the broader research study.

Thank you to those who have contributed to data collection and project management for the Creative Writing | Neuroimaging Research Study. While this is a separate venture, without it this book would not exist. Thank you to Paris Lyons and Dr Benjamin Slade for continued discussion about art and science as it relates to traditional research endeavours but also, or perhaps more so, as a way of being-in-the-world. Thank you to Professor Tom Johnstone and Dr Will Woods, Annalaise Takla and Nathan Kristian, as well as Dr Rachel Batty, for contributing to the broader research project in various capacities. Thank you, Paris, as well as Fanny Suhendra, for your labour in showcasing these works via the ScAN website. For the significant task of collating contributions and images for a text-based publication, thank you, Benjamin. For generous financial support, thank you to Professor Tom Johnstone | SNI, as well as the AAWP. I deeply appreciate the combined commitment of SNI and AAWP, enthusiastic supporters of transdisciplinary, open and collaborative research practices—organisations who take an avid interest in the intersections between diverse disciplines, in this case, Arts/Science and Arts/Health—considering the ways we can work together not only for the future for our fields but for a better world.

Thank you to Shane Strange, publisher at Recent Work Press, for publishing this collection and, more broadly, for your wild generosity and steadfast support of the AAWP community. Who knew, Shane, when you agreed to discussion over a glass of wine at the poetry event in Adelaide, many moons ago, that I would pester you so incessantly? I certainly had no idea that you would respond (then, and *at every turn*) with unwavering generosity and calm hilarity, providing publication pathways and thereby facilitating opportunities for us to gather as a community of practitioners.

Thanks, and deep reverence, to each contributing author. I hope you find as much joy in this collection as we experienced in engaging with your responses. In this book we have prose and poetry that is connected by ideasthetically imagined shadows—it's too much in the way that intersections in feeling-thinking *are* too much—the way we meet in untamed spaces, as felt presences bridge otherwise unlocatable space and time.

Finally, my inordinate gratitude to Dr Eileen Herbert-Goodall and Professor Jen Webb—for agreeing to come on board as co-editors, for your meticulous attention to detail and your unfaltering commitment to the integrity of this book. Above and beyond, thank you for the editorial sisterhood, sharing all manner of everyday stories as we progressed—*precious* and *utterly delightful.*

References

Freud, S. The uncanny. (2016). J. Rivkin & M. Ryan (Eds.), *Literary theory: An anthology* (2nd ed., pp.418–430). Blackwell Publishing. (Original work published in 1919).

Nikolić, D. 2016. Ideasthesia and Art. In K. Gsöllpointner, R. Schnell & R. K.Schuler (Eds.), *Digital synesthesia: A model for the aesthetics of digital art* (pp.41–52). De Gruyter.

Ricoeur, P. 1978. *The rule of metaphor: Multi-Disciplinary studies of the creation of meaning in language* (R. Czerny, Trans.). University of Toronto Press.

van Loon, J. (2020, November 16–18). *Creative writing as nourishment: The political philosophy of Corine Pelluchon applied to our field* [Keynote address].25th Australasian Association of Writing Programs Conference, Griffith University, Queensland, Australia.

Weaver G. 1983. Gordon Weaver. In R. Shapard & J. Thomas (Eds.), *Sudden fiction: American short-short stories* (pp. 228–229). Gibbs Smith.

Image 1: Movie

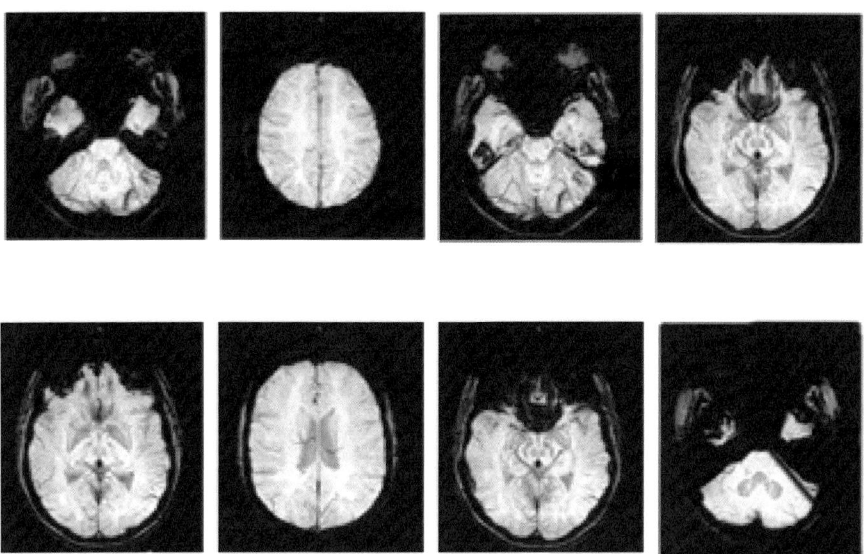

Still Living in My Head

Katharine Coles

1. I grow used to the way I come to
Myself then go in time, as one fire

Detonates another, ignition
And spark, idea's charge

Lighting a path and laying
Its own land. Feel an eye

      2. Scanning; will I ever know
      How to read what may go

      Missing or wrong or what
      Structure makes the abstract

      Work when thought becomes
      Mist or a kind of breathing? If

3. The world arrives as it does, un-
Curatable, piecemeal and incurable

Flash at a time, to me
It repairs into whole body

Where I forget to see myself
Thinking. So my rooms fill

4. Windows with delight and air
And hold dark corners

Tight, and this other
Thing, alien and full

Of shadows, could also
Make pleasure a kind of space.

Smile

Paul Hetherington

The mind looks back with smiling efflorescences. But it's serious work in there, the darkness being lit every moment of day and night and coins of thought constantly minted and multiplied. If you travelled there, you'd be dumbfounded by the terrain and byways—like Marco Polo—and by spilling lakes and waterways; dusty mountainside highways; the variousness of customs and laws. You'd arrive at what you believed was the emperor's citadel only to find it was the keep of a minor noble; you'd search further into wastes and distances but come to an impasse. New roads would stand in the place of old roads—where once you could cool your feet in a stream, now you'd be channelled toward a forest's bird calls. You'd turn back to the citadel but it would be gone. A sudden slant of sunshine would cross the landscape like a smile.

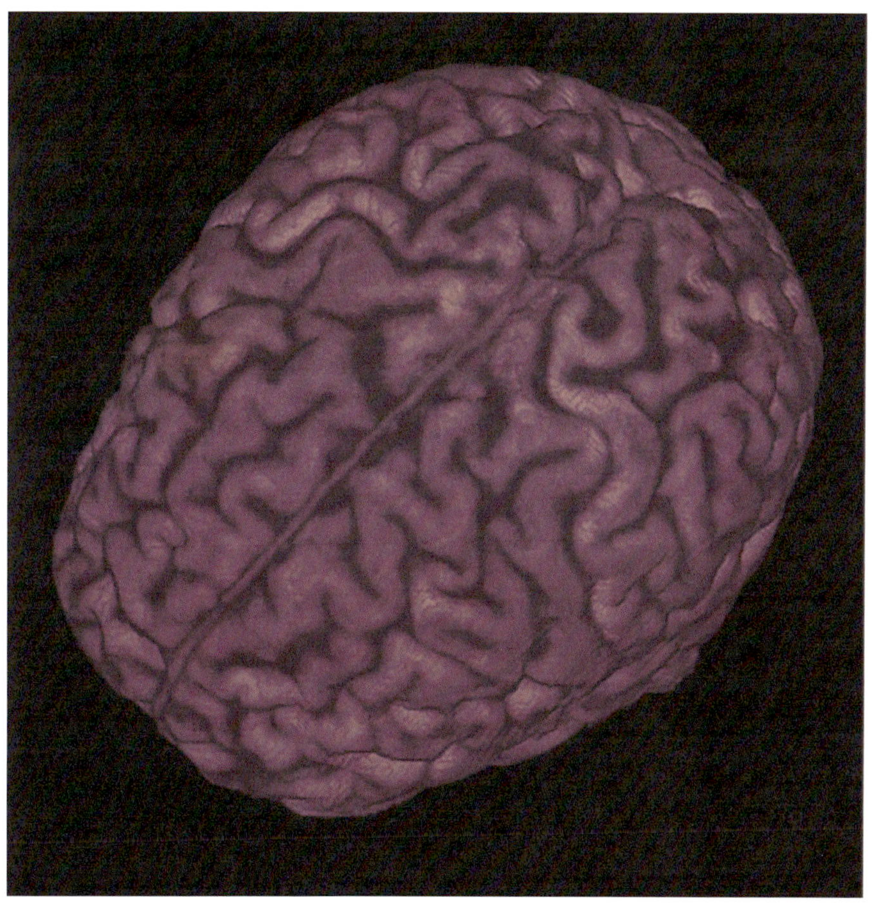

The Canals of Venice

Sudesh Mishra

In my brain, I think, I see the canals of Venice. I picture a gondolier dipping an inky oar as he passes under a bridge into a garden of sighs. The vision is counterfeit and it fills me with disgust. I turn disgust into an object of contemplation and come up with a trope: a cranium crammed with corrupted flesh. Maggots browse through both hemispheres, exhaling wormholes. I pass dreamily through one into an astral frogspawn. I begin to grasp the aesthetics of honeycombs and catacombs. I remember the taste of memory and its testament to rust. When I was six, I got hold of a clump of purple yarn and unravelled it speedily. I wanted to see the end of it, its limit, but the more I reeled it out, the clumpier it grew in my grip. I never riddled it out for the life of me, but the child did. Spin, my dying brain, your deathless yarn.

Planetary Nebula

Cassandra Atherton

In an airbus's aisle seat I slowly get drunk on whisky, contemplating the last of things. I'm not haunted by ex-lovers, but I remember the first time you bent me backwards over the bed and enfolded my body in yours. In corner rooms of four-star hotels, we watched the moon cycle through all its phases as points of starlight combed my hair and brushed your chest. You say we can't always live in this state of flux—as if I can turn off the heat as quickly as a Joni Mitchell song vanishes in an airport lounge. But I understand endings. I might be 650 light years away, riding the back of the Helix Nebula, but you are standing in the ultraviolet of its dying glow.

Image 3

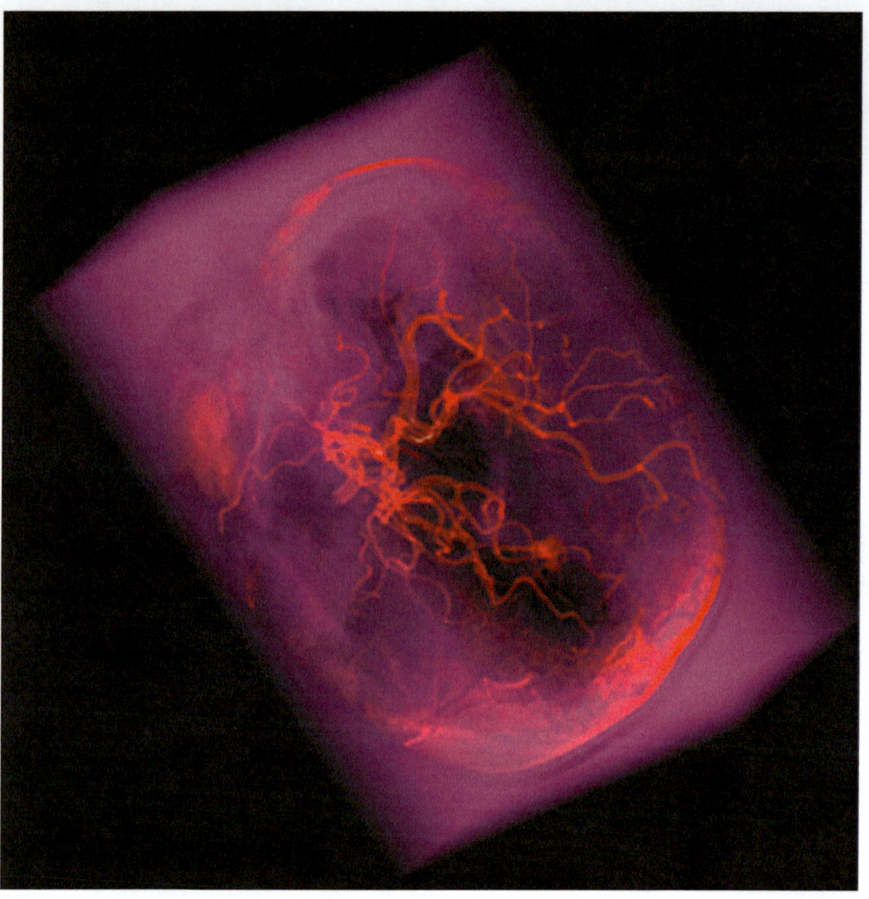

Untitled

Shane Strange

When Julia asks I think
'It's difficult to think right now.'
It's the drugs and all that.
I want to begin by talking about folds. About folds
within folds. But this
is lightning. In the pink. Sunset
sometimes. Flesh two layers in.
The colour of pregnancy tests
of watermelon, of guava. I see
an Aries-ram-head-left-horn-eye-socket.
I don't know what's good anymore.
It's the drugs and all that.
I see a shadow foetus. My head feels
like a drop of tar. Tessa says,
'When I stopped taking the drugs,
my brain came back.' I think
'Might this be purple?'
R=222 B=0 G=222, #db00db, C17 M100 Y70 K5
What does purple mean?
Or pink, or red. I don't know
what's good anymore. It's the veins
under a closed eyelid. Why do veins
look like lightning? Illumination,
like neon. A headache in the gaudy light.
Or are these roots? Why do roots
look like lightning?
Cerebral gyri and sulci—folds
within folds. It's difficult to think
right now. It's the drugs
and all that. Are we reduced
to phenomena, reaction and observation?

Gemma says, 'You'll get through this.'
Like lightning. Like the tresses of a spindly dress.
Like roots drawn through the ground.
A falling. A folding. We are
reduced. What is it
to understand? To fold one hand
against another? Am I asking too much
of myself? These are the facts:
beautiful and temporary and luminous.
I don't know what's good anymore.

Fireworks

Katrina Finlayson

Someone's letting off fireworks in the dry scrub at the end of our street. Kids, maybe. Sound carries further in the still, warm night air and the sharp popping cracks sound close, easy to locate, but really, they could be anywhere. It's thick scrub, hillside carved by steep bike trails, rust-coloured dirt now stained black by shadows, pale streaks where moonlight slides through stringy treetops.

The day's noise and drama have faded into a soft pile of sleeping child beside me on the couch. Body surrendered completely; one arm flung high, and one plump foot pressed against my bare leg. Maybe there are dreams beneath those heavy eyelids. This golden head is a room with no doors. I wonder whether that deep mind dreamed inside the roundness of my body, or if dreams began later. My body knows how much it has given to this child in three years, but I recently read somewhere that, from as early as two weeks, foetal cells can move across the placenta to the mother. The cells embed in organ tissue, finding new homes in the mother's body. They become like the cells around them and can even repair damage. Scientists have found a person's DNA in their mother's brain, decades later. Maybe this child's brain is part of my brain, fresh electric thoughts sparking colour in my dreams.

Many years ago, when we'd just moved in, I called the cops about the fireworks. Sounds dangerous, they agreed. I don't know if anything came of it. I never called again. Once, smoking a midnight joint on my back deck, I saw a helicopter with search lights circle low above the scrub, but there are always more kids and more fireworks. Tonight, I hear the echoes of danger through an open Saturday night lounge room window at the front of the house, as my laptop glow falls softly across the smooth, sleeping face. It's not even eleven and I'm reading the same sentence over and again as the words swim. I'll carry the small child to bed soon. Our family has changed in big ways since those back deck late nights: one life created and one life lost. The big old rundown house breathes emptiness around the shape of our two bodies. At dawn, the rooftop crows will comment on my nostalgia again, but tonight is all about dreams and fireworks.

Image 4: Movie

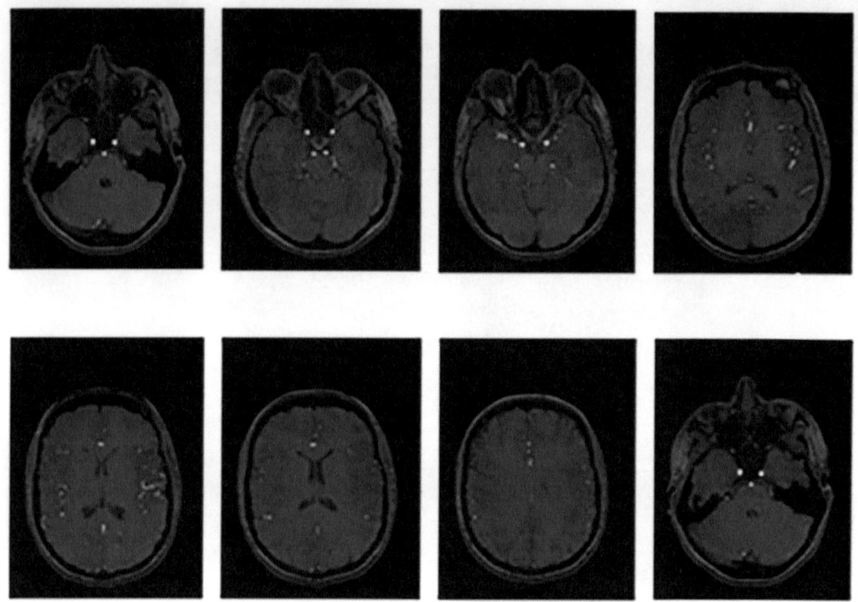

Untitled

Julienne van Loon

I am aware of a watery filmic image, as if observing a dream in those moments before waking.

I am looking at the ocean, distracted by the white froth at the top of each wave, the way it is propelled forwards and back, sometimes dispersed right up to the high-water mark along the beach, and sometimes recaptured, before being sent around again, again, again, in those beautiful but insistent cycles. Dispersed. Reclaimed. Dispersed again. Those white flecks, how they carry things, how they pattern our days.

Time passes, my attention shifts, and I become witness to a darker energy, emerging from beneath, as if from the stomach or the heart. It balloons up, taking up all of the oxygen. While this darker, deeper shape is present, it's hard to focus on anything else. Acknowledging it makes me swallow.

But this is it: this is me. This is where I locate myself now, deep in the undercurrent, the kind that used to bowl me over as a child of five, when I tried to stand sentinel on twiggy legs, up to my chest at the edge of the mighty Pacific. How it frightened me then, with its forceful energy, so much larger than me, as if I was nothing, as if was merely flotsam.

But here I dwell now, away from the spectacular flurry of the surface, away from the distracted, fleeting attention of the casual observer. See how I come to life, take shape, transform, as if from chrysalis to butterfly? This is me.

You know I am here fully for a time. You witness it, too. And besides, it is also how things have reached fullness, then I begin to recede. The cycle calls me back. There will be new flotsam, new froth, reappearing at the top, patterning new days and nights for others. Meanwhile, I have come into fullness. Perhaps I was only fully present for one breath.

We know each other, don't we? You have your own pattern. I have mine. There are differences, of course, but we are so similar, aren't we? Perhaps that is why I love you. But of course, you know all of this already. You are ahead of me, as ever. And, I am telling you nothing new.

I am beneath, and receding, aware only distantly now of a watery, filmic image, as if observing a dream.

turning

Quinn Eades

I've been listening to the same song for weeks I've done this all my life played and played a song until it is all of it in me until it is all the way in.

In the car on the way to school A says not the sad man again and I laugh we change the music she looks out the window brown eyes open open sings under her breath sings into a warm wind.

There are too many points of light I can't do anything quickly anymore a breath is infinite is a shallow a shudder I am tired it is more than tired I can't keep my eyes open I hear seconds counting out measuring what's left smoke another cigarette weigh up immediate relief against a truncated life make a bargain with no one let me have this let me have these small intermissions where everything is about breath and heat and what I can hold inside my body and for how long wait a bargain means I offer something in return so it is not a bargain it is a plea a please a let me be witness be writing let me stand on this caldera's lip larval sulphuric let lungs survive long enough to shout.

These hands of yours do so much more than hold we show off our forearms and fists flash them at each other in passing in the hallway in the wet dusk everything I thought was an entry is a tunnel we tunnel in to the other we go dark and liquid all our bodies a deep red pulse a tunnel pulling in a backwards well he teaches me to laugh in the ends of a world.

They told me weeks ago the curfew the five-kilometre line the no visitors to my home was gone but I am still here writing sleeping worrying I do everything from a couch.

I have been like this for years I have a body that won't let me up some times I have been vomiting bile for 11 months the only things my stomach lets me eat are weetbix and watermelon and ice.

I don't go outside the sun hurts I am too tired to dodge and duck I am still at home bare footed soft fisted around I circle around around make a tunnel move quietly quietly in.

Image 5: Movie

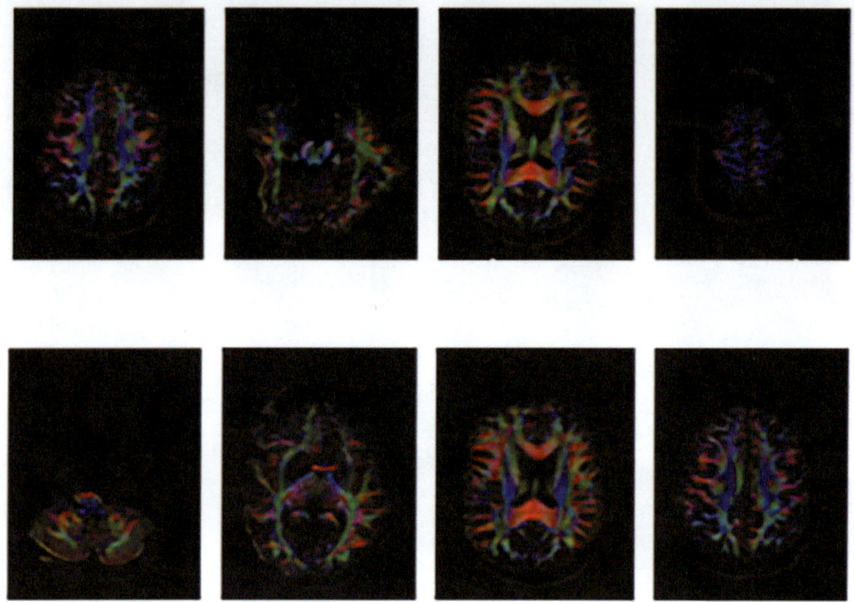

This is a Photograph of You (for JP)

Jen Webb

Your face at the north-facing window and behind the window
Borealis shines, billowing multicoloured scarves, its invitation to
the dance.

You dance pas de deux, him going in for glissade, you a jeté,
both of you stumble on landing but no matter, it's just a tap on
the edges of consciousness, just a ripple in the pool, and you
dance on step pivot step till your feet kick up rainbows in the
startled air.

I observe, from my watch house; I will not ask you to step out
of the vehicle; I will not ask you to surrender your licence; I will
dance with you, back and forth in a tireless loop. Determined
that we will find the gold at rainbow's end.

When I was Joan of Arc

Katharine Coles

young, needing a bath, running hot and cold.
When I spoke my truth to power and raised
Armies with a flick of my wrist. When elect
-ricity moved my body forward. However does
Fervour appear? In error, in a flash. When
Painters wanted to paint me and poets
Sang my praises, when I imagined
Nations bent to my will or to God's

Whatever it was, when I was all my own
Sex and needed nobody else's
Touch to illuminate my body in
-side out. I mean, where did that time
Go? If I survived it. Almost in my head
If I didn't consume myself with flame.

Image 6

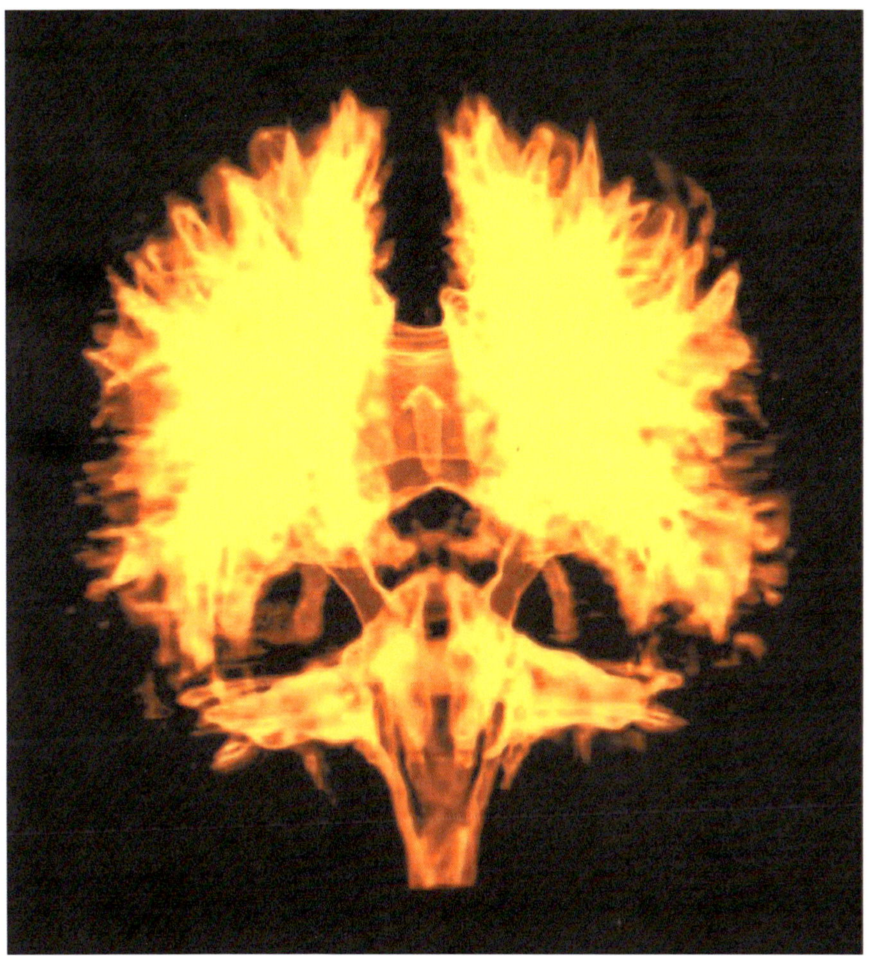

Orange

Julia Prendergast

Look at that beautiful orange dress, I say, standing still on the
footpath and turning to my adult daughter. I shift closer to
examine the webbed lace, like an orange daisy chain, running in
all directions.
You could pull that off, she says.
I have wondered, on many occasions since, precisely what
it means to pull-something-off. Is it a pass or something else
altogether?
Orange memories—bonfire flames in the wayward wind—
relentless returns, endurable deficits, irreconcilable extremes …
Tell me it's true for you, too—the flaming rift
today's riddle, yesterday's embers.
I know you feel it, too.
Tell me again what we might do to each other—it will ignite a
memory, thirty years new—the boy with the marbly biceps who
scoured me orange.

For a Long Time Now I've Been Burning

Sam Meekings

For a long time now I have been burning.
Flecks and ashes spray from my suit
as I walk to work. I hardly notice it now.
Maybe it started with my shoes
smouldering, a small flicker, embers nestled
between my toes. I brushed it off. Petty
slights, parties I wasn't invited to, a passed
over promotion. Later
snaking up my ankles, flames leaping
from the pleats of my trousers.
A loved one disappearing. It seethes
and pops, leaves my skin like crackling.
The news each day a different spark.
Sometimes someone notices and
reaches for a glass of water,
a hydrant, an extinguisher, but I tell them
No, don't worry. Not even a river or sea.
I am burning, always burning.
And besides, I hardly notice it now.

Image 7: Movie

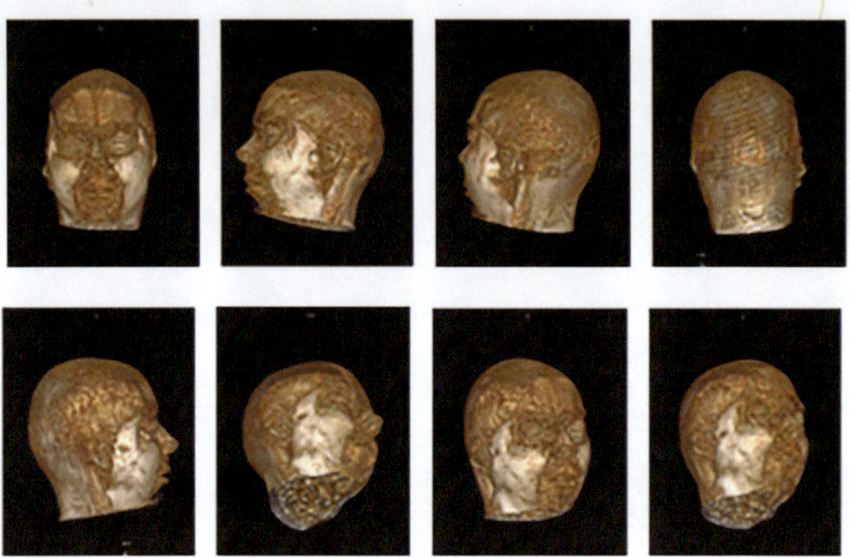

Disney to Acquire The Bible Ltd

Luke Johnson

Continuing its successful strategy of
delivering exceptional spiritual content to
audiences around the planet the
Walter Elias Disney Company has
recently agreed to purchase the Bible in
a simple stock and cash transaction which
promises to combine a world-class portfolio of
character-enriching content such
as the immensely popular New Testament series with
Disney's unique and unparalleled ability to
'shift a shitload of product on a global scale' said
a spokesperson for the company's marketing division who
also labelled the deal a 'truly historic moment the
biggest day in the history of religion but
a bit of a disappointing outcome if
you're a diehard fan of the original series still
stuck on some quaint piece from the 00s where
it's puppets cutting the heads off other puppets for
a hundred and twenty-five minutes running and
in all that time no one even gets their insides melted with
a laser or green-screened onto a river of
really realistic lava but
we're somehow supposed to believe it all actually happened? well
just you wait until you see this new trailer that's
been released for the upcoming John the Baptist film in
which you ain't never seen special effects like this it's
like you're pretty much actually literally there' said
this spokesperson representing the marketing division of
the Walter Elias Disney Company which
operates out of an abandoned amusement park on
the other side of the Pacific Ocean or

'A long time ago in galaxy far, far away' as people will no doubt come to think of it some two thousand and twenty-one earth years from now.

Pike

Shane Strange

Pike-free Trojan
asteroid

Cauterised, animate
ghost

In the machine
transparent

Skull the skin
that holds

The hunting deaths
and failings

To recognise you are
elegant

with blazed curled words

Image 8: Movie

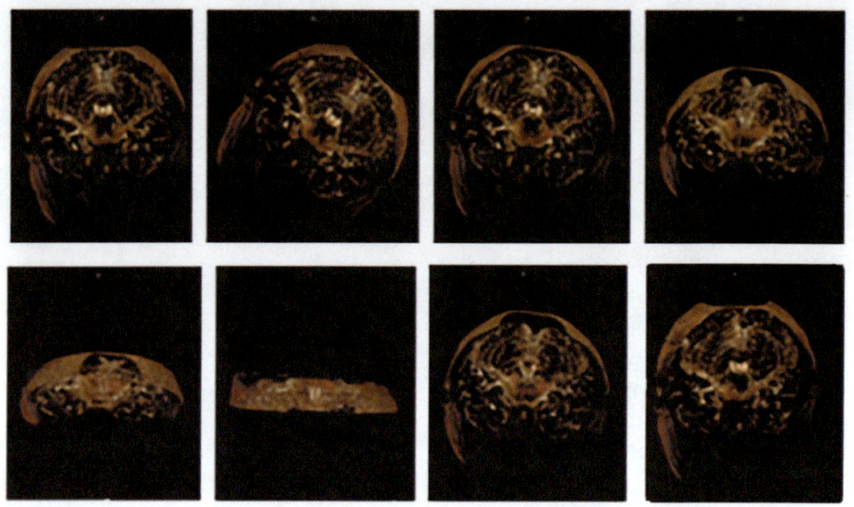

The Flights of Bats

Paul Hetherington

Thought swerves through images as a bat accelerates through air. You stand in memory, your dripping shirt brown from dirty river water; air and sunshine colliding; a smile lifting your mouth. I'd hold you as I did when you spoke of thought as knotted and tangled thread; when our love was umber, arms linking shadowed synapses with nerve and world. Our tensed bodies were skin-listening antenna and, as swarming feeling dragged us into air, night had the colour of dark words. 'I'm there,' you said, sensation expanding like the sudden flight of bats, sending ultrasound, tonguing and hearing, sensing gardens and movement, finding in echolocation the fetching shapes of night and body.

Jangle

Cassandra Atherton

Silvery timbre, the vibrations resonate along the curve of her ear and flutter down her neck. Lips pressed to the embouchure, he serenades the quiet. He watches her react to the long flow of air and standing wave patterns. But the tambourine remains silent in her hand. Staring beyond the moment, she is imagining her hollowed spine resting horizontally in his hands.

Image 9: Movie

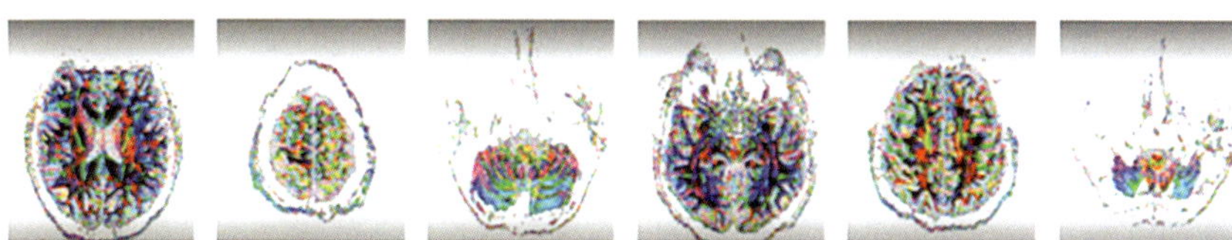

Avocado

Cassandra Atherton

I squeeze all the avocados in the supermarket. Some get a quick pinch at the top; others I pick up and, as they sit in my palm, I sink five fingers into their rounded bottoms. Most are hard but occasionally one is mushy and the dry skin stretches under my enthusiastic thumb. I prefer Haas with its knobbly purple-black skin but I'll take a glossy green Shephard if it's ripe. When I come to the end of the display, I start the process again, weighing one that's too hard against one that's too soft. When my husband asks if I've finished feeling up the avocados, I take the soft one to the self-checkout, placing it on top of my groceries, making sure nothing bruises its flesh. On the drive home, I imagine cutting its stone belly open, using the knife's blade to remove the shiny pit. I've decided to peel it before putting a coddled egg in its womb. I'll encourage the two halves back together, roll it in breadcrumbs and deep-fry it. The silky orange yolk will flood my plate when I cut it open—dark green, warm flesh covered in eggy bread. I unpack the car, wondering if I should add hot sauce or cracked pepper. As I take the shopping bag out of the car, the avocado is nestled on the punnet of raspberries and, as I open the front door, it rolls across the top of the bag, landing on the concrete step. It's completely flattened on one side. I pick it up and the skin bounces back, but there's a hollow underneath. I go inside to make scrambled eggs and smashed avocado on toast.

Turning

Willo Drummond

This persistent undoing. Pendulate
    folding, ceramic
      bowl of cerulean knowing. [Fragile. This Way Up.]
I see your face in there. Shadowy
    spectre threading all
    vision. Certainty
turns in a day. Cells transform
    between *nice to see you*
    and *later*. On Friday:
firebrick only (going forward). A fierce
    determination. By Tuesday:
    tourmaline, the only truth. I witness
an insistent spin
    into myself. Collapse the mould
    to begin. At the wheel
a [re-]turning, and all of us seeking
    our own hands in the dark, imperceptibly
    enacting   departure—

Image 10

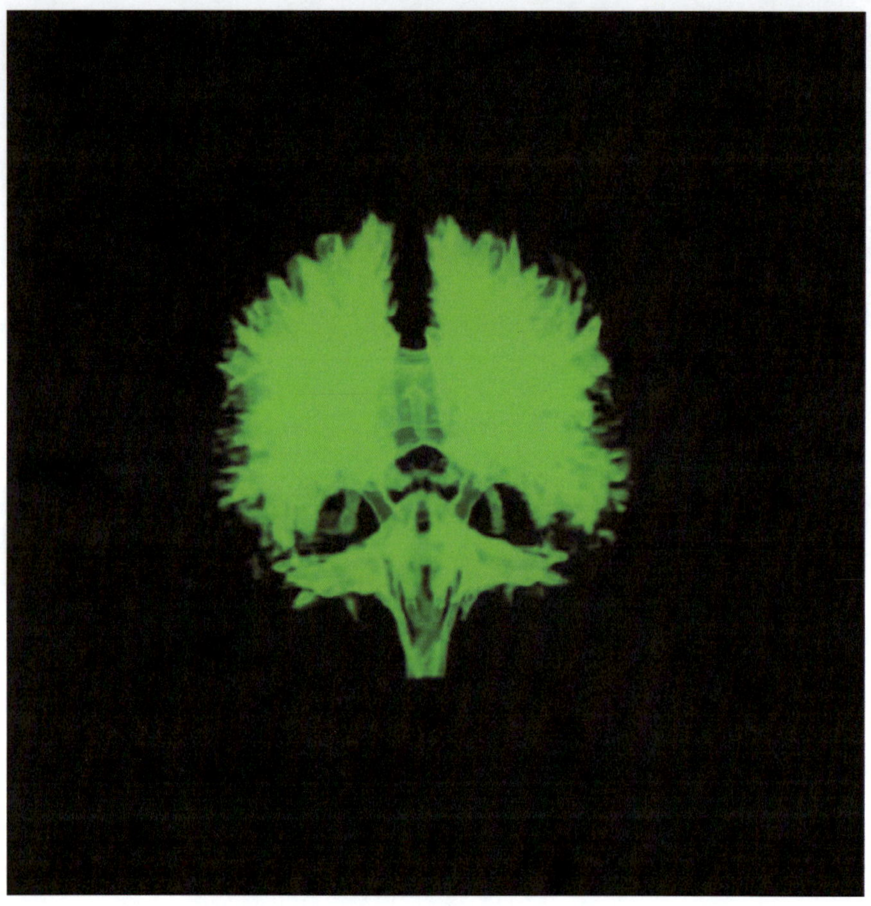

The Greening of Neuro-Humanities

Gay Lynch

Bright-coloured scans best signify neural activism, during which, oxygenated blood rushes right and left. The machine clicks and roars, when volunteers puzzle, pun, choose pics—prefer a house or face?—and optical allusions address right-sided stress. Loud green dye makes intensity lurid or abnormal—a glitch in symmetry's stitch—a surprise effect. Brain scans span like wings and lungs.

I visit Piccaninnie Ponds, where nitrogen-rich algae, effloresces in lacy, drifting green ellipses. Grows like ideas, in karst and coastal fen; resembles spineless brain pics, laid head-to-head. Affect or effect? I see algal mats shaped like lungs. Or water wings. Divers can die in ponds, tensions surfacing, worse than left-right brain fundamentalism. Indiscernible grief lurks in sinkholes, buries itself in 'Chasm'. Lofty ceilings in 'Cathedral' uphold human joy.

Corpus Callosa fatten in surges of traffic, ignited by cognition, logic. Keep compact when thousands of left brain synapses fire. In brains and algae, green needle strings form and filament, regenerative impulses overlap. Simple to compare air, water, blood, cyanobacterial blooms—the kind that sicken mammals— with creative surges. Too simple.

Aquanauts equalise hemispheres of pressure. I watch neo-brained pond divers, their extremities bleached with age, propel their rubber faux bodies, through the vivid Cottee's-Cordial-green algae. Smash, plash, on, in, under, water. Tension and transition. Pre-consciousness the loci. Corpus callisum spasms. Left rules right. Right, left. Feeling/thinking, temporal/transcendent. Ideas slide like liquid, like water, always all ways.

Limestone solutions clear debris, enabling divers to seek clarity in the deepest water, eyes-wide in atavistic terror. Better than panning body cameras, those feelers on their heads, wavering, willing, like heat-seeking penises. Same blokes, once swam in utero, glide below now, fired by ancient awe. Data and instinct fuse. Disperse anew. Calculations, cell sortings, classifications, intersperse with bubbles of absent-minded and ecstatic play.

Bungandtji girls dived here, practical, hungry. Wrung eel necks, in bunches of twitching fibres. Writhing bodies slung around their shoulders. Caught creatures evolved to think two ways and survive in fresh and salt titrations. Storied and sang those girls during skilful kills. Clever all at once, old way. Pickled, and steamed eels. Seared and charcoal-smoked, those white flesh delectations. *Koo-ngap-urn-ine* pond.

Green gives balance, Kandinsky said. Speculation that smaller corpus callosa found in creatives augments the generation of strangely connected ideas, likely provoked my descent into brains and ponds. Marsupial swamp antechinuses lack this organ entirely but their pond life is simple. And shorter.

Chernobyl 35 Years on

Jeri Kroll

The second pandemic year still harbours luminous terrors. I stumble through weeks pretending to cope, while memories divebomb without warning, nest in my mind and breed. At midnight despair swoops along currents of sleep, only coming to rest in the morning gloom. At least the pathetic fallacy can't bully the weather. Rains begin as predicted, the sun retreats as expected, yet winter will end, the gardening show guarantees.

And thirty-five years on, I read that Chernobyl proves there is hope for the planet. In the exclusion zone, flora and fauna baffle the experts, refusing to disappear. Two hundred bird species have returned, disregarding the danger signs. Albino swallows nest in deserted barns, tawny owls feast on voles and tree frogs and swans glide in cooling ponds past the crumbling reactor. Building codes embedded in their genes, beavers reclaim the landscape, while foxes, wolves, elk and bison make new ancestral tracks through a thousand acres. But what about hawks and eagles that sweep across borders? Do they mate with unsullied neighbours? What legacy do they leave in fledgling bodies? Have all these animals bested human survivors?

Is every story then part truth, part metaphor, or Rorschach cards foretelling a toxic future? I'm left to calculate the half-life of my aging brain and, before it's too late, try to cross the alienation zone, hoping to reach a humane world. But those radioactive images still agitate the dark, and all I can think of are birds of prey coming home to roost.

Image 11: Movie

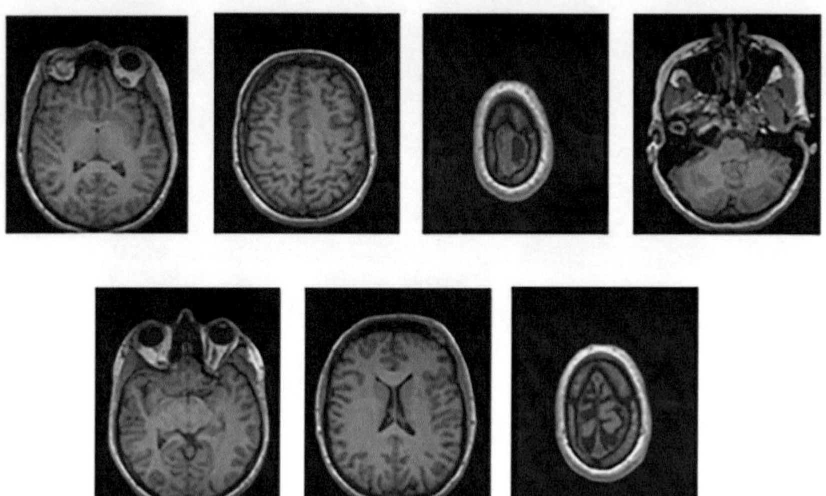

Who is This Strange Being?

Nigel Krauth

'*Who is this strange being that is the creative writer?*' (Kaufman &
Kaufman 2009: xix)

This is the first editorial sentence of *The Psychology of Creative
Writing*, a Cambridge University Press publication of 2009. It reads
like James Cook might have thought as he stepped ashore at Botany
Bay: 'Who are these strange beings that are Australians?' Except
Cook didn't think 'Australians' because he didn't understand that
he stepped into an inhabited territory with its own languages,
paradigms and understandings.

Writers' brains are their major writing tools. It has been so
since writing began. Unsurprisingly, writers have studied their
own minds through metacognition and have studied the minds of
others as best they could by observing from the outside.

*

'*Catch yourself thinking…/ Inside skull is vast as outside skull…/
Mind is outer space…*' (Ginsberg 2003)

Ginsberg's poem sends us hammering through outer space as
if we enter Kubrick's star gate in *2001: A Space Odyssey* (1968).
And why not? Our minds are as deep space as deep space itself.
Neuroimaging slices away and couches forward momentum in
Disney-style animation, but where are we going, and what does
it mean?

Writers may think about brain activity more than normal people
do. Writers may recognise the mind-universe better than others.
I may wish for an atomic scale journey through my brain similar
to *Fantastic Voyage* (1966), but neuroscience has not provided it
yet. We have the Disney version already, but not the real thing.

*

'*Exterminate all the brutes!*' (Conrad 2021)

The enigmatic, traumatised, white ego-figure Kurtz, in
Conrad's *Heart of Darkness*, has come to represent the deepest
thought-producing area in the mind of the Western white male. The
statement Kurtz made is appallingly racist, fuelled by centuries of
colonial practice. Conrad observed alarmingly that there's a jungle

place, deep in the white male mind, where truth gets forged for white guys, so they think.

I write this on 15 March 2021 as women gather around the nation and arrive at Parliament House to demand a change in the mind-work of Australian males. The Prime Minister responds by saying that similar protest marches in other countries are met with bullets. I can only think that in the deepest jungle point of the PM's mind, Kurtz is there advising him.

The unexplored galaxy of the human mind waits while neuroscience and creative writing attempt to investigate it fully. We are still strange beings.

References

Conrad, J. 2021 [1899]. *Heart of darkness*. Available at: The Project Gutenberg eBook of *Heart of darkness* by Joseph Conrad. https://www.gutenberg.org/files/219/219-h/219-h.htm

Ginsberg, A. 2003 [1986]. *Cosmopolitan greetings*. Available at PoemHunter.com. https://www.poemhunter.com/poem/cosmopolitan-greetings/

Kaufman, S. B. & Kaufman, J. C. 2009. (Eds.). *The psychology of creative writing*. Cambridge University Press.

Passerelle

Paul Hetherington

The mind looks back, as if with eyes. Yet, despite this dive
into memory's tidal extravagances, the waterways of Venice
are hidden behind the Biennale's colours and shuttered rooms.
Undulations tug at your image; you're paired with a distant
cathedral; you stand near mosaics that illuminate a wall with
saints and apostles. You've pushed past the queue, saying, 'I must
see it.' We've already watched contemporary paintings jostle and
listened to news of warfare's destruction of shrines. Now, you
want to place your hands on the old images, as if the past might
be channelled through the body into mind; as if modernity's
carelessness might temporarily be stayed. Evening stretches
through windows; the mosaics dive into shadow; an attendant
shuts the heavy doors. Water begins to query the piazza

Image 12: Movie

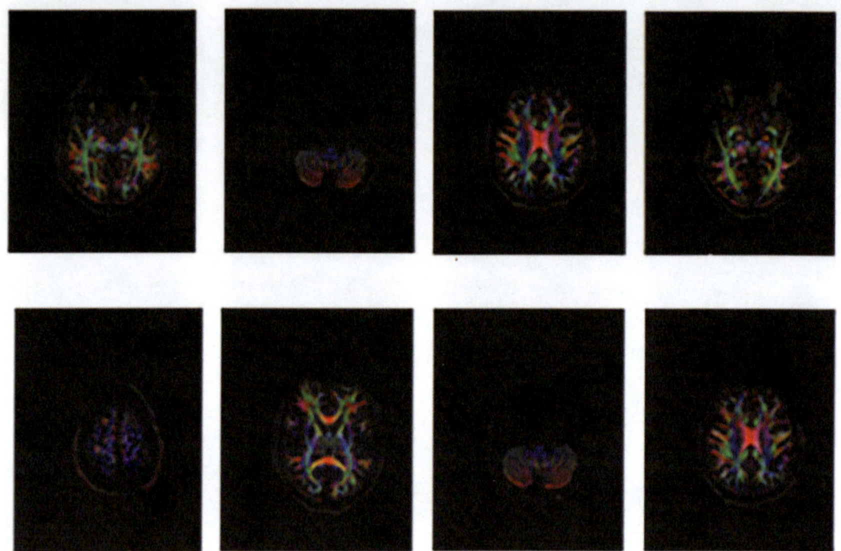

Transmission

Nicola Redhouse

This is where we close down/
            ^

this is where we merge/
            ^

the beat is in the heart stop/
            ^

the flood is in the mind/
            ^

the pain is in the brain of the tussle
when your mouth moves
on mine/—boom boom/
   ^ ^

the muse of the muscle in the words/
     ^   ^   ^

the fuse of the light in the chemistry/
     ^   ^ ^

the fire of the lit is greened/
     ^   ^   ^

the black of it is shot through/
     ^   ^ ^   ^

look at that!/
     ^

the same in the synapse/
     ^   ^

of the babymother heart/
     ^   ^   ^

There is where we went soft/
                ^

there is where we part/
            ^

on the left the word is cut down/

^

on the right you get the hard/
^

the way the salt cuts the way the song silts
^   ^

in the wrong start you have the
^

long hits/ he's in the strong threads/
^ ^

you've got the short straw/
^

it's on the hot side/ the hand will with-draw/
^   ^

the signal gets there/
^

the signal comes first/
^

you'll need to meet here/
^

where we join up/
^

where we touch hands/
^

in the dark part/
^

in the close down
^

it will go
fast
^

The Third Kind

Tom Evershed

Endless ranks of alien craft flashed like stars. Each salvo sent their silver fire lancing, dancing like lightning, splitting and reforming. It seared through space, crackled around his ship. He shot back lasers from his eyes, taking down two of the craft.

Mum twisted in the passenger seat. 'Fancy a cookie, darling?'

He ignored her. Car headlights zipped by, the illusion broken. He narrowed his eyes at the streetlights and the aliens loosed their rays once more.

'Little brat,' said Scott. 'He's still sulking.'

'Should have got a babysitter,' said Mum.

They travelled on. He imagined if the aliens abducted him. The boss alien would roll its eyes and gnash its spiny teeth; but they would still fear him. If he promised not to kill any more aliens, they might free Mum from Scott and make her back how she used to be.

They drove into a tunnel. Red taillight drones led into its yellow blush; then white striplights hurtled them into hyperspace. A vehicle screamed by too close, coruscating blue lights like exploding alien attack craft. The tunnel flashed in every colour. Space was a kaleidoscope.

On they went to their destination. Disembarking, they joined a throng moving with purpose through the dark. Lanterns hung from branches and the path was edged by fire. From the borders, fleshy leaves groped. Illuminated trees scratched at the stars in green and red and ultraviolet. Angular limbs flickered and vines coiled.

He saw a man selling devices that twirled with multi-coloured LEDs. Tugging Mum's hand, he pointed.

She said, 'Can I get him a windmill?'

'He doesn't deserve it, Kelly,' said Scott. 'He's been a little shit all day.'

'Pleeeease, Mummy?' he said.

'Sorry, darling.' Her eyes were sad. 'You have been a bit naughty.'

He pulled his hand away. 'It's not fair.' He frowned. 'I hate you!'

Scott moved towards him and he bolted. He dodged between strangers' legs. Fires cackled. Mum called his name but he dashed into darkness.

Stumbling from the path, he hid behind a tree and pushed his fists into his eyes.

'You okay, mate?'

Looking up, he saw an unfamiliar face, all smile and beard.

'You want one of those toys?'

Sniffing, he nodded.

'I've got a bunch in my van. Come on. We'll get you one.'

He looked around for Mum.

The man proffered a hand. 'Come on, mate. What are you waiting for?'

Image 13: Movie

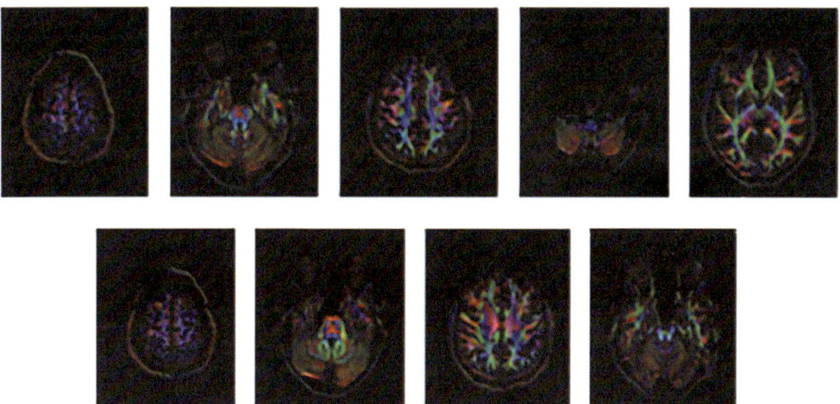

Body, Not-Body: A Brain Scan Response in Three Case Studies

Shady Cosgrove

In the video, he's more handsome that I'm expecting. Receding hairline and an earnest jawline. Tender. Something about the angle of his face makes up for the cheap tie. He's in a room with oversized white tiles and a locker—or maybe the edge of a water heater—just in frame. He's not a small man. He's mentioned this, his weight, but it feels irrelevant now. We aren't even bodies, I tell myself. But his pants are around his ankles, and he's holding his cock. He is words and images, processed through retina and brain, but when he looks at the camera, I am both seen and not-seen.

—

Mardi Gras weekend, Central Station. We've missed the last train to Wollongong and my girlfriend eyes the track, biting at her nails. I'm crouched down, staring at the brown tiles now—the colour offers both motion and safety. I stand up and toe-heel along the yellow line; the straps of my shoes cut into my ankles and my green leather skirt has twisted around. I've been drinking bottled water and high-crying most of the night, so much joy falling from my face I can't catch it all. I'm fun-shouting at the vending machine now, trying to explain the post-structural subject to those apathetic snacks behind the glass, but maybe they're right. Who needs a PhD? My girlfriend glances over, and it's obvious I'm shouting: this, right here. This is it. She shrugs—but I've figured it out. The universe has cracked open.

—

The baby is asleep and even if he wakes, I've jammed the headphones in as far as they'll go. Noise cancelling. My feet are bare on the floorboards and the wood is solid, unconditional. It's Aretha and Florence and Dolly. Respect and men and work. I could be anywhere, eyes closed, feet thumping. I'm jumping with the beat, arms overhead, hips shaking. A faint reflection follows me from the window. I'm exhausted but energy surges up my legs. A gift. I'm pulling off my shirt, breasts leaking through the hefty bra, but whatever. It's a meditation and I'm bassline and voice and spirit.

Breathless

Catherine McKinnon

She's walking, deep in the forest. The path thick with blackened bark, sticks and branches. Thin yellow shoots push through leaf matter and spiral towards the sky. Sedge and bracken grow between bushes newly layered with tiny white buds and banksias whose burnished flowers leak honey into the air.

A lone bird cries out.

In the distance, coming towards her, she sees the man. The same from the other day, same time too. Like the other day, one hand holds a long bone. She is determined to make eye contact.

He smiles as they draw close and she nods in response. Blue eyes. Nose rather straight, soft at the end. Lips, almost full, pleasantly shaped. Bleached hair, dark roots. Wearing a puffer jacket, navy blue, and jeans. But it is the bone she is drawn to. Less than a metre long and flat at each edge where the joints should be. So perhaps not a bone, but bone shaped, bone coloured. Or a bone that has been sculpted. On one of the flat ends there are three distinct lines, etched in. Could it be a tool? What for? Measuring? No. She cannot think why he might be carrying it.

The trees above rub across each other, making cat-like screeches. A friend once said; women have a nose for predators. Always trust your instincts.

Once they have passed each other, she walks faster, but keeps looking back. The path swerves. He disappears. She breaks into a run but is soon breathless. Not fit enough. She half runs, half walks, keeping alert, looking back along the path, but out into the bush too, because he could double back and surprise her. She is thirsty now, her throat raw.

Next walk she will change her route. Come an hour earlier. It bothers her that this is necessary. Frustrating. When she hears water falling, she slows. From the waterfall it is ten minutes to her car.

She laughs then. Idiot. All imagination, probably.

Wind hustles the leaves above, the whoooosh calming, not frightening. As if there is a presence moving through the forest, protecting it. The faint warble of small birds and then the bright song of a honeyeater.

She breathes deeply. Winter is ending and spring is coming.

Past the falls, she sees a shadow form on the path ahead. Someone emerging from the bush.

She picks up a stick …

Image 14: Movie

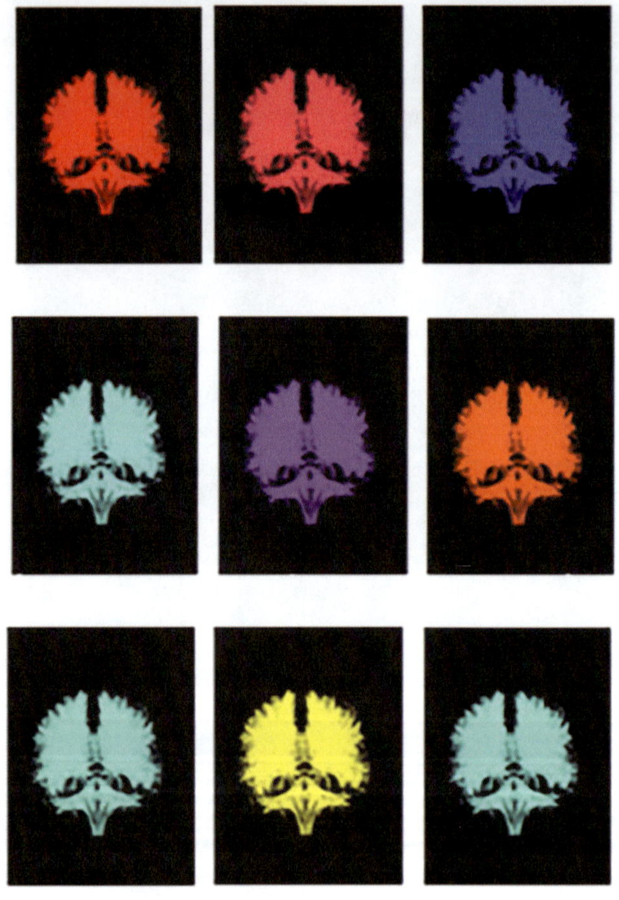

Body Mapping Inside the Arachnoid Disco

Willo Drummond

Life is jumping at the Callosal Commissure
longitudinal fissure, luminous
hall of mirrors. Citrus days / splice
indigo nights, oranges

and apples paint hemispheric
fields. Always more than
ones and zeroes, in this fine philosophy. I
and *I and I …*   *anybody … no one*

to: think, feel, hear, see
the nerve! Remember: trace, move, transpire
(Right [Ctrl] left   left [Ctrl] right).
It's all about

'aboutness' here,
cakewalk at four lobed disco; constant
cartography catching the essence of everything—
all night long—

Past the junction, emergence is full
of fluffy hope, the flush hues of a landscape
like a salmon morning;
love, lust, longing, languid

days lace across
mater, through matter (*I and I* matter
without choosing to matter).
A matter of mater

this matter, a spattering
of technicolour, light fantastic
tripping cellular jelly.
Shapeshifter: omniscient

town-crier of two-way dance, teller
of tales, collector of story
chemical body whisperer.
Lyrebird of corporeal

communion, *I and I* mimic
each flow of body weather
move with the music
of the spheres, spongy

cauliflower calling:
I am home (let me tell you)
I am here (let me show you)
I am.

Notes: With acknowledgement to Denise Levertov's, 'People at Night', Rainer Maria
Rilke's 'People by Night', and Lionel Richie's All Night Long.

Dreaming in Colour

Deedle Rodriguez-Tomlinson

Recently I dreamed I was

    watching a feature on TV about

the phenomenon of tall sea green grass

    woven into human forms

waving in the wind.

    A man in a red, white, and blue

shirt turns to the camera and says:

    I can cure your disease.

In another dream, a man who reminded me

    of a gay friend back home in Manila

had canary yellow hair streaked

with the natural jet black of his own.

    Monarch butterfly colours.

In the dream we were helping

each other escape.

    To where, I don't remember.

From whom, I can't recall.

And in a dream not my own,

the cousin

of a dear friend who

perished in the North Tower of the

World Trade Center on 9/11

dreamed he stood before her,

smiling, told her not to cry.

She dreamed he was happy, at peace.

She dreamed he gave her a vision,

the last thing he saw:

a steel white wing coming out

of a bright blue sky,

glinting in the hot September sun.

Image 15

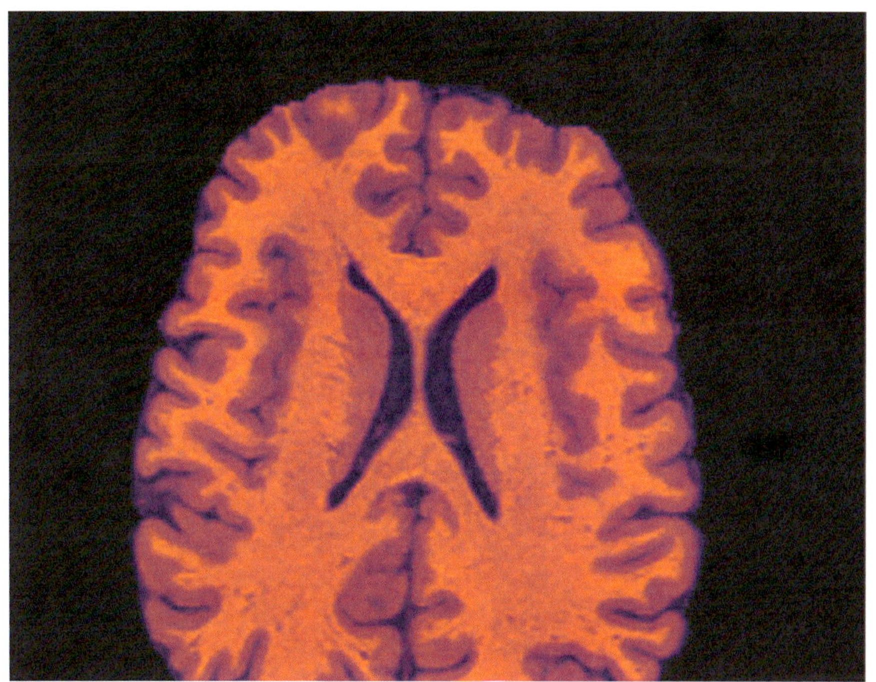

Brain Clock Face Scan

Katrina Finlayson

An easy task.

(You, doctor of words, fat completed thesis on post-apocalyptic fiction, theory of endings.)

A young doctor, crisp shirt and sedate tie, sits facing you in a small, fluoro-lit cancer centre emergency room. He hands you pen and paper. Asks you to draw a clock face.

The clock drawing test. A simple name; so significant. There are other common cognitive dysfunction screening tests. Count backwards from one hundred in sevens. Your name. The current year. The Prime Minister of Australia.

You draw a lopsided circle.

Fine.

(Slurred speech this morning. Wild and confused, about the sunlight in our bedroom, my concern, my request for crisp sentences. I drove you, cautiously, urgently, to the hospital.)

You write numbers around the circle's edge. Everything is orderly from one to six. But then the others all try to squeeze into one quarter together. Eleven wanders away, twelve acts bewildered, and I swallow panic. I glance up but the doctor's face is hard to read. Tangle my fingers; suppress an urge to correct your drawing. I desperately want you to get it right.

(We fell in love to a soundtrack of drunk poetry and draft essays read aloud at 2 am. More recently, it's been *New York Times* crosswords in a chemo day treatment centre: think about 23-down, my love, instead of the multiple attempts to guide a needle into tired veins. Who even are we without clever words?)

You frown as you draw clock hands. Two lines fight each other over which is the bigger one. Arrows point in odd directions.

(You alone don't yet seem to realise it's all gone wrong.)

And now you notice something isn't right. You look from clock to doctor, eyes wide. Turn to see my face.

(I hide my fear.)

But the doctor assures us it is (hopefully) temporary. You are speaking clearly again, seem to be making sense. Vitals within your usual range.

We can go home (rest and monitor).

Two days later, a machine scans your brain. The report says nothing unusual can be seen. It was a glitch; maybe a build-up of chemotherapy drugs, maybe a toxic effect of the lymphoma. (Nobody really knows.) What's important is that the clockwork mechanisms of your brain are once again moving.

A snapshot image of one second of your mind.

Symmetrical. Beautiful. (Terrifying.)

Shape of lungs, coral, clouds, a Rorschach inkblot, a Mandelbrot set.

The violent violet dawn of your life. Your atomic amber sunset.

Tick. Tock.

Rhodes

Julia Prendergast

We arrive in Rhodes in delirious darknight, a hilltop road beside the church, more like a wide footpath.

I have no more ideas, says the cab driver.

We shift to the floodlit shopfront of Yasou's Souvlaki, pull out our phones. A motorbike approaches from the steepside—*Yasou's* in white cursive script along the black belly of the engine.

We're lost, I say. *From Australia.*

I show him a photo of the house, zooming in on the green gate.

I know it, he says.

Daniel straddles the back of the bike. As the bike-light fades I wonder if Yasou will kill Daniel, send his brother to rape me. I see it in fast-time, until the scene is broken by a patch of road that appears to be moving—a guts-out cat, limbs paddling, eyes like tinned lychees.

Jesus-fucking-Christ.

Shining my phone-light on the rocky embankment—loose lichen shifting like drifting seaweed at low tide. I'm fuckeyed— longing for the rockpool sea.

Did I imagine the writhing cat? Guts like maggoty brain matter.

Why do we fester in each other?

I loosen a boulder, carry it closer. *It's okay darlingheart*, I say. Strobe-lit, I drop the rock on the cat's head.

Image 16

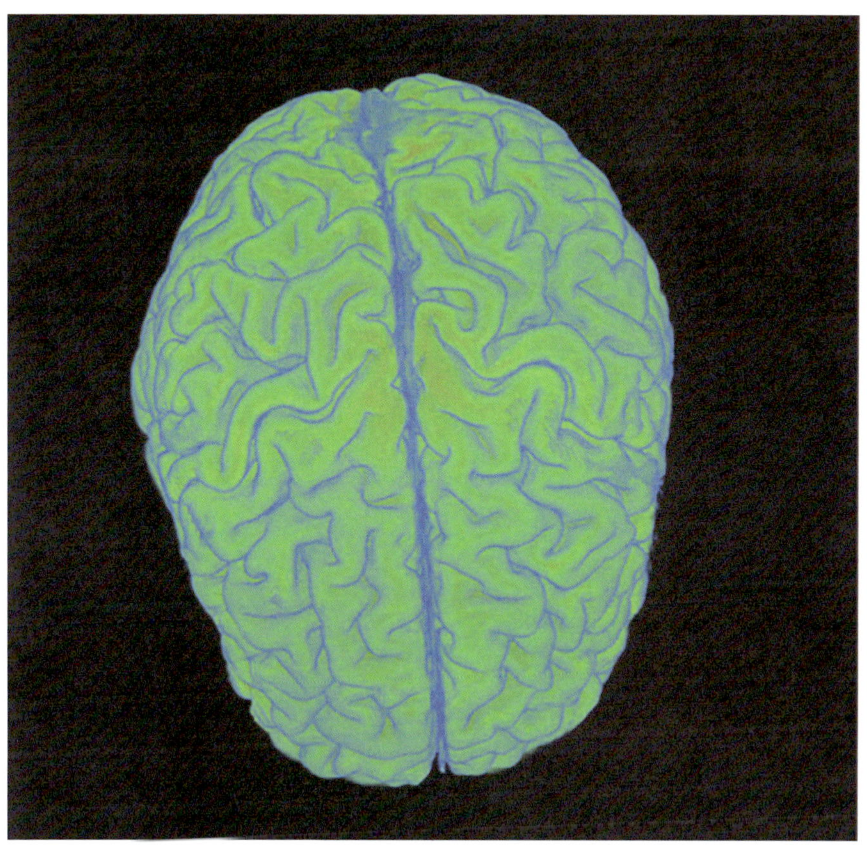

What's in a Name?

Eileen Herbert-Goodall

The woman can't remember her name. The man, who claims to be her husband, calls her Lil and says it's short for Lilia. She's certain this name must belong to someone else, an impostor maybe. But if so, then who is she?

The man calls himself Doug.

Supposedly, they've been married for thirty-two years.

How can that be possible?

She stares at the ceiling, trying to recall—yet again—the series of events that brought her here. Her thoughts are a looping circuit and end, inevitably, where they began.

In her mind's eye, the woman sees herself slumped against a wall. The man named Doug crouches, staring into her eyes. His mouth moves but she can't grasp anything he says. She hears only a rush of white noise, a constant buzzing that emanates from somewhere deep inside her brain. The buzz remains faintly detectable, even now.

How much damage has been done?

Her eyes swivel as she attempts to anchor herself, to allay the anxiety creeping beneath her skin. Cables sprout from a nearby monitor, connecting with soft pads that are, in turn, attached to her chest. Her heart can't be trusted to sustain its rhythm. The doctors claim she was lucky not to have suffered a cardiac arrest.

She doesn't feel particularly lucky.

The man named Doug says the accident was caused by faulty wiring in their washing machine.

Apparently, it happened in the blink of an eye.

The doctors can't be sure whether her confusion is temporary, or a more permanent condition—it's too early to tell. Injuries incurred through electrocution can be complex and difficult to ascertain with any exactness, so they say.

The man named Doug likes to talk. He says she had been a teacher of literature, a professor no less. Is she still a professor, given the present circumstances? Or has all that shifted, along with the very foundations of her identity?

Answers remain elusive.

In any event, she suspects things will never be the same.

The woman turns to see a vase on the bedside table; it is filled with tall, white flowers. She concentrates, trying to recall their botanical name. Words rise to the surface of her consciousness—bees, pollen, rain—but instinctively she knows none of these are correct.

Her eyes well as she looks towards a shaft of sunlight that tumbles through a window and spills across the cold, grey floor.

Topography

Jessie Seymour

Split the middle; force your way through the gap
and find sweet, tender insides waiting there.
Dips and valleys splay out on a green map
as mountain rivers flow and scent the air.
Narrow, rocky streams, rapids, banks so steep
that standing is a game already lost,
and sliding down stones, dirt, and roots less deep
is certain as a bridge already crossed.
A seed cast away to grow or shrivel.
Water splitting earth into mountain streams.
Walnut pulp in salads, lips uncivil,
cutting into other social machines.
Drops of water, seeds, and time. Just some time.
To shatter, to grow, to break or refine.

Image 17

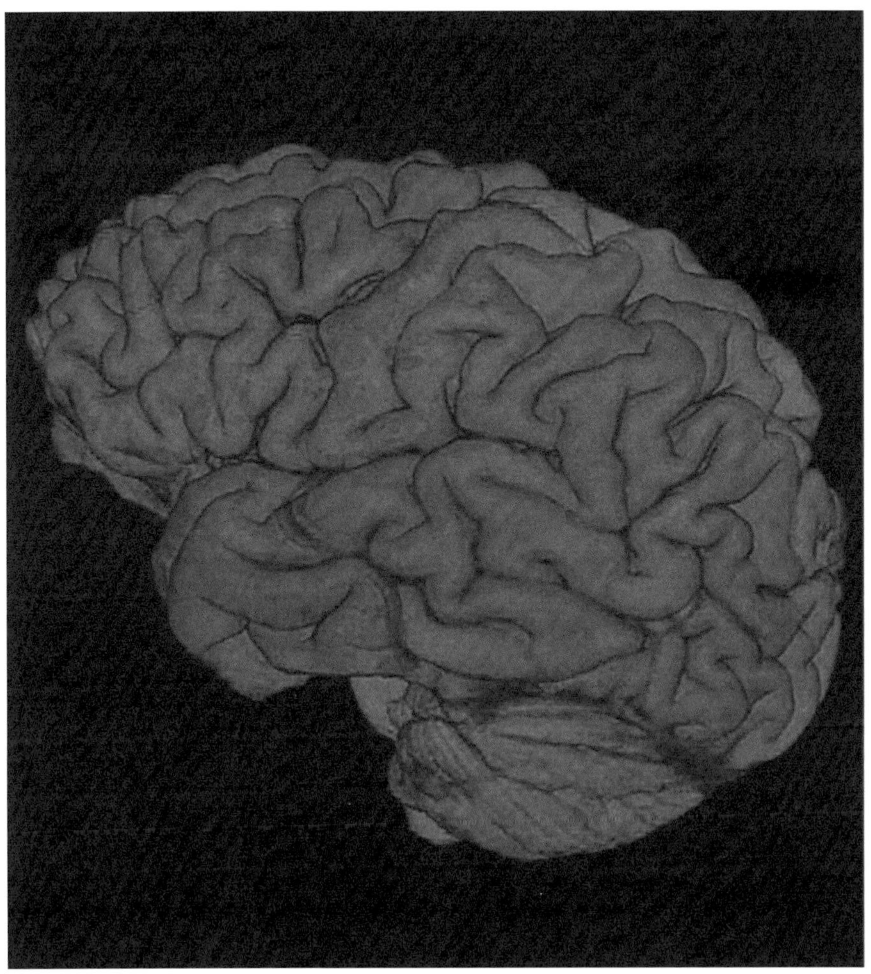

Purpling

Daniel Juckes

The steamed-cabbage look of it starts the suspension of belief. And perhaps ends it, if I am being frank: there is no way this crinkle-cut globule, soft and bruised, could swell with all of who someone like myself happens to be. Even the mushiness of it is offensive—like the parts of your body which fold themselves without intention, or even those that dimple despite all efforts to the contrary. Yet.

Something about the image rejects even the idea of the organic: I am unable to imagine this thing beating, throbbing, or pulsing— and I cannot trace in my own version of it (the one which sits inside my skull) all the swirling mechanisms of life that should be there. Instead, it hovers—jar-kept or dangling—and is inhuman by disassociation. Though.

There is no doubt it is the seat of things. That it produces, despite the bloated disconnect that exists between the dream and fact of ourselves: the gap that persists in each of the ways we convince ourselves against softness, or set up in opposition to gangling insides. (These can only revolt us.) But.

This thing, too—the origin of all anxiety; of all that is felt and thought and sought—still beguiles. It lulls, maybe because, while being both distended and less-dimensional than it should be in the flesh, it somehow remains cute; seems slight; is toylike. This.

Suggests a lilliputian grandiosity. An unimaginable, imagined contradiction—a force of endless aeons, manifested as in-built curlicues and grey complexity; a doubled, tripled, en-billioned bodyless object. That.

Tells time. Sings songs. Writes books. Dwells; computes; remembers. Settles a body in the space of itself and within the space of a universe; which allows brief comprehension. So.

Is undeniable, while being impossible to believe. But there still. And doubtful yet, though ticking and turning and squeezing endless impressions. With.

Nothing to keep it from stopping except for the wearing down of itself.

Matryoshka: In Utero

Sue Joseph

They stack on my shelf, woman nestling inside woman.
Hiding until unwrapped; undone; opened. Vivid, multi-
coloured and Russian; my ancestry. Peasant jumper dresses drape,
diminishing in size.

Inside.

*

In utero, she is an idea; a notion; a perhaps. Then she moves, she
grows, second by second by minute by minute by hour by hour
by day by day by week by week by month.

Months.

And arrives into my arms, the notion a truth at 12.10 pm on
that day in that week of that month.

That year.

Soon after she arrives, the room is full—three offices full, with
people watching and touching and speaking, near. Flowers and
grapes and chocolates and baby jackets and bootees and picture
frames and balloons. Teddy bears and books and candles.

People gather and stay, for hours. And hours. Tag teaming.
The noise and laughter and awe and excitement are infectious. The
adrenaline courses and the ecstasy of a magical feat—something
achieved by millions of women for millions of years—seems all mine.

And then they are gone. Nine hours.

The first moment alone (but not) I look hard at her. And she
looks back, hard, staring unseeingly. But surely, seeing.

I feel a chill as she squirms. And struggles; begins to whimper.
Big Ben chimes nine.

I have no idea what to do.
The sudden stillness of the night;
the silence shattered by that clock.

I have no idea what to do.

My trepidation.

And then … I remember this sense like it was yesterday: a long
line, a procession of women standing behind me. Toweringly tall

and straight and strong, disappearing into the distance, getting smaller but there, definitely there.

For aeons.

I feel them, holding each other, up. Holding me. Up. Blanketing and warming.

Enfolding me, as I enfold her.
I sit up straight in that bed oceans from home, holding her.

I know these women; their cells course through my body.

I know these women; their knowledge pours through my pores.
I know these women; they dance and dally in my dreams.

I know these women; their shared strength sometimes saves me.

Their laughter buoys me; their sensibilities define me; they travel with me.

All their wisdoms are mine.

And hers.

Are ours.

In utero we imbibe understanding; we learn a universe, our first classroom; we fit like Matryoshka. We weave our magic and conjure life, and we know.

Image 18: Movie

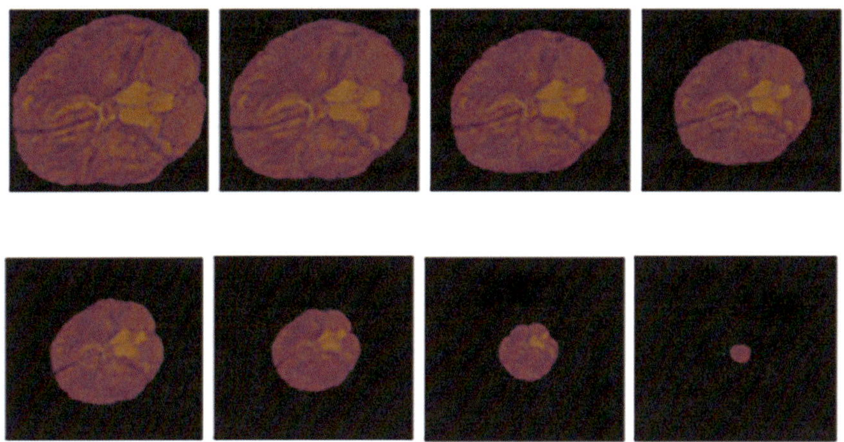

Freefalling

Julia Prendergast

You are here in your gone-ness.

Your freefalling a becoming.

I replay the memories in colour so I don't overlook what I mustn't forget.

That it's possible to love deliberately—when you're freefalling—when the ground is suddenly gone.

> You make a run for it, kitchen to bathroom.
>
> In the midway, in the 'living' room, your head thwacks floorboards—mottled veins, purple, spreadeagled.
>
> Orange vomit sideswipes your face like a backslap. It pools on the floorboards, glistening in the afternoon light—catching purple like a rainbow …
>
> Misguided hands, blood orange slippage—thoughts scramble, orange-purple.

Now I write it—*Now*, I see.

Back then, you were already here, in our tomorrows, even as the suffering turned you sideways.

Champagne Supernova

Dominique Hecq

Starlight, annular. Self-luminous and thermonuclear coils in a nest. Shot silk. Alive taffeta. Scales, feathers, down, fur, skin. Pinkish brightening against the jet-black sky. Implosion. Compression. Explosion. Spicules. Your eyes, red-rimmed, hurt with gaseous light unlighting. Spectroscopic pulsation of pinks and reds. Slow whirl of carmine, vermillion, *giroflé,* red lead, scarlet pink, fuchsia, baby pink, rust-speckled traces of brain matter. Swirling cloud of hydrogen, helium, carbon, neon, oxygen, silicon. You plunge into your own dismembering body. Rise up to the surface. Cool down. Plunge again, *inwardoutward.* Cicadas scurry through your *bodymindsoul,* carnation-darnation chills. You breathe in tantric fashion when what you need is an antipyretic, analgesic, emetic. *Pffffff* … Fast slow entropy. Hundreds of billions of years in three little seconds, snuffed. Three caskets in stellar atmosphere. *No, Doctor, this is no hallucination. This is the* real real. Life leaches away from you. Tubular bells. Church quiet. A whiff of incense and black sun … *Gegenschein.* Light curve. Crepuscular rays. Green flash. Twinkle. You sail ahead of *timenotime* into the dark bubbling out of gravitas. Radiate your own heat. Blow apart in a brilliant anti-anthropic stellar body dispersing on the other side of the eclipsing pillars of creation, purple lake, ultra-deep charcoal shades. The Dead Sea *Asphaltum.* Stardust, afloat.

Note: The title of this piece is in homage to Oasis's song Champagne Supernova.

Image 19: Movie

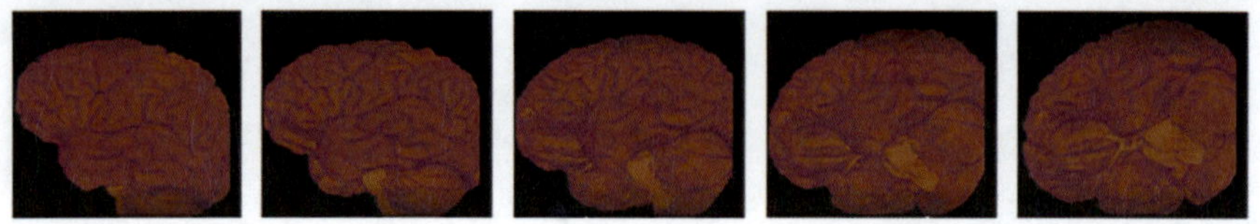

Brainwork

Joshua Lobb

I'm not Tintin. Orbiting the moon in my chunky orange space suit, a deep-sea diver in the ocean of space, spinning into an infinity of adventures, fearlessly flying into deepest darkest wherever: wild west America, Stalinist Russia, the tangled jungles of the Amazon. And now the moon. I remember the picture from the book: a full page of the craterous expanse, the black empty sky. A speck of a figure. *This is it!* he cries. *I've walked a few steps! For the first time in history, there is an EXPLORER ON THE MOON!* The gravity is lighter there. Your head spins. The captain would rather stay in the cigar-cocoon of the rocker, but grudgingly clambers down to the grey sand. Tintin and the captain head off in their lunar tank across the lumpy surface. They follow a groove on the surface; it splits into a narrow valley, worn down by an infinity of moondust. The captain spots a crack in the valley wall, an opening to a new adventure, a cave. Tintin and Snowy venture out in their orange deep-sea space suits. Snowy strides ahead and falls deeper into a crevasse. Tintin follows. As he drops into the unknown, he cries, *Into the hands of fate!*

I'm not Tintin. Not even Captain Haddock, refusing the adventure, but grudgingly going anyway. The gravity is heavier here. Headier. Under the rumples of the duvet, hiding from deepest darkest everything. Nothing ventured. Trying to work up the courage to open the door and face the dusty air, to step into a yellow-lit supermarket, to climb into the cigar-cocoon of a bus again. The lumps of crowds, the ocean of bodies. My narrow strip of life round the block, an adventure of one foot in front of the other. Avoiding confrontations with breathing human faces. The tightness of fear. Tangled up in the orange and purple darkness of my own spinning brain. Avoiding all hands at all costs.

The Rabbit

Christine Howe

Years later
when he was off his medication

living alone in a cave in the bush
he remembered the rabbit—

the way it emerged
from the clay

in his fingers
chalky fur

drying pale on his skin
sloping ears bent up and back.

Back then, art
was still part of the curriculum.

Her nose arose unbidden
her limpid eyes met his

and, as other kids spaghettied under tables,
farting, calling each other names

he helped her scrabble free.
She entered the kiln

one lonely beast amid a platoon
of mother's-day pinch pots

and suffered the scorching heat
with no complaints.

When she was released
she was a tougher version of herself

burnt umber and split
right through the heart.

Image 20

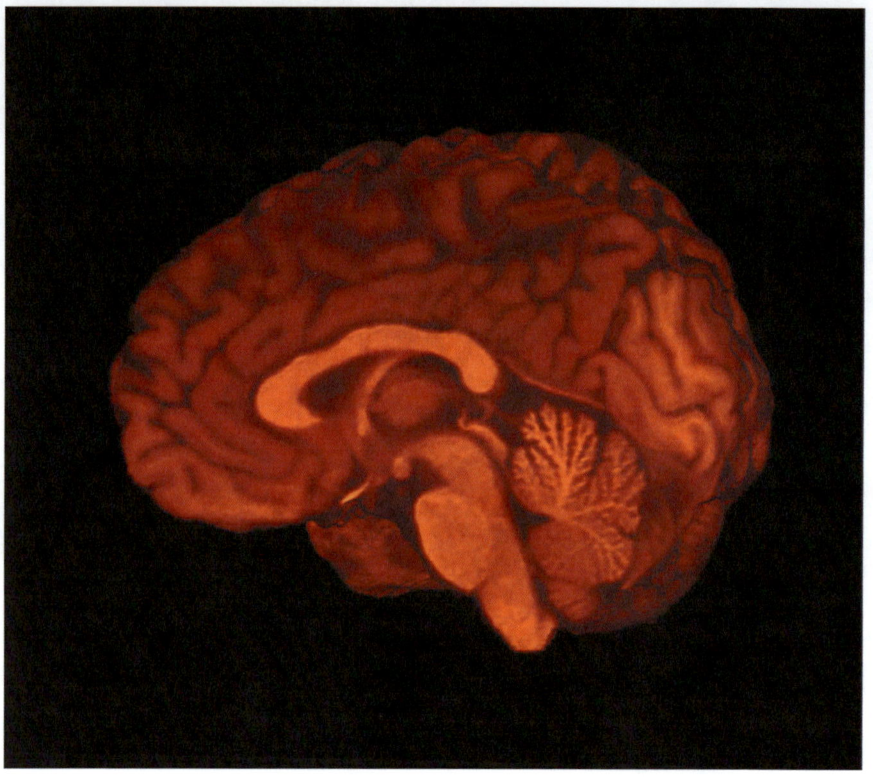

Neurowomb

Kay Are

And at last one day it slipped out, twin
and compass rose to the brain: my womb,

mind's rhyme but also seasonal respite
from its reason. Once departed I missed less

her upturned scales of justice,
ovarian weighing pans dispensing

grinding fervour direct
to the lumbago, her stubby fists on my eggs

colliding with every bloody thing
as she backed out and fled. I missed more

her coiled idea: reproduction inside my body
of the cast that made my body

inside my mother—the cave that mirrors still
my sleeping shape and from which I both

did and did not escape. No sum of rationality
delivers that kind of poetry. Now

my reproductive labouris motored by
my brain: feebler twin, it tenders mere document

of the decoupled organ, saying there is only one
lovely uterus and every woman has it, or had.

Still Life

Stephanie Green

Arrayed against darkness, these vestiges shore up what seems to matter as the tide ebbs away. Red fronds of coral, dried sea cabbage, the pink interiors of empty shells, scalloped treasures gleaned from undulating waves that, captured here, can never decay, nor allow us to forget. Gathered from an ocean garden, what passion or justice is recorded in these still remains? Destruction and power are as nothing to this vision that can never betray. In us, you exist as belief in the inner life, the charged possibility of thought. In you, we exist unblooded and unafraid, as if we lounged on silk embroidered chairs, straightening our powdered wigs and ruffled collars while we wait for musicians to come in from the antechamber.

Now the performance is over and only artifice remains. There is no glimpse of fierceness or frailty, no hook tearing through skin and scales, no red upturned crab clawing desperately through the net. With this brief, quiet seizure, how softly we clock the dead passage of time, and cling to the promise of reason amid the clash and fall of failed civilisations. In this moment, earth itself seems an empty pearlescent shell. Here we need not see spilled viscera, nor swallow back against the thick scent of decay as the dying ark runs aground. For what once was fired with fury and desire, still time scours to inanimate civility, leaving us only this one bright reminder.

Image 21

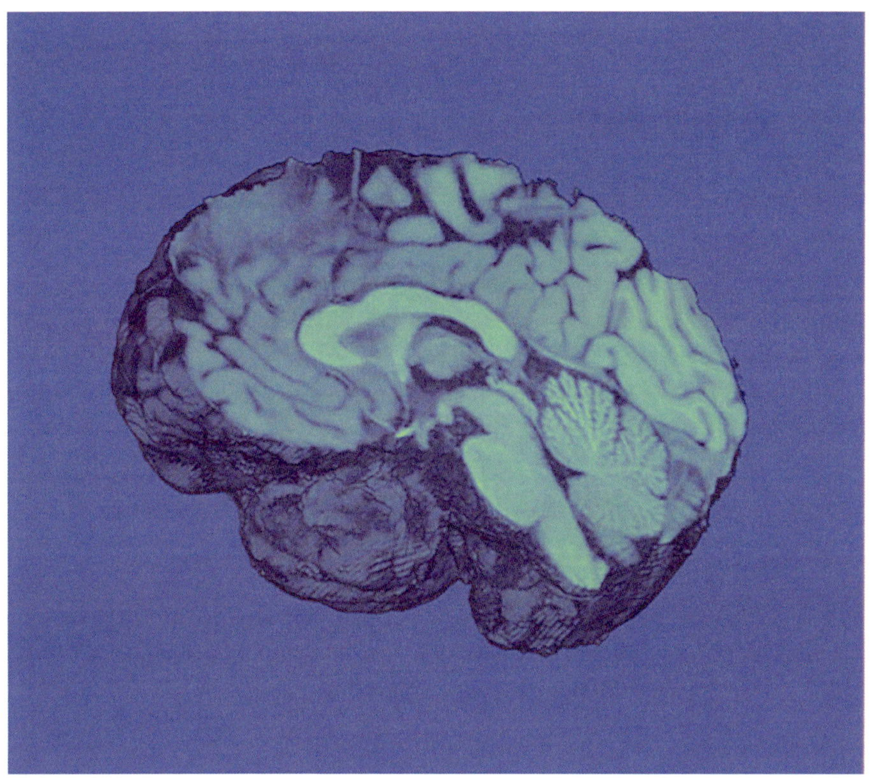

Untitled

Patrick Allington

One day, I looked into the ocean—you can do that these days—just in time to see the last caper on earth make its journey from land to deep water. Its time had come, after nearly a decade of floating alone in a jar of vinegar at the back of someone's fridge.

The last caper bobbed about on the surface of the water for a while, gaining weight, gaining salt, catching some run. Eventually it began a steady, though hardly graceful, descent. It's a reliable bud, the caper: by the time it reached the bottom, it had adapted to the currents and the cold and the dark.

The last caper was no trendsetter. The last blue whale was the first to go, although admittedly it was already ocean-dwelling. The last cigarette butt soon followed, flicked from the hand of the last smoker. The whale and the cigarette butt became an item: some say it was expediency or loneliness or desperation, but love is love.

Since then, there have been almost daily descents, resulting in very few problems. The last crocodile broke etiquette, though no actual laws, by attempting to eat the last goat as they went down together. The last goat took it in its stride. 'I would have eaten the crocodile,' it is reported to have said, 'if it would have let me.'

The last box of popcorn panicked the day before it was scheduled to descend. Fearing it would turn soggy when it hit the water, despite assurances to the contrary from officialdom, it coated itself in several layers of varnish. The Committee of Last Things ruled that it was now a replica, and an ugly one at that. At great expense, the committee recommissioned a movie theatre to make a new, authentic last box of popcorn.

There is harmony of sorts at the bottom of the ocean, a sense of shared purpose. The last caper misses the solitude of its jar, but it knows that it is better to be stuck in yet another inane conversation with the last lion and the last sea lion than to be sitting like a green pimple atop a steaming bowl of pesto, waiting for the fork of death to scoop you up and dump you down some human's throat. And the caper likes being the last of its kind—the gravitas, the grandeur.

Twelve or More Brain Facts in John Cage's Thirteen Harmonies

Tim Tomlinson

(in)Sufficient memory imprint

to transfer

to reach

    two colours

two hats, with sounds

    whatsoever

the Impossibility of

        identifying/recognising

similar objects, forms

seeing is forgetting the name …

    again,

      however

worry the object, do something to it

a single category, a generalising

    mechanism—

    a unique

      normal with

no central constant form

    leaves the work

it becomes

a language enjoyed

    without being understood

nonabstract abstractions

    the mind already knows

light snow

What I am calling poetry is

bound up with

the telephone

or the aeroplane

silence symmetry zero *ich*

is never capitalised

Image 22

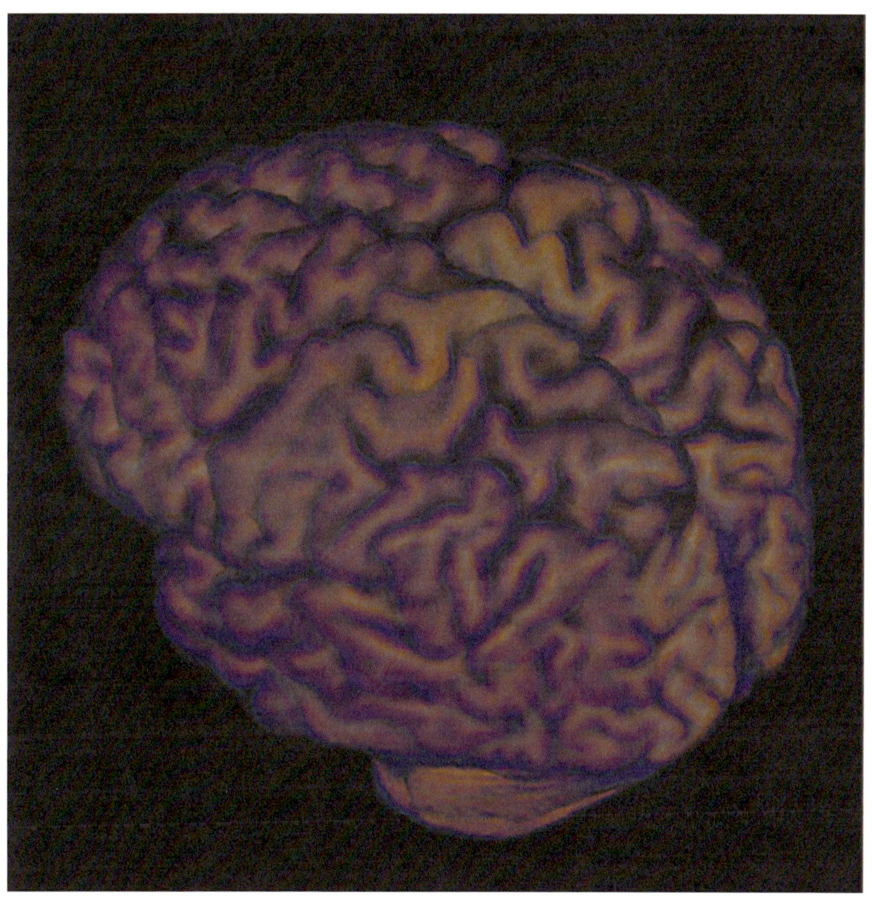

Imaging the Future

Jeri Kroll

Could this be my brain,
snug in its casket of bone,
a golden deep-sea coral, inscribed in purple,
suspended in perfect black?
My brain first fed on words,
rocking in a liquid cradle,
as voices sang to me.
Only when my eyes unglued,
my mother's face took shape,
could images begin to sketch their truths.

Decades on I thought my mind
was written out; I'd spent my stash of words.
This year of solitude's revised us all.
Plagued by memories,
I've ached and sweated scrolling back.
What rivulets of passion or despair
flooded through these days?
And yet the present finally dammed the past—

the paddock's breath that shimmers in the morning,
the night's sheer black that still admits the stars,
the whirrs and clicks of lives I cannot see,
the growls and squeals of everything nonhuman,
and all the sighs and rages of the winds
that never hold their peace.

And so this is my hope, perhaps my last—
that age has woven fissures
delicate as these;
that purple dye's more beautiful

because it has to fade,
and I can flicker as the voltage drops,
the light dims, the heart calms.
Until that final pulse,
let words remain the bridge between the folds,
recording what I am.

Kim

Donna Lee Brien

Kim was born in winter 2006. If you make the 'one of our years equals seven for a dog' calculation, then she's just about to turn 105.

But that's not quite right. She is decidedly stiff in the mornings, almost completely deaf and very grey, but there is nothing wrong with her eyesight, and she still loves her beach run. She swam in the dam until the first frost of winter just a few weeks ago, gobbles up anything chicken, and does most of what the younger dog does. Just for less time.

I found an online calculator that is based on comparing DNA aging in both Labrador Retrievers and people. When I put her age in, Kim came out at 74. That sounds much better, but I have to admit that Kim is not a Lab. She's finer and leaner and blends the gene pools of both smaller and larger dogs—an elegant brindle mix of Staffordshire Bull Terrier and Great Dane, but no retriever. Confirming this is how she loves chasing sticks and balls, but only very rarely brings them back.

Another recent version of these estimates suggests that the first year of a dog's life is equal to fifteen human years. That makes sense, as during that year dogs grow from squirming newborns to being able to have puppies of their own, although, just like for human girls, this is not recommended. Their second year of life is worth an additional nine of ours, meaning that two-year-old dogs, often wild with reckless energy, are akin to young adults in their early 20s. Then, for each additional year, four or five of our years are added. This makes Kim equivalent to somewhere between 76 and 89 years old.

That sounds about right, but I know that, in general, larger dogs live significantly briefer lives than the smaller breeds. I locate a chart that has figures for small, medium, large and even giant dogs, and with Kim on the lower end of large, her age is valued at 93. I don't like that at all. Plus, the chart only goes up to 15, which was the most terrifying information of everything I found.

Living on a farm, death is part of our everyday. But every loss hits hard and I can't imagine life without Kim. Instead of worrying though, I've decided to stick with her 15 actual years and my hopes of us celebrating at least a few more birthdays together.

Image 23

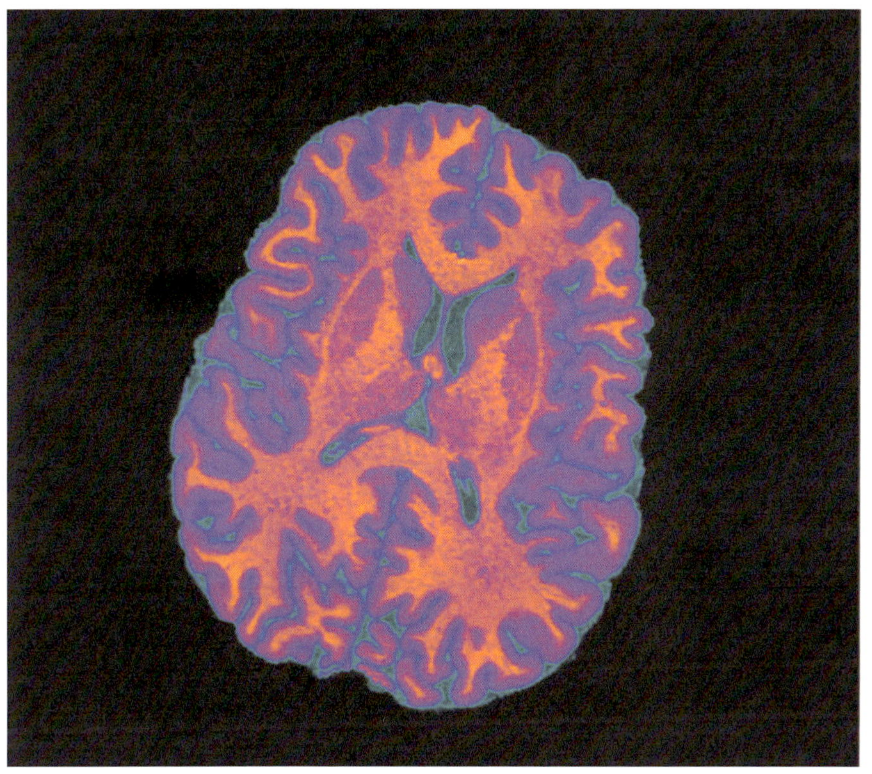

Sense/Making

Amelia Walker

Make more sense, you told me.

Unsure what sense meant, from what to make it, I opened my dictionary, which in turn opened into multiple senses, but no recipe. It offered judgement, based in wisdom, fact and practicality—understanding. It offered words, too, of sensing: sound, taste, touch, smell, sight, fright, lust, love, motion and emotion; a sense of fun, of humour, or occasion; of right and wrong, South from Sky and good from better, among other directions; of waves, tides and their rises; moons and stars; rhythms and dancing; sense as experience, as knowledge and/as body; sensuality; intuition; what we know without knowing how we know; sense as common; connection; a shared sense; binding.

All these senses seemed parts of longer dreams recurring differently in the minds of countless sleepers across endless eras. I decided I'd piece their parts together, make something for you—something in which I hoped you'd see sense.

I took the many words and reworked them. I turned them into cards, with which I built houses, countless houses, and then towers, halls, stations, malls and cemeteries. I made a small world for you, presented it with pride.

You glimpsed briefly, then smashed the lot down.

Try again, you said.

This time I went straight to the source. I pressed my ears to beehives, gathered their buzz, stewed it behind my eyes, cried nectar for you to drink.

You spat and grimaced.

Then I undressed myself for the ocean, let it sing through my insides and out. From sheets of foam, I made up a giant bed, soft and waiting.

You would not lie down.

I grew wings just to feel them clipped, busted limbs to know the how of healing. From ground feathers and bones, I fashioned sculptures of hearts—moving sculptures, really beating.

You barely looked, refused to touch.

After that I rode my bicycle across snow-covered beaches, slept inside mountains of sun. I ate to know tastes and starved to taste more. I sat in sound and danced with quiet. Time came and danced too, gifted me a sense of loss and thus gratitude for everything still left to lose.

I tried to share all this with you. You shook your head and turned away.

Finally, I stopped and asked,

What is sense?

How can I make it?

Your mouth opened—wide, then wider. From it rushed a freezing tide of silence.

Untitled

Jen Webb

You wake to find yourself lost. A trace of day has snaked beneath
the covers, trees revert to grey, early birds stretch their wings
and you squat, a frog beside cool water, to wash the night off
your skin. To the south is a roof you recognise, to the north that
familiar hum, you are home or close to home, all sides in sync.
You think you might stitch a path from here to there, a tapestry
made of height and depth and time. Sun is higher now, and the
first flies touch your face, tentatively.

Image 24

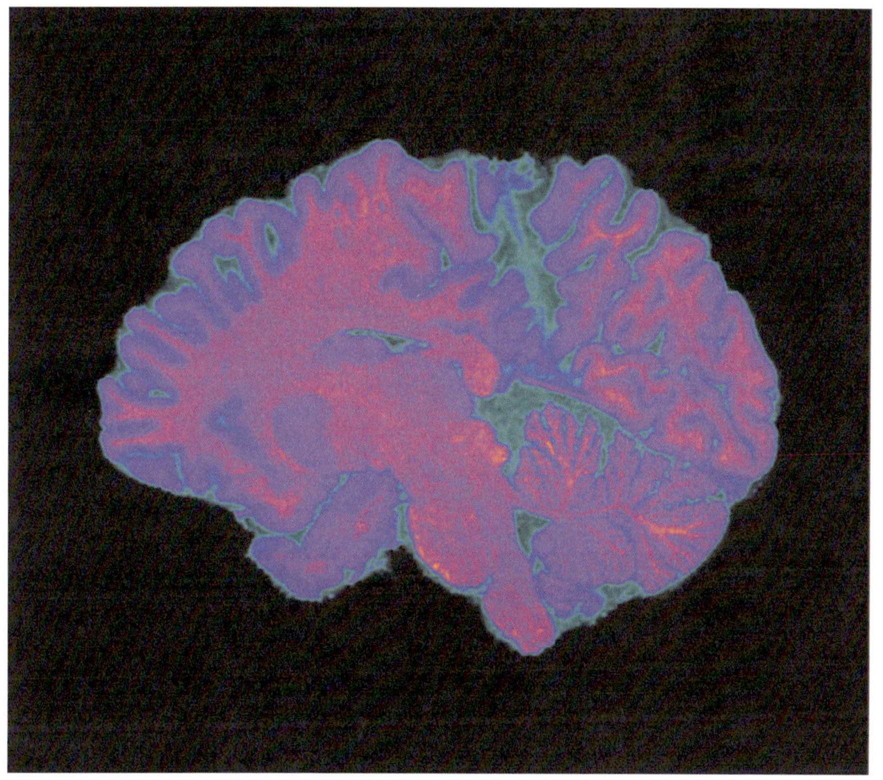

Sucked Into my Floral Veins Like Fresh Data

Antonia Pont

we went blinkered into that forest, lured
by haemophilic figures, night-ploys playing dumb
at the threshold of what we call 'empirical'
old trees & greyed 'gorithms, left in the wake of human passing

the way a creature sees: in streams of hyper-
intelligent code, reading our spindly, pointless arcs
of proof, falling like fake-rain, like sprinkler-intel
—you might thereby navigate a frozen night

in dream-dystopias that accumulate
to tell you what you are—but still …
nodes of leaf-ing, real exits, present themselves
& you escape into sideline stains

into viscosities lying beyond the scope
of your registered terminals—Delicious Darling!
I clasp your liquid ribs & your ghost-colours
peel back in a thrill of silent shedding

(dried layers made from all our system errors)
to the wet, magnanimous ground & now! hot
organic thoughts stack up in lines of perfumed binary
—all around: matter to make undisputable fire

we all watched clouds from aeroplanes (in that era)
traversed terrible nights, our lobotomies in full swing
(touching skin pads to rectangular eyes)—I named
close to your face this precise program: scrutinising

(you were teetering, a tight bud of tears)
I named, refused & brushed its blossom softly off:
mere bruise, then went out (cardiac flight
down cool stairs) to smell the recent snowfall.

Somewhat of a Loss, After
'The Broken Fountain'

Autumn Royal

'God made me a businesswoman'—Amy Lowell

Oblong, its jutted ends round into the stained basin
fixed against the bathroom walls of the flat I'm contracted
to, built in 1968. It's currently 2021—
a disposable training pad for my puppy is placed
beneath the sink. I can't afford a patch of green
for her soils—a backyard as it's commonly known.
My stagnate water is not in a pond or a broken fountain,
but in the toilet bowl—and yet I care, I do care, or I try
to care in opportunities for horizontal reflections
as I sponge the bathrooms owned by people who pay
me to care for their children, like my own mother,
this mirroring revises my chances to have already had
the baby I was told I would have, and how could I ever
afford someone like myself to care in the way that I do.
My desire trails purple and red fuchsias dripping
from marble urns, the heavenly highs and lows of a spout.

Image 25: Movie

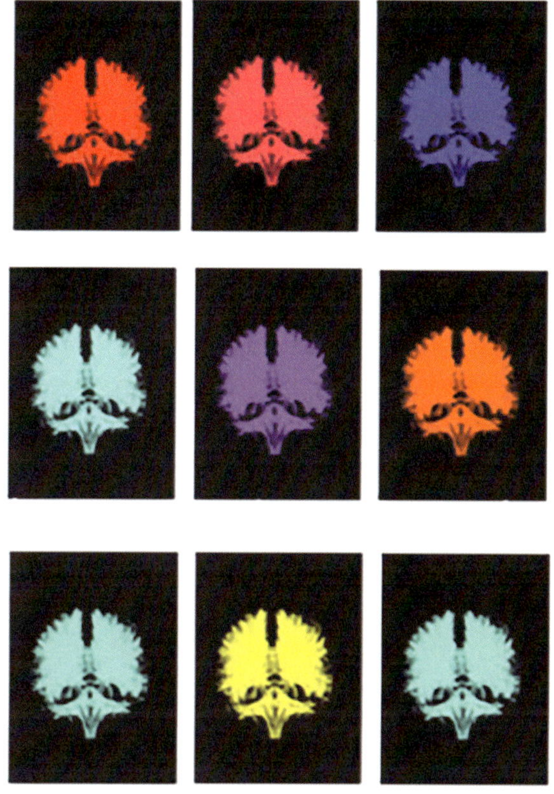

Red Tree

Nathan Langston

A red tree. An ancient autumn oak by the graveyard at sunset. The bone yard is on the university campus and the colour almost hurts to look at. A supernatural colour. I sit on a gravestone and can hear the school bells playing the evening song. A light body of breeze shushes through the boughs above like a beautiful language I cannot understand.

It's my freshman year.

Today I went to my class about Shakespeare. The professor is finding inventive ways to make these incendiary texts boring and lifeless as dust. I sit in the back of the lecture hall and read ahead. I find Hamlet in a graveyard.

Let me see. [takes the skull] Alas, poor Yorick! I knew him, Horatio, a fellow of infinite jest, of most excellent fancy. He hath borne me on his back a thousand times, and now, how abhorred in my imagination it is! My gorge rises at it. Here hung those lips that I have kissed I know not how oft. Where be your gibes now? Your gambols? Your songs? Your flashes of merriment that were wont to set the table on a roar?

My next class is Human Physiology. First, the professor wheels in the skeleton of a short woman. Then he begins to pass around actual femurs and an actual human skull. I gently run my fingertips over the surface between the ocular cavities where shining eyes once saw. And then the professor had us put on gloves and tenderly handed me an actual human brain. It was shocking—simultaneously lighter and heavier in my palms than I could have imagined.

An entire life happened here. Every memory, every dream, every joy and grief, every sight and sound and smell and taste and touch, every idea, every day, every laugh and fear and hope, from the moment of birth until the bell of death, had been housed in what I held in my hands. A soul once perched in the mortal boughs of these branches and sang.

Who were you? Where did you come from? Where did you go?

I stumbled lab to library, dormitory to dinner hall. People were everywhere, laughing and fighting and making out. What are we? And then here, to sit on a tombstone with an actual name and date. Above me a red oak tree. But there is no red that is as red as blood.

Red Brain: Red Games

Gay Lynch

Red manifests in amygdala and Mars. Over slow summers, furious flashpoints, fast fires. Scrubs ignite. Flames rampage right to the sea. One billion Australian animals burnt. Seven hot global seas: ours on record. Rivers rise, houses capsize; hard to measure on an MRI.

Human brains, heavy with clever dread, weigh down newborns until one year hence, set on their feet, they snatch and jerk their own weight, balance on spine, shoulder, toes and perambulate forward for another decade, before inhaling newsbytes.

Amygdala alerts us, beware the bear, Krasny, Russian-red, hot beauty, latent heat and reckoning. Like Red Guards; worker blood, Rus people, Ruthenia. Red October, Romanov red. Soviet, Rubra.

Putin, puttin' a toe 'cross a red line, to where nightingales call out sweet, ready to die, despite or because of a red button. On these terms, so-called West ready to let 'em. Whose book of revelations, foreshadows this fuckening?

Who engorges on the colour red? Military money multiplies? Red-ragged by industrial complexes, red-faced men playing with morte. Raise your hand if you're in. End game. Exchange your queens.

Boomer-fuel sky high, real-estate through the roof; XYZ, Alpha no stable shelter, just doof. Like Jesus, who survived Herodes Magnus's census and sword. Unlike people smashed in Mariupol, fleeing beneath a blood moon.

Amygdala, red hot—Covid alarm goes off. Even asymptomatic brains shrink up to 2%. Bad weather precipitated by Donald, Joe, Scomo, Vlado, these hungry, thieving red foxes. Red-bum monkey allure, not ovulatory, phallocentric fear of power lost.

Do you believe greed pees blood or that lies light up your arse, explode your brain, dilute good red, combust over patriarchal curses, that wrathful horsemen trample all the hope, of getting out of this one?

Image 26

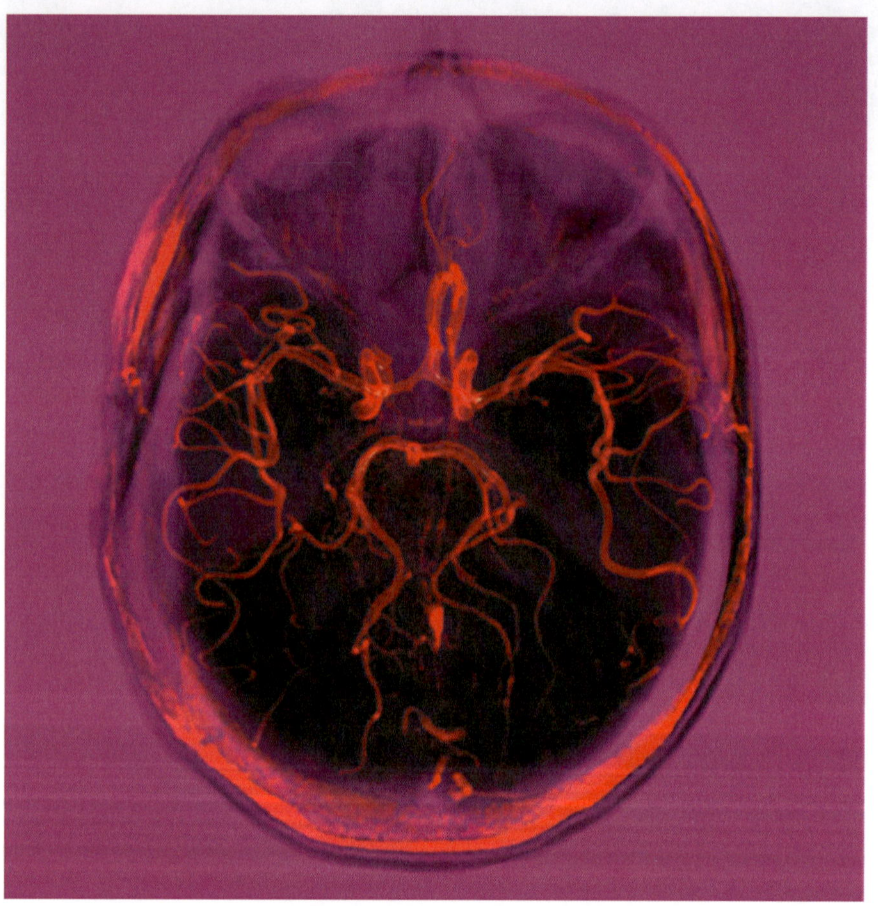

100

Boundary Lines

Rebekah Clarkson

Her eyes are perfectly symmetrical, black and small, like polished stones. I won't meet her gaze—resolved as it might be—though I know she wants this. Beckoning with her chin, boring through me. She wants to speak to me and this is the only way: quick shot with her eyes, imperceptible shake of her head: No more, she will want to say. Desire slices through the wind, skates over the brittle grass between us. I won't look into her eyes. Look at me, she implores, look at me. But I won't.

I stare at her leather boots, laced tight, peeping from her long skirt, hemmed in dust from her walk across the paddock. I imagine unthreading those laces, lifting her calf to rest on my knee, pulling the boots up and off, her naked foot, and then the other. The thought of her feet in my hands catches the back of my neck like a current, shimmies down my spine, electric. I close my eyes for a beat and travel her body, secretly in my mind's eye, up her legs, her soft white thighs, closer, closer, her stomach, hips, up, up.

I open my eyes, her face a blur in my periphery, the sun lighting up her hair. Her lips thin, wide, turned upwards, so slight—if you covered her eyes you would think her smiling, but if you covered her mouth, you would be surprised by how stern. Her eyes and mouth are in juxtaposition, so she is hard to read.

But I can read her. I know what her mouth tastes like.

Her husband is here, his hand firm on her shoulder. His fingers thick and clammy and I know this because she's told me: her skin crawls with his touch, moments after he moves away.

His lips are pink and full, closed, framed by a close-cropped beard and moustache.

He wants to talk about the fences. And so I wait.

Not Easy to Die

Julia Prendergast

I wander the street near work, looking for something to buy you.

I stop in for Pho because it will satisfy thirst and hunger and sweat-out a mild hangover, adding extra chilli and Thai basil because it will help me decide if I can see the year out in this lobotomising job.

I lost sight of what I wanted. I'm not sure I can turn it around.

I shouldn't have thrown the plate …

As I shred the plum-coloured basil, I notice the soup man, hovering, fingers knotted together.

Holy basil, ah, he says, in meditative singsong.

Shuffling toward the counter, I spy the beautiful plants—miniatures, all different species, arranged in tiny painted pots on a wrought-iron stand near the register.

Do you make these? I say, looking at his childlike fingers. *So beautiful*, I add.

Holding the shiny black pot, I see my fingers reflected, running my thumb along the spear-shaped leaves—purplish and smooth, slightly transparent, fine red veins exposed.

I hand the pot to the plant man. *I'll take this, please?* I say. *And the soup.*

He holds the plant at eye-height: *Not easy to die, this one*, he says.

Perfect, I say.

Image 27

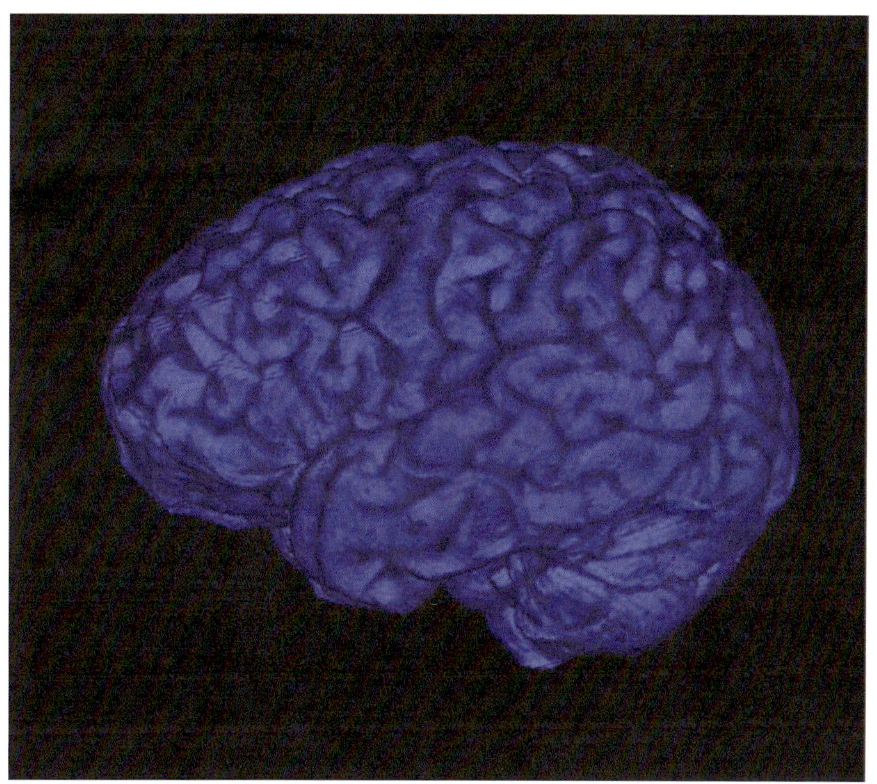

Untitled

Graeme Harper

First brain, you say, because you have five? What then are the colours of your others? I imagine a planet bright all the time. A candy world. But what colours do you dream? And how does one brain relate to the other? Had I known we'd discover you deep there in the sand, I'd have prepared some welcome. And only in your dying breath did I see what blue thoughts you had, what red feelings you wished, what green beliefs you sought to share. Up there, dark, starry, perhaps there are others. Like you. Like us. Like another. Blue-brained, green-brained, together, sharing colours, in brains, hearts perhaps. Coloured hearts, each one having many, many and one. The colours of connection. Blue brain, yes, and others, many coloured, more thoughts, more time even. How human this all might be.

Brain

Frank T. Simes

Electric blue brain
with your fiery weaves,
empire of the body,

will you not disavow
the heart's hunger
to bridge the yawning

gulf, to be taught
gently to waltz over
the fen as the music

transforms into rain,
to not gild memory's pain
with soulless dissection,

for raw feelings need
no thought, nor moral
explanation?

Image 28

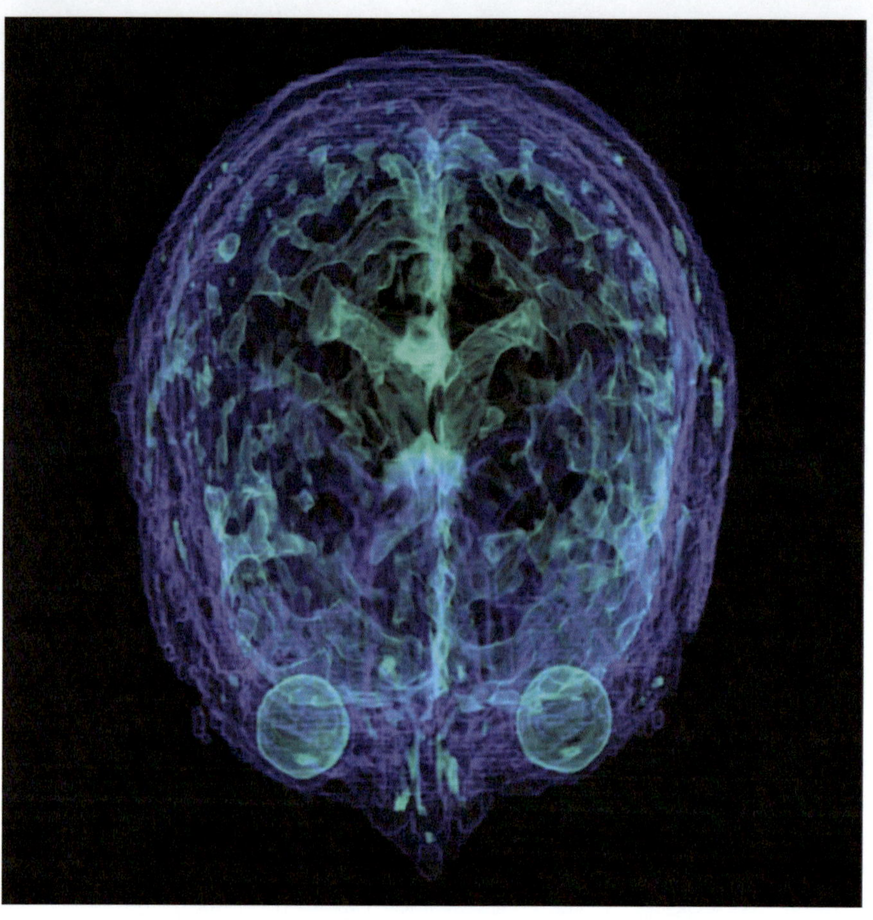

Where the Tree Begins

Rose Lucas

in the electric
        blue of brain and
cord   and artery
                where quiet communities   bustle

rhizomes of   reaching
    synapse
            to synapse   and chasing
through flickering filaments

like an expanse of night city watched
from a plane's small window
        its territory of what is seen and what
is not

an incipience of energy   studded
on velvet black—
        in the eye of this azure field
a tree

might begin to
        unfold   coiled
possibilities of green   hidden
encodings   of stem and leaf and

blossom   delivered   into sunlight
        that airy space   a trepanation
of light   and breathing
a clot of roots—

the wonder of what flares
                    and sparks
and vanishes
            swallowed   in the crook of darkness

Twinklewinkalling/Aseptic Perception

Dominique Hecq

Lilac and jasmine in the air. Indigo. Violet light of a grave-lit moon. Black motes swirl in iridescent blue. Whirl, twirl and settle on your name. Jay—from the Latin for Gaea. You always wanted to fly, but have been grounded a lifetime. God knows I tried to change the script. I look for all twinklewinkalling gone. A Rorschach is what you left. Cold blade lips. A palimpsest of bruises. Vacated are your emerald eyes. Winter is in your mouthless mouth. I imagine your dreams, realities, nightmares, suffocations. Once you told me in your waking life you flew. Despite the grounding. How you feared falling off bridges. It was vertigo and agoraphobia took your breath away. No angel wings here, though they say they are always blue. How many times can you die? I zero in on the black hole of the question mark. No breath. Your throat, cinereous grey, is lined with needles. A thimbleful of bluish light. A chrysalis. Cells twitch, uncurl, zizz out. Fizz beyond imaging, beyond the apocalypse of bloods and tissues, beyond the wildest imaginings. A noose dangles, lonely; motes whirling in the luminescence of day—a drama you staged in air and liquid desire for yourself only.

I extinguish those go-get eyes. Welcome a winged victory. I want to believe there is an absence of hate love in this pandemonium. This blue pestilence. This soaked paper aeroplane with a broken wing grounded for all eternity next to the angel of history. They macerate in octopus ink, the plane and the angel. Sombre tones seep through the monochromatic scheme only a maniac could have devised. A paranoiac godlet from IMAGING, say something spawned by Les Chants de Maldoror, a reverie that moves associatively and appositionally to cover and uncover the most extravagant images and proclamations of abjection. Say it! Declare imminent hostilities. Grill some brains with mashed sardines and anchovies. Grill us, squashed as we are in this corset you call a room when we are meant to explore the limits of painting. Assassinate poetry. Resurrect prose. Only to describe, define and affirm the visible. Portray. No. Poetic physiology is not the physiology of living creatures, though minds unmind after blasted hearts. Nothing is d'après nature. Eat that nothing mixed with blitzed green chilli, coriander, lime juice, olive oil and absinth. You'll see what I destroyed. Taste what I mean.

Image 29

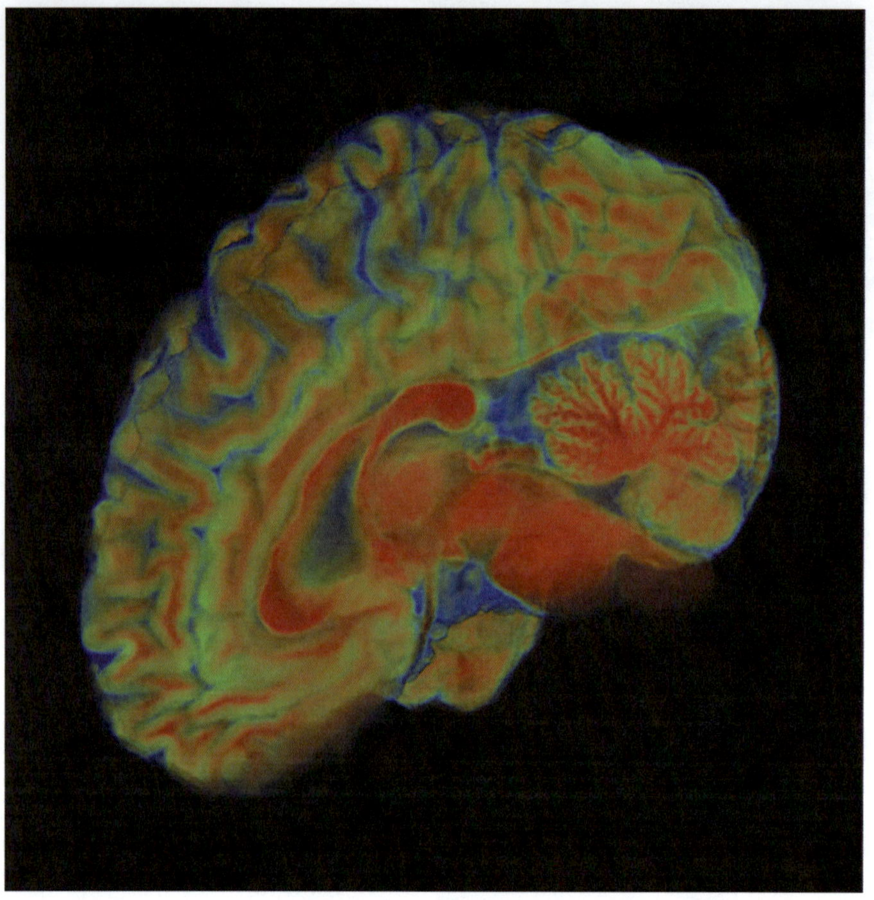

The Weight of Thought

Ravi Shankar

Atop the snow-tinged massif of Monte Rosa,
some 9,000 feet above sea level, there's a lab
named for Angelo Mosso, a 19th-century Italian
physiologist who invented a machine based
on a simple premise: all brains need more
blood the harder they work; he felt it possible
to measure the rate, even map it on the page,
like a topographer using elevation contour
lines to show the depth of the ocean bottom,
the height and steepness of mountain ranges.

Non parlo italiano but I do know the Nebbiolo
grape and Marcello Mastroianni taking a dip
in the Trevi Fountain in Fellini's La Dolce Vita
and I know Satan, still buried up to his waist
and bat-wings from the impact of his comet
plummet to the lowest circle of hell in Dante's
description from the last Canto of the Inferno.
If he was truly once as beautiful as he is ugly now,
when he raised his brows against his Maker,
well is it said that from him proceeds all grieving.

I'd like to keep you on my desk like a chunk
of red coral for a paperweight. You would feel
so smooth, cool and tonic against my forehead.
When we die, rather than float from our bodies
to the Bardo, or getting ferried off to Limbo,
we each just shrink into the superdense gem-
stone essence of our lives, our every choice
crystallised as inclusions. Then we live out
our afterlives on display in an intergalactic fossil
and mineral shop at the dusty edge of time.

Utter the mantra of pons and medulla, cerebrum
and occipital lobe, cingulate cortices and fossa.
Remove the slow linear drifts prior to the fast
Fourier transform, but don't smooth out the data.
Serve it up in its raw form, neuronal stimulation
uncoupled from other signals such as respiration.
Āścarya in Sanskrit means miraculous; the name
Monte Rosa comes from an Aostian patois word
roëse, or 'glacier'. Each mark that presses down
from behind my eyes shapes a singular luminosity.

The Fire Inside Your Head

Michael Salcman

Here lies consciousness in the brain stem, its power plant
of energetic fibres travelling up towards the corpus callosum,
this picture captured in the moment of wakefulness spread
to both the right and left brains, just above the blushing red
fingerprint of a small guided missile computer or tree
(your cerebellum) tilted up from its basement, and everywhere
spent energy washed in the blue sulci between the red-green
forests of curving cortex, where crystalline fluid bathes
the brain clean of exfoliated toxins and metabolic spillage.

On our left, the heavy frontal lobe looks planted, facing down
as if the head's engaged in an acrobatic flip, its owner
tumbling on a floor mat or reaching for the lowermost bar
in a qualifying gymnastic stunt. Or else this head is bent
to a research bench or at a writer's desk in a concentrated instant
of thought worrying over an equation or rhythmic sentence.
We can never know whose brain this is or what our alternate self
is doing but share in its creaturely pride, having painted the scan
with colourful flames to highlight our machine's mysterious activity.

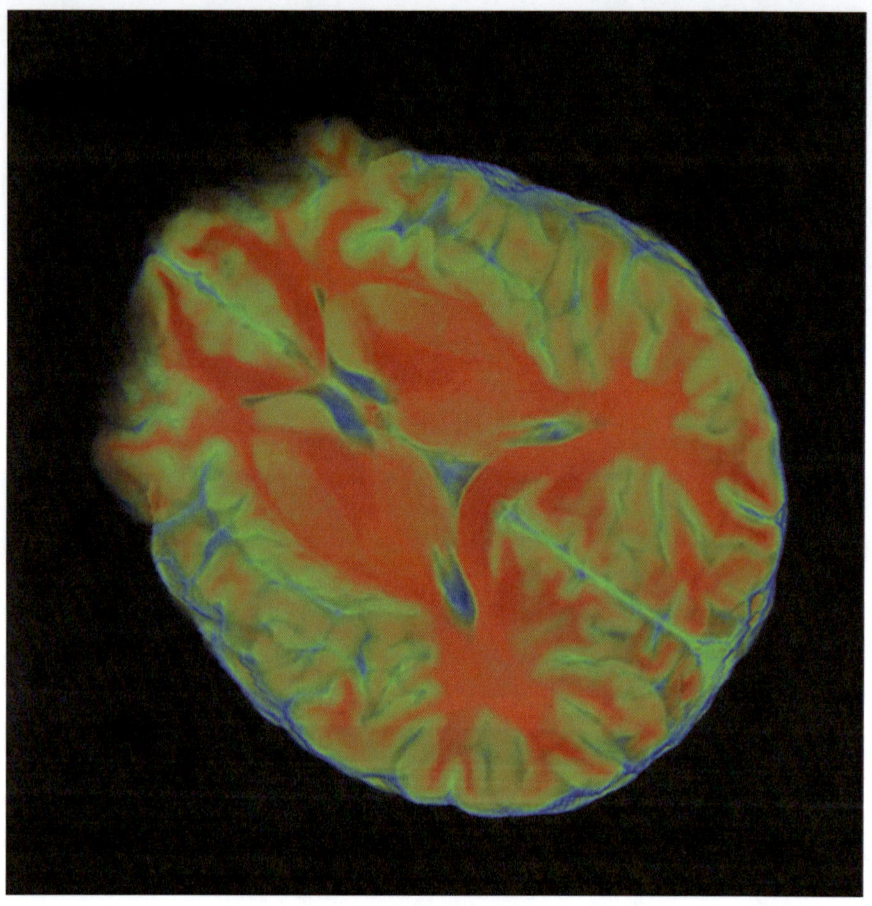

Blue

Deedle Rodriguez-Tomlinson

I see unbloomed blue iris … beautiful blue iris like the ones I saw at a flower shop on Second Avenue near my apartment years ago … so many years ago yes, blue iris tips wrapped in orange tissue paper … the ones he promised to get me he promised you know because of what he did the night before but he got blue-dyed daisies instead at the corner bodega because that was all they had that was all they had he said when he handed them to me here these are for you I'm sorry about last night okay I wanted to get you blue iris but there weren't no blue iris today okay honey no blue iris but that's okay right honey what what you don't like 'em tell me hey what's with the long face c'mon gimme a break yeah yeah I know you wanted the ones up the street in that fancy flower shop but come on honey the price it's outrageous look you know I don't have the money be happy I took the time to get these so take the goddamn flowers okay they're blue flowers same difference take the flowers honey I said take 'em before I grab 'em and throw 'em in the garbage you want that huh is that what you want is that what you want 'cause I'm going to do it god help me I'll do it 'cause you don't deserve flowers you don't deserve me and you should be happy someone loves you cause no one else will. Now put the damn flowers in water and get dinner ready I'm starvin' over here and—what what you're cryin' again?! Look I said I'm SORRY okay—now can I have some dinner PUH-LEASE!!! Look I asked you nice okay I said STOP CRYINGGGGG look at you blubbering you disgust me! Okay—THAT'S IT! Gimme those damn flowers I said GIVE IT TO ME!!! NO? Okay outta the way—Boom!—down the garbage they go GOODBYE to no good piece o' garbages. There—no more flowers no problemo so no more cryin' okay awright okay you know what forget about it forget dinner forget I even came home. I'm going down to The Marlin. You better be done cryin' by the time I get back. Ungrateful bitch.

Yes. That's what I see—blue iris tips in orange tissue paper.

For the (Fossil) Record

Deb Wain

My mind is full of the ancient, segmented bodies of trilobites
in a way that it hasn't been for years—their various forms, their
parts and patterns. Not since my undergrad in environmental
science and Palaeo101, not since the boyfriend who majored
in studies of fossils and soils, pursuing Earth Science which I
mocked by only ever referring to it as 'dirt studies' or 'playing
in the mud'. I pushed away, maintained a stridently independent
identity, ensured survival. I walked away, towards a major in
things-still-living and a minor in linguistics. I secretly found the
long-dead things fascinating and now those hardy little world's-
first-arthropods have invaded my brain. Their many pairs of
legs scurry around my head, exoskeletons clicking against any
hard surfaces; their many pairs of lungs steal the oxygen of my
thoughts. Tri-lobe-ite: three lobes, but not in the way you might
think, not head to tail, not cephalon, thorax, pygidium. No,
they're named for their central axis, the two pleura either side, a
lateral movement. My brain is supposed to have four lobes and it
makes me wonder which one they've consumed being spawned
at the advent of predation, well-adapted to withstand adversity,
resilient.

They're not actually extinct. They're living, alive, a life in all
their glorious diversity in the sea of my imaginings, swimming
through cerebrospinal fluid as easily as the ocean, burrowing
into grey matter like silken sediment.

Image 31

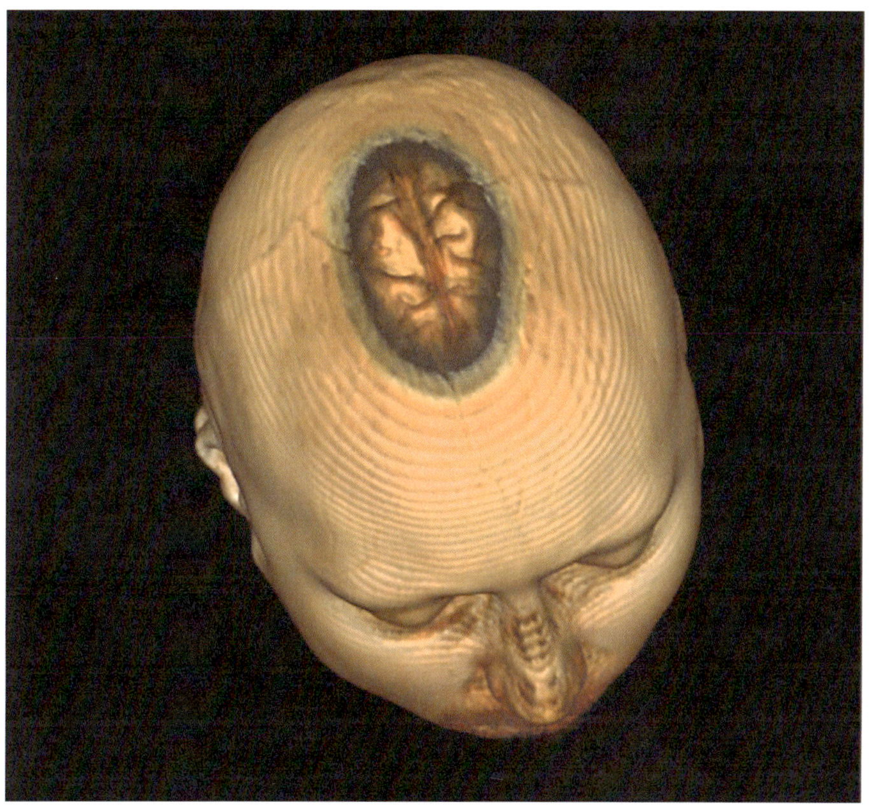

Opus 23

Tim Tomlinson

In the back story there's hair. Hair and a scalp. But it's just a rug, really, thrown over a trap door. In the back story, there's a skull, intact. A skull in full. A skull was something to get out of, which he managed to do quite well most Thursdays. There's a lull in his skull. Isthmus be his lucky day. In the back story there's a story. Got a good reason for taking the easy way out. I think a no I mean a yes. Uh-oh, here come the abstractions. In Opus 23, Schoenberg … oh, fuck it. One side looks at the other side. They're the same. Between thought and expression, the middle way, the three uses of a knife. The pope died and everything was cancelled. And you know what? Amma git me a hammer. If you could read my mind, oh, what a tail my thoughts would smell. Comes a time when you're drifting too far from the whore. I want a girl just like the girl, etc. Did I tell you that my bed's on fire? So let us go then, you and I, through that aforementioned trap door (cueing us up some Amboy Dukes). Oh, big nuthin'. I got two bottles, one liver, and nine counties to cross before sun-up. You with me? Welcome to my vicious campfire. Hey, true fact: Ringo is Mr Tambourine Man. The faster you go, the rounder I get. Ted Devil takes a free ride, heaven never treats you like yourself, and, I mean, who knows where the time goes? See, I got this rig that runs on memory. I remember this one time, long before the stars were torn down—you might've heard about it except you weren't even born yet, were you? So let me tell you what: we're gonna fuck this sleep mode, fuck the adagio, cause easy's getting harder every day. In fact I wouldn't be surprised, now that I think of it … ah shit—hold on, it's Amazon Goddamn packages).

Now where was I?

Pagudpud

Deedle Rodriguez-Tomlinson

When I am lost
in thought
find me.

Peel back the
top of my head
and find me

back in a dream
I had last night
of being in

water, in a
boat on water
just before a storm

and then recalling
something a
Hawaiian poet

said:
Ola i ka Wai—
Water is life.

Find me back in
2015, standing on the
edge of the northernmost

tip of the Philippines,
on the shores of
Pagudpud in Ilocos Norte.

Seen from outer
space, the Philippines
is a dog lying

on its side. I imagine
I am standing on its
head. I bury

my toes in the
wet sand, waves
around me breaking

then receding. My
father is watching from
a van behind me.

Even now my father
watches, but from
a higher place.

Spirits, they say,
use water to speak.
My father lives

in dreams, his
voice somewhere
above the

hiss and sizzle
of sea foam. If I
listen close enough

I hear him.

Image 32

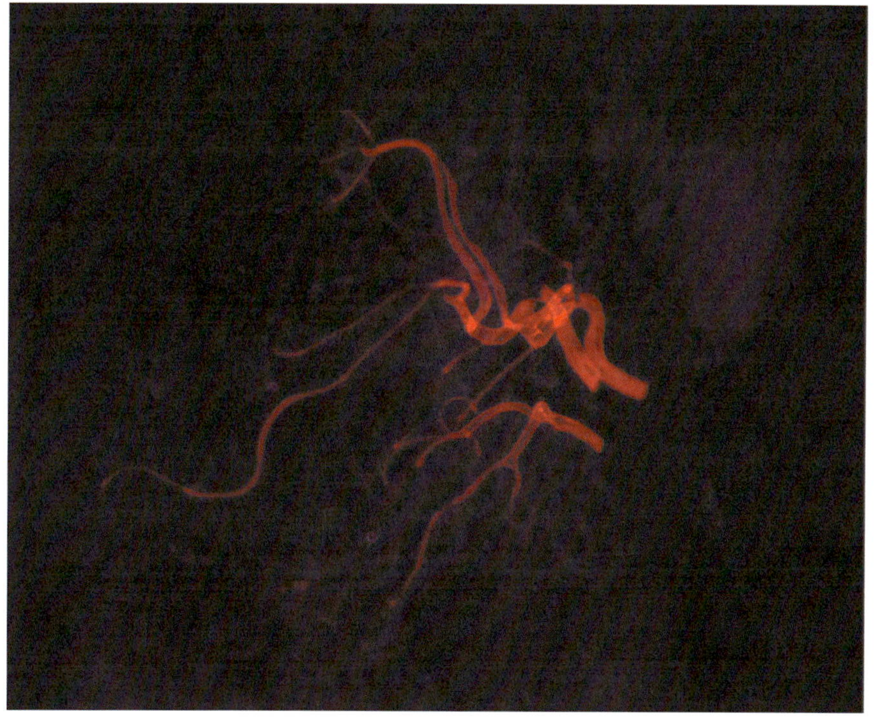

Sea-Song

Julia Prendergast

I say: *Let's make our own way, today.*
Perhaps I add the word *separately.*
I want to stretch my arm out of the car window, blast the sea-song on repeat, belt the chorus at the top of my voice—I want to sing it on loop like a clawing memory, spinning my wrist and curling my fingers to the instrumental riff—

—as if I'm back there, night-dancing in sea-licked air, the spindly-soft grass against my calves, my skin seething and drawing in on itself, sweaty salt-tongued-madness.
Charybdis was a sea monster—later rationalised as a whirlpool. Before she displeased Zeus, she was a nymph.

Fuck this thinking. I merely suggested that we part, for a day.
Your eye, you say.
The blood vessels in my eye have burst—smatter-shot in all directions and spark-lit like fine red kelp under my eyeball's glassy pane—bristling beneath your torchlight gaze.
It's nothing, I say. *A trapped bruise. In the eye the blood has nowhere to go.*
I don't care for your displeasure.
I turn away—I can't see you, anyway—my pulverised eyeball thrashing with underwater kelp snakes. Coiled clusterfucking inversion … There is nothing shiny, here.
Of course, Charybdis exploded water. There is only so long we can suck it in and hold it there.
I want to sing the sea-song over and over, again, until I'm beneath the surface and what never happened feels real—until you're here with me, in the cool-heat of underwater blood snakes.
Let me give in and be asked nothing in return.
Let this snakeblood longing settle into my memory-reel like a long exhale, like the relentlessly sighing sea. As if my memory is a form of snakeskin.

Castle

Paul Hetherington

Thought is a branching worm,
riddling as it constructs, making
the mind an impenetrable castle.
You visit after many years and the
worm is writhing in its rooms—
back and forth, like some ancient
Lernaean Hydra. You stand away
from its miasma, holding your
map in front of you, determined to
find a carpeted hall you remember.
The Hydra eyes you as you climb
the steps and, when you come to
a courtyard, it stands before you
refuting every way forward, like
a punctilious philosopher. You
know that it's primarily made
of language, but there are dark
associations you can't read; and
scenes you won't interpret. Later,
you'll try to describe its shape but,
by then, nothing will be clear—
though you made it inside and
found fires burning; though you
read books in a vast library. You
recall being taken to a high attic,
beginning to write as the Hydra
climbed through your mouth.

Image 33

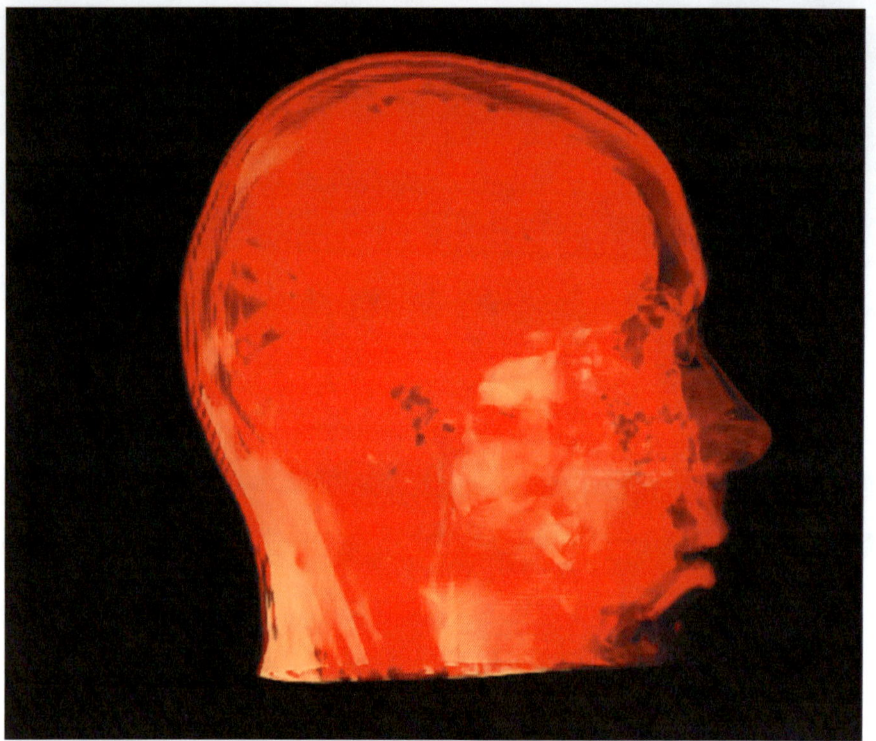

Punishment

Shady Cosgrove

Vinny's your conscience and I'm your imagination. We climb over each other inside your brain, up the monkey bars, circling on the tire swing until we throw up. We've been drinking again and curfews are in place—but fuck that dog-world-cage. The takeaway shops across the road have been dead for months, and the petrol station's locked up. They call this an apocalypse but I'm hoping that's just spin for protesters who wanna raid supermarkets. Vinny says bricks are too heavy, and I agree—but maybe we're complacent. We found someone's stash buried in the cricket pitch—a case of wine, big hunks of cheese—and we're working our way through another bottle of red. I'm giggling. Shh, Vinny says. He's hanging off the slide, eyes caught on the horizon of your frontal lobe. He's worried you're going to find us, worried you and your police officer monkeys are going to kick us out. Yeah, probably, I shrug—but everyone knows you're an arsehole and I'm the one you'll come for first.

Taken/Not Taken

Alan McMonagle

What I notice is the shuteye. These nights I crave some shuteye and at the same dread bedtime because I know sleep won't come easy, if at all. Friday night, not long into the new year, and there's a Bowie celebration that gets me past the midnight hour. Classic clips. Vintage footage. Songs. I pour glasses of red and affect a singalong. Blue, blue, electric blue, that's the colour of my room. Documentary over, I scroll channels and suggest a late film to my partner. Too late, she's already bedbound, sleeping pretty. I find something passable, a so-so comedy set at a writers' retreat somewhere in rural England. Nearing three, don't care how the flick ends, and I'm scrambling to cue up something else. Comedy. Quiz show. Nature trails. Where is that train journey that lasts for thirty-six hours? Nothing doing and besides I'm getting restless. Twitching in the chair. I pace circles round the sitting room, the kitchen. Need some air. Open the patio door and offer my helter-skelter self to the four am moon. Why not go a little further? Jacket on and take to empty street. Out onto the main road, down the hill, past the sleeping hotel, pace circles round the roundabout, continue to the end of the road. Home again and try to sit. Nothing doing. Still twitchy. Stand at the breakfast bar and start again into the Jonathan Coe novel The House of Sleep. A main character hasn't slept in fourteen years. He's a film reviewer and early in the book he attends a week-long film festival, watches without sleep 134 films. This miracle of artistic endurance lands him an entry in the Guinness Book of Records. Impressed, I entertain the notion of having a go at outdoing this fictional feat. If nothing else it will while away future hours as I line up the 135 films I will watch, paying particular attention to the final, record-breaking title. 6 am. Move the chair in front of the tv. Sit into it, grip the arms, not so twitchy now, grateful for fleeting reprieve. What to watch, what to watch? Remember the Marilyn Monroe documentary I've recently recorded. Who do you belong to? Marilyn is asked. I belong to fear, she says. Fear of being taken, of not being taken.

Image 34

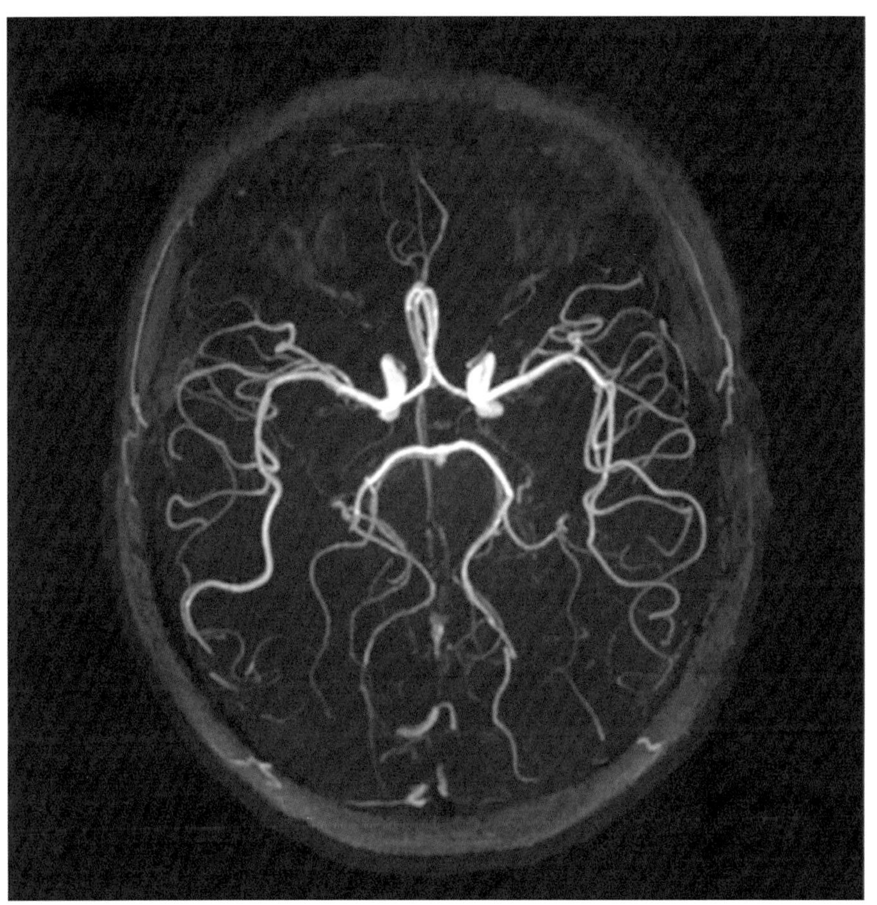

Untitled

Barrie Sherwood

When I asked for a picture of you,
this isn't what I had in mind.
I'd thought you'd send a winter scene, bundled in your coat,
or at some landmark, smiling over your shoulder.
I almost hoped for your bikini, though I could hear you say,
My tummy … on film … no way.
Now I'm staring at this cross-section of your brain,
its activity, apparently, mapped in white lines.
I've put it up on my wall, I sit gazing long into the night.
(They can be coaxed, the images in black-and-white.)
They spiral from the centre like cursive
written by a stick pulled from the campfire.
They fizz, these tracers, to the furthest limit,
ricochet against cranial walls and come corkscrewing back.
Fuzz of friction. Arabesque of lightning.
(Can there really be laws to explain each curve?)
Is seeing penetration? Does desire cast its own light?
I'm not writing for an explanation, the anatomy or the chemistry.
What I want to know is what was in your mind's eye
at the moment this was taken.
Is this a picture of contentment? Is this fear? Laughter?
Passion? Your grocery list? Your holiday in Thailand?
A new bicycle? A pear tree? Climax? Or just a sneeze?
Is it yearning? Is it me?
I'm sorry, it's been so long I'm hoping for traces of myself,
I want to see my hands, your lips, our feet,
the frisson, the tremor, the release.
I should know better. It's only more code,
white lines against the black. I have to interpret,
describe, a web of meaning, a web of signs.
I need a drink. I get up from my chair …

But see, there! Just when I looked away—
how alive—how kinetic!
Fleeting into every corner, a ferret of light.
It wants to break out, complete the circuit, find a way.
I'll bet your eyes were open when this was taken.
I'll bet your eyes were shining.

Carol Burnett

Nicola Redhouse

Carol Burnett
P something; something P—
I'm pretty sure it's on Tuesday—
reading this book called
Murakami writes about it
what is R into at the moment?
said I would get back to her
The family legend of when
it's music from Beethoven;
Murakami?
An Italian place, served cold meats.
Stood on a pigeon!
My grandmother forgot
Walk down Streetview and
I'm pretty sure I've told you this but—
La Paloma—
It was bloody Spanish!
that American comedian's name
Girl in my art class; had depression.
Once in my twenties a friend—
You might recognise it.
For three whole weeks—
the only story I remember well.
Then, in the middle of the night—
like a deflated basketball
Or was she Canadian?
But it survived!
Woke my grandfather to exclaim
I think it was a pigeon?
Carol Burnett!

Image 35

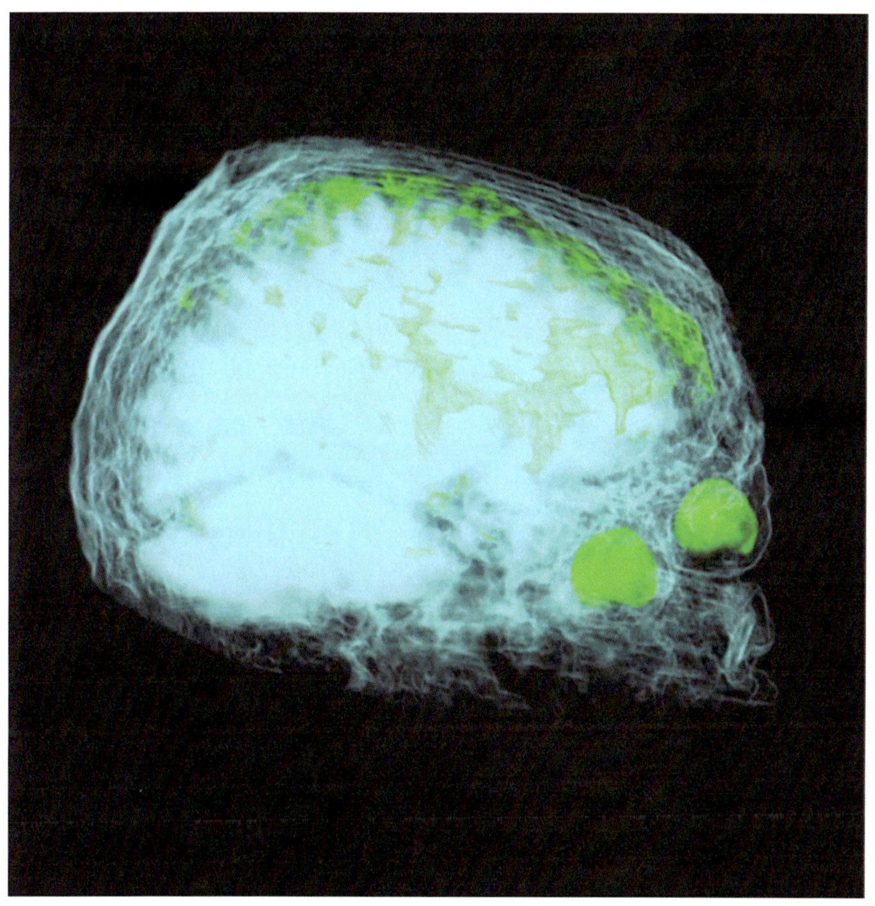

Aqua Profonda

Dominique Hecq

When I wake, I see not the sky's artistry shooting through time in
a swarm of equinoctial colours pinking the dawn, your radiant face,
eyelids enfolding teal eyes and twilight, but your body moored to
the edge of aquamarine, turquoise, peacock blue

    Taste, smell, hear, touch the air looping and whirling
    desire drowning the night
        heartbeat a swell between us
           after a long-held breath

    Blueberries, aniseed, rebetiko, emerald blue spangles
        between water and sky
           seagulls pecking meringue clouds
             the bridge between us dissolving

I forget I am coming
    to, kneading rock into Eros
        shapes on the shore

        O deark dear K amid the glow of day break
          skull a blank page I name aqua profonda

And, yes! I rise from Botticelli's shell as you scallop words like lip,
ear, wing and brush philtrum, columella, cantus in the mist.

Notes: There is a now famous 'AQUA PROFONDA' sign at the Fitzroy
Swimming Pool in Melbourne. This 1954 sign is listed on the heritage register
for its social significance due to its association with Australia's post-war migration
program. It was originally hand-painted as an initiative of the pool manager who
was constantly rescuing migrant children from the deep end of the pool.

The sign also achieved iconic status when it appeared in Helen Garner's 1977
novel *Monkey Grip* and the subsequent film. Playwright Hannie Rayson also
created a play named *Aqua Profonda* in collaboration with students from North
Fitzroy Primary School in the late nineties.

'O deark dear K amid the glow of day break' is a twist on a line from Milton's
'Samson Agonistes'.

Ghost Ship

Katrina Finlayson

We don't know much about the old white and blue hotel, just that it's favoured by sea captains. An uncanny vertigo filled my body the minute we landed at the island airport, and I exhale as we drive the rental car into the small carpark. I'm unbalanced and nauseous.

On the side of the building, this poem, in typewriter-style letters:

> Three flag-swept days.
> Ships monstrous and transitory.
> Heroes I could not captain.

Up wooden stairs, a narrow hallway leads us to our own sea captain cabin. I open a whining wooden sash window to let in salt air from the harbour at the bottom of the street.

Our travels here are our own kind of Odyssey. Looking back, I think we knew this could be our last holiday together, that the shadow following was getting closer. We ran towards the raw comfort of art.

After many Warhols and Ai Wei Wei works at a big waterfall-fronted gallery in Melbourne, we have come here, to sea-cradled Hobart, to visit a rich evil villain's lair, riding windswept at the bow of a boat across black water, to a museum of sex and death.

Deep underground in ominous caverns, we visit an Egyptian tomb artwork in a tiny room, and vertigo almost pushes me into inky water surrounding a stone slab path. I crawl, hands and knees, back to the door, and our laughter silences fear.

The next day, we drive to the top of a mountain. Icy wind and rain arrive with us. We peer out from anoraks at fog creeping across mossy rocks and walking trails. City and sea lost somewhere far below. Driving cautiously back down the narrow winding road, we listen to the Velvet Underground sing about a perfect day.

On the last night, we visit a sea-themed restaurant. We share a foul-tasting cocktail from an oversized tankard shaped like a parrot. I look above your head to a painting of a shipwreck.

Nostalgia is dangerous when you're adrift in rough seas. Now I'm a lone sea captain, tied to the mast of a ghost ship as luminescent green mists swirl around me. My ears are plugged with wax against siren song, but I still feel creaking timbers and the sway and crash of enormous waves. Salt water in my blood. The wind and stars carry old sailor names. White knuckles hold tight to bright spots of memory. It's been three years since I last saw land.

Image 36

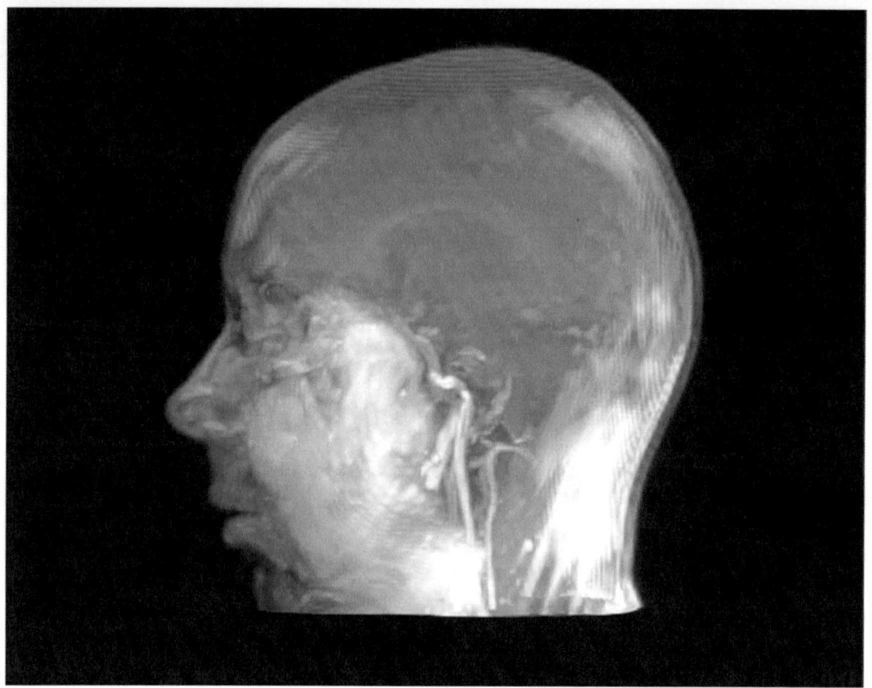

tunnelling

Quinn Eades

The body is a tunnel is tunnels is tunnelling where tunnelling is acrossness is never down or up because the body is all ways a tissue a tunnel net that goes in every in no direction.

By the time I am home from the hospital the rosehips are waiting to be harvested along my front fence the fig tree has lost its fruit and leaves the bats have left even the bold as fuck possum that trawls my fence line has disappeared.

When the bats were still here fig tree gobblers teeth shredders I met you. You messaged me on an app you had kind eyes a smile that reached them but the last man who messaged me on an app came to my home and I could not get him out for I can't tell you how long because decimation because digging in far enough to tear apart tunnels takes years takes an hour takes a body takes a no a no a no a no a no.

Before hospital I am laid out flat I am night sweats I am soaked sheets pyjamas changed five times in the night in the radiating pain in expulsion expulsion expulsion. I cannot speak I am unvoiced I am tunnelled in shivering foetal submerged in the violence of a body fighting what comes in unbidden, what we cannot get out.

You arrived with a packet of biscuits and we sat in my backyard and drank tea and I did not disappear. You were kind and gentle and when I drove you up to the station we kissed, awkwardly, at the red light.

At the hospital you are with me. Needles into tunnels drugs and fluids into veins scope through anus into colon tunnel hunting. What is here that should not be. What is the body fighting. How much more fluid can we lose how many more inflammatory markers can we gain which symptoms do we ignore how do we empty this bed.

A week later I am home the figs are gone you are still here. You are warm and gentle and handsome and we tunnel into each other in the aftermath and I do not I do not disappear. You are tunneler and tunnelled as am I. We hold each other with fists and forearms, with throats and mouths, spiralling in and through bodies, with love.

Overthinking

Dominic Symes

your kite's getting wet in this thunderstorm, mate
but hey, when it rattles—that's the key, the piece of string, the pitch:
white noise   if it's death by a thousand electric shocks you want
consider me scuffing my socks on the carpet as we speak
perhaps it's being phone-numberless in the unexplored country
finger protruding like ET's peering into a cave's dark depths   at least
this is where my mind goes   electricity   firing over synapses
we know more about the creatures at the bottom of the ocean
the ones with the single dangling modifier bringing death whose light
forever exceeds them   we know more about the anglerfish than this:
why moonlight symbolises romance, and not knowing, fear
knees trembling before a blackboard, Twombly shifting across its surface
like a cloud of chalk dust which finds its way into vacant nasal cavities
if not going in one ear and out the other   some resonant hum
I consider stars pin pricks in the mute black contact sheet of sky
attestations of love so urgent the pen goes through the page
as translucent as vulnerability   transparent   positively glowing
the ability to hold their stare as your partner's eyes
are burning a hole into you with the knowledge that they've known
all along

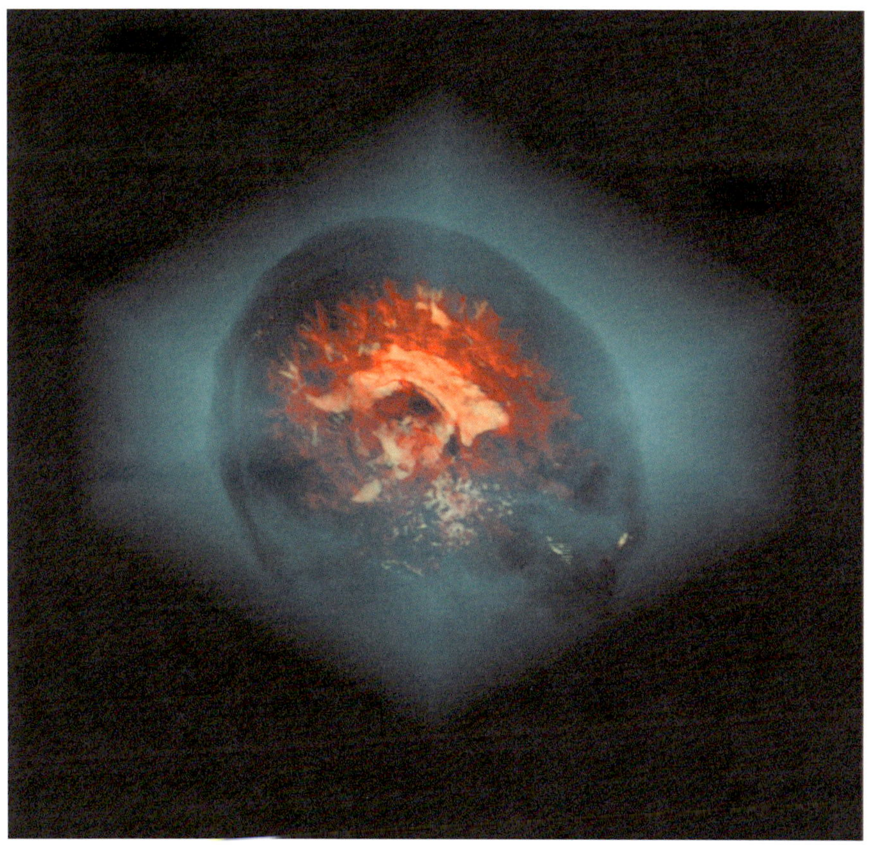

Slow Burn

Deb Wain

On the morning my sister, Libby, left it was already hot before breakfast and the Stilson's hayshed burnt down. It sometimes happens—hay bailed wet can spontaneously combust, burning slowly from the inside out.

The night before, she and Daddy had been shouting again. I held my hands over my ears, wanting very badly not to hear it all again. Good bloke … Look what you're wearing … What can you expect? After five days of the same words, I could almost mouth the next response along with them and I wished, in a way that I hadn't wished for years, that Mama was still here.

Libby didn't cry in front of Daddy, not after that first night when he found her curled on the couch with a cushion clutched to her chest like an old teddy bear. He hugged her and called her 'pet' until she said it was Mr Stilson.

'But he …' I watched Daddy's face change. 'But he's a good bloke. He never says nothin' crass to the barmaids.'

Libby pulled herself away. No words but she looked at Daddy hard.

'He never ducks out on his shout … He paid me when I helped get his hay in.'

When Libby found words, she flung them like fistfuls of nails—the big ones that Daddy used to build the chicken coop. She pulled her denim jacket tight across her chest and clomped upstairs still spitting nails down at Daddy who could only think to say, 'I won't have it, Liberty. You keep yourself nice, goddamnit.'

When she saw me sitting on the landing, Libby stopped. She put her hand on the top of my head and her voice went from hardware to toasted marshmallow—a bit crunchy on the outside but gooey underneath. 'Get back into bed, Beth. And never, never go to the Stilson farm, okay?'

For five days Libby went out drinking and came home to fight Daddy. She was burning slowly. But her hand was cool on my head as she smoothed my hair when she slipped into my room that hot, hot morning. She kissed my forehead and whispered, 'Never, never, okay?'

I nodded and she got up off the edge of my bed.

From the landing, I watched her hoist her backpack onto one shoulder and put something small into her pocket. She waved up to me then closed the door behind.

BBQ

Julia Prendergast

'Ungrateful cunts,' he says, pointing the tongs at his children, mostly grown now.

The plural use of the term lingers on his tongue—a very slight whistle, *cunce.*

He doesn't yell and this satisfies her as much as the positioning of the steaming tongs, moving from face to face.

Back in the day there may have been a hurled fork, a fist in a wall. Both and more.

Today it's remarkably calm and she wallows, sponging the dishes in too-hot water, the woodsmoke marinade steaming around the kitchen as if there were a roast in the oven, as if the dinner was in-promise, as if they were another family.

She's not much of a dishwasher but she takes the steel soap-pad, working deliberately, shifting the greasy charcoal from the hinge of the tongs, rubbing at older muck, too, until the tongs spring open, and the hinge screw is set swirling in a whirlpool of briny water.

Image 38

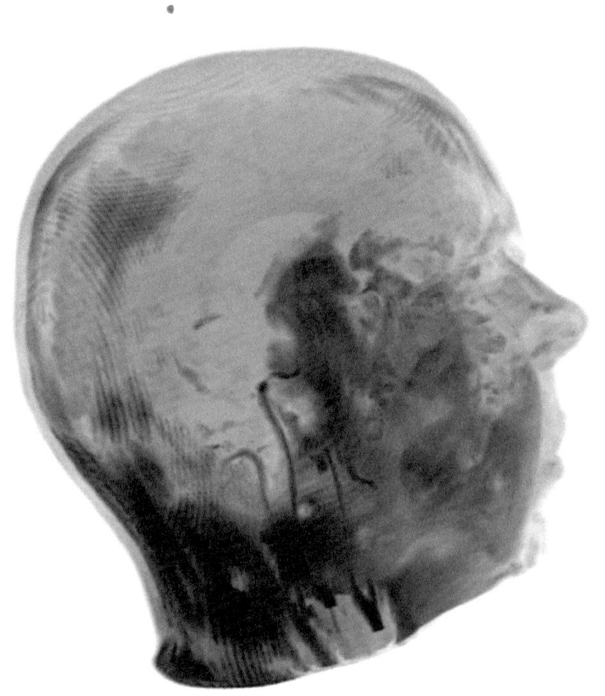

Time

Julia Prendergast

I look up at the wooden clockface.

I'm seated on the carpet with the other children. Our teacher moves the clock hands manually, explaining how time works—the big hand and the small hand, sometimes wide apart, at other times close.

Time is always moving in circles, she says. She looks out of the classroom window and I look, too. I can see the shifting gum leaves, like tongues.

Turning back to the clockface, she takes hold of the ticking hand, spinning it so it touches the small black lines around the edge of the circle. She passes me a real clock. *Listen*, she says. I hold my breath and listen to the clock's whispery heartbeats.

We barely notice the second hand, she says, *but it is there, nevertheless, moving time forward. Tick-tick-tick. Softly. Like a paintbrush*, she says, stealing another glance outside.

The gum leaves sweep the windowpane in soft gusts.

She shifts the big hand to a quarter past. *See how the small hand moves*, she says, *when I shift the big hand*. She looks at me directly— time is a circle song. I tap it on my knees with my paintbrush fingers, looking into her eyes.

She says: *When we get to half-past, it becomes something-TO rather than something-PAST—29 minutes-to and so on*, she adds.

I raise my hand. *Can it be half-to, I ask, instead of half-past?*

No, she says, and sighs.

But I wonder …

At half-to you are on the way to the hospital to have your stomach pumped and I'm sent to school to learn time.

Later, you are crisp and new-clean in your bed and you explain— not about the pumping, about why it was necessary.

I glare at you with a quarter-to eyes.

Years later, I understand.

At half-to my baby's head is crowning and I say: *Get out. Get out.* The midwife says, *Nearly there, Honey. Don't push. BREATHE.* I'm inside out—I can't tell the midwife that breathing is automatic, like a tick-tock song. I meant for *her* to get-out. *And him.* Both of them, with their half-past words.

Many years later, I understand more fully.

I'm sorry, I say, sighing.

You're dead so you can't answer—nevertheless I hear you and feel your breath against my cheek, half-to, your words marking time.

Quantify

Nicola Redhouse

I'm paying attention to affect felt at the edges—
this will be my raw data.
But lately grief or joy, surges of weightless emotion
overcome me unexpectedly, leaving
no edges at all—the way black holes are both empty and full;
I hear about a philosopher who became docile with factory work;
an astrophysicist who is chasing an interstellar light sail to find other life;
and there are no edges; surges of weightless emotion
as the body feels on a rollercoaster, falling
as dizziness has overcome me recently,
turning in my sleep, my mind left behind in the dream
hitting my skull, disobeying inertia—
and this anonymous image of personhood,
this brings the surge too; to reduce
a whole life to a grey scan—this is sad to me;
but equally sad is how, again at the edges, you see the ripples
like fingerprints
like something only capable of being made once.

Image 39

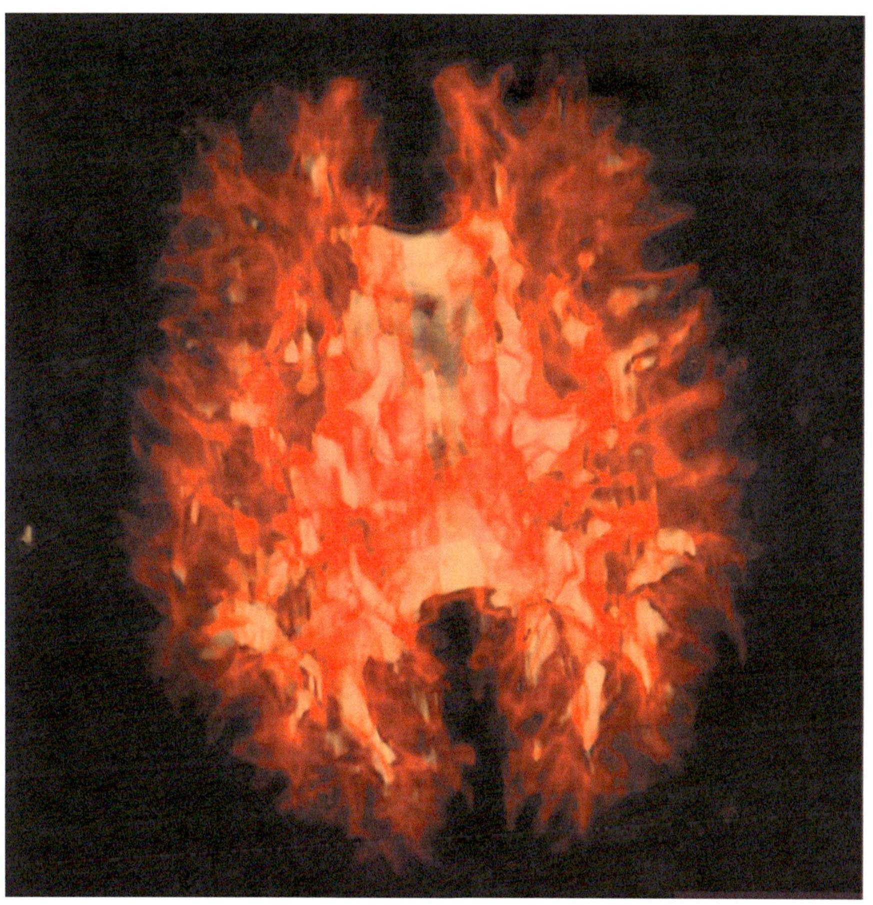

Firesky

Julia Prendergast

We run, weaving between ironbark gums in early evening. The amber sky is misleading.

It's cold. We talk despite our foggy breathlessness.

So suddenly dark, you say.

Don't start with the solstice. I know your spiel by heart—the shortest day of the year—the day of least daylight—the darkest day.

The sun as north as north can be, you say, as if we're stuck on loop, as if a year hasn't passed—the same fern gully and clay tracks, bark and moss layered like a juxtaposition.

Some places have festivals, you say. For death and rebirth.

I spit into the wildgrass.

Another month before we reach the peak of coldness, you add. *A month after solstice—*

Please shut up, I say.

You blast the running app, marking our lap time.

Shut it off, I beg.

I hate the running app. Who cares how our form compares to yesterday, ten minutes ago, last month?

Why are we so afraid of the dark, I *mean* the silence …

The next day we run early in the hope that things feel new. When we reach the deepest part of the gully, there's no sign of Melbourne suburbia. Wet earth, brittle bark, spiralling birdcall—time in yesterdays.

Clear dew shines purple in the morning light—spindly green leaves, glittering with purple crystals.

I stop, reaching toward it. Against my fingertips it's cold water.

You, too, have stopped.

No sign of rain, I say. *How is it possible … ? But don't answer. It's rhetorical.*

There's more energy escaping from the earth than being absorbed by the sun. Do you mean entropy is rhetorical?

Purple, I say.

My calf spasms. I shift to the closest tree. Our tree. I arch my underfoot against the exposed roots, glistening like sweaty thighs.

Six months ago, we lay here like teenagers, a blowjob in the summer dusk because what was the world coming to?

Treetops clawing like hungry fingers. Firesky.

I Don't Know What I'm Looking at

Patrick Allington

I came to understand that there was a creature living inside my wood heater, gazing out through the glass door. The creature was made of skull-sized pieces of red gum, maybe/maybe not sustainably produced. I say creature: it was just the head. Oh, technically, it occasionally had limbs made of kindling or newspaper shoved inside a toilet roll, the headlines of the previous day flashing by and instantly gone. But only the wood face endured. The face and then just the nose, as indestructible as a squid. And then came a new piece of red gum, a new face, a new nose.

I undertook to keep the creature alive. It was the right thing to do. The whole house, the street, the side of the hill, the suburb became smoke-infested. Too bad: I kept the creature breathing into spring and right through summer. Look at me, standing my ground against 45-degree afternoons, ignoring catastrophic fire danger warnings for the good of my creature and all creatures.

The neighbour's child went down with asthma. The family stood on my doorstep, mother, father and child, telling me that my smoke was to blame and begging me to do the right thing by the community. What about the right thing for the creature, for the earth?

The child heaved on an inhaler, maybe/maybe not for show. The father threatened to call an ambulance. I suspected he only did it because he thought the emergency department would have better air conditioning than they had at home. I myself had excellent air conditioning, which I ran at full blast at all times, what with the fire going. I invited the family to come inside, a touching gesture if I do say myself. I gave the child a glass of lemonade with ice and the man a gin and tonic and the woman a bottle of Cooper's Ale that I'd been saving for myself.

I sat the family before the creature and I asked them to look, to really look, and to understand, to really understand, that my fire must stay lit. The parents sweated and sipped their drinks and glanced at each other, some secret silent language. The child told me that he could see a dinosaur in the fire and that everybody knows that dinosaurs are giant frogs and that frogs can breathe underwater and that they can jump so high that in the old days people thought they were birds.

'Did you learn that in science, mate?' the boy's dad asked.

I looked for the frog, that day and the next and the next. I'm still looking. It's possible the boy is right. It's possible we're both right.

Image 40

Conclusion of Phase 4 Study Meeting all Primary Efficacy Endpoints Demonstrating that Purple Vaccine BLT1984 is 95% Effective Against 'Belief that the Universe is Made of Stories' (BUMOS)

Roanna Gonsalves

The Coalition of Experts & Governments (COEG) announced today that, after conducting the final efficacy analysis in their ongoing Phase 4 study, their vaccine candidate Purple Vaccine BLT1984 against 'Belief that the Universe is Made of Stories' (BUMOS) met all of the study's primary efficacy endpoints. Analysis of the data indicates vaccine efficacy rate of 95% ($p<0.0001$) in participants with and without prior BUMOS infection, measured from 7 days after the consumption of *Game Of Thrones* Season 3.

It was noted that contrary to the conclusions of previous studies, BUMOS affects not only females, but males, those who reject the gender binary, and some species of sea slug too. The observed efficacy in adults over 25 years of age was over 94%. A safe dosage range was unable to be determined for three subsets of this demographic: imitators of John Clarke, fans of Muriel Rukeyser, and writers of satirical fiction. However, these subsets were later deemed to be ineligible for this study on account of them comprising entirely of Low Net Worth Individuals.

Data demonstrate that the vaccine was well-tolerated across all populations with over 43,000 participants enrolled. No serious safety concerns were observed other than the detection, in the offspring of participants, of a more virulent strain of BUMOS now known as BLT1984 (ToastED). In response, Phase 5 of the vaccine development process will enhance genetic sequencing by submitting participants to the compulsory memorisation of the Periodic Table backwards with all consonants de-activated. Methodological similarities with Hemingway's Theory of Omission are purely coincidental. In the rest of the population, the only Grade 3 adverse event greater than 2% in frequency was fatigue at 2.1 % and the spontaneous composition of stories that reject the three-act structure at 4.57%.

COEG is confident in its vast existing cold-chain infrastructure to distribute BLT1984 around the world. The (thrice-vaccinated) COEG Chairman is unreachable for comment due to being inextricably immersed in Midnight's Children (25th Anniversary Edition). Consequently, it is expected that the COEG Treasurer will shortly announce the successful conclusion of negotiations for a five-book deal with Penguin Random House based on this dramatic period in human history and COEG's crucial role in it.

..., screaming

Daniel Juckes

> Brain frazzled brains, pickled brains, putrid brains,
> fickle brains / Giant brains, shrivelled brains, vile
> brains, crippled brains / Runny brains, yummy
> brains, mushy brains, get your brains / Lovely
> brains, steaming brains, eat your brains, buy my
> brains
>
> Jam Baxter, 'Brains'

There's no end to this, the eye seems to say, and to stretch as it says it, plucked and pulled forward from its dock as though tweezed or teased with fingers—like piano-played notes on rotation. Somehow false. Looped. Mechanic. But pictures don't lie, so that must be the shape it takes: tapered and conal at the lens, as if trying to escape, while all that's thick and glutinous behind where the light gets in attempts opaque defence. No wonder, given the cloud-dust and sparks which throng in the back, and manifest as galaxies dumped small-scale, or like movement gathered; as fingers, bicycles, handcuffs, bones, and as cave-walled creatures. Whatever, you can see them better in black and white, where they are even more striated; incensed; where they flex as nightmares, memories, and inhibitions gathered to attention. As the electric-opposite of shadows, and at the behest of the smoky, marbled medulla, which rises like a fist and sits close to the place where a mouth should be, screaming.

Image 41

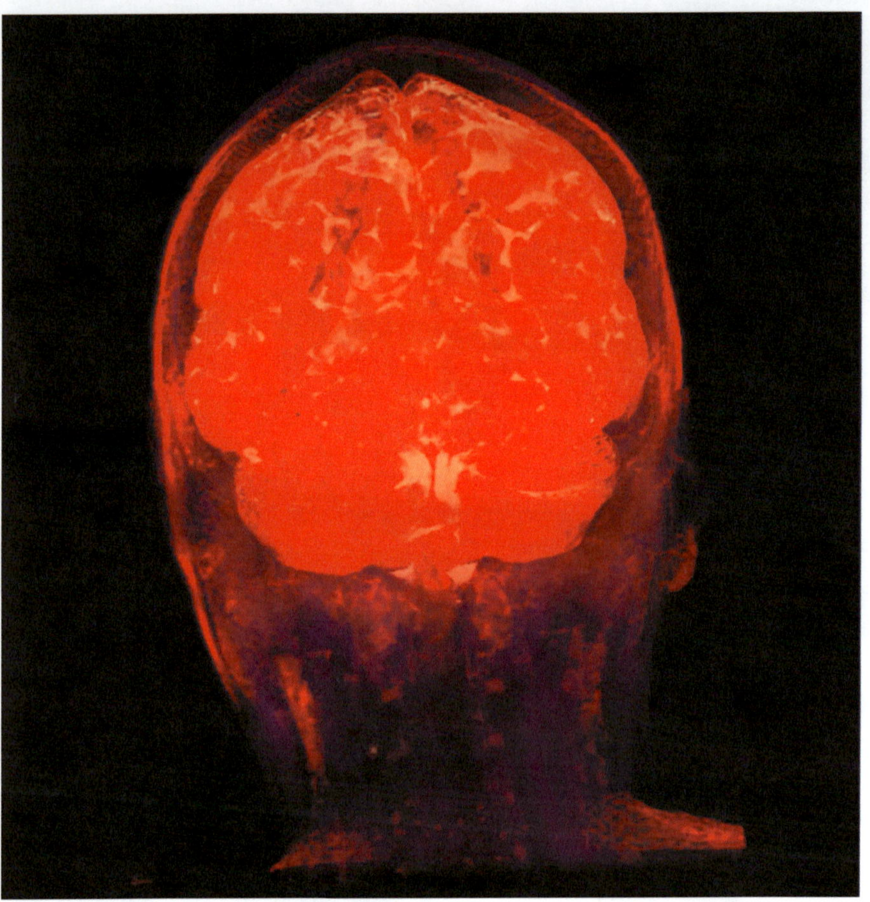

The Stranger

Maria Takolander

There is someone behind me, so quiet I cannot hear,
so quiet they must be breathing with me.
Blood rushes through my veins, turbulent with fear.

Blood, bright and urgent, is crowding my ears,
crowding a silence that is panicking me.
There is someone behind me, so quiet I cannot hear.

If I turn around, would it simply appear,
or would it take violence to show itself to me?
Blood rushes through my veins, turbulent with fear.

If it was your blood surging this loud and severe,
would you turn around or flee?
There is someone behind me, so quiet I cannot hear.

Its power is obscene, that much is clear,
from the way it gloats over goading me.
There is someone behind me, so quiet I cannot hear.
Blood rushes through my veins, turbulent with fear.

From Mars the Earth Looks Red

Ravi Shankar

Under the seams runs the pain—
I think that's the autobiography of red,
Anne Carson, but being too lazy to fact—

check, I declare the allusion with confidence
nonetheless, because so much of truth
is in the telling like (and unlike) how much

of our eating is in the smelling or how little
of our movement is in our dwelling.
In this cortex colour-by-numbers use beet-

root red … no firehouse … no rubicund … no,
the limitations of language writ large mean
no shade of syllables will flame ochre

as mineral hematite, as carmine as ground
up cochineal bugs, as definitive as a stop sign.
Mental magma bubbling up fissures of tissue

to issue heat, light, misunderstanding.
Seen from inside the skull, we are all the same
(and different) because there's no veil of skin,

no history to distract us from the perpetual
motion machine. Until lub dub stops. Red
light / flat line / floating like a helium balloon

above the top of your skull, looking down
at yourself thinking again about how under
the pain run the seams. No, wait, the seams

run the pain. Rising lava underneath wobbly
beams distracted by too excitable tulips
imported from a country a lifetime away

from health. What's red without Sylvia
Plath? Without Madame Monet in a Japanese
kimono? Without Mark Rothko, No. 301?

They are all dead now, but their chilli pepper
flames burn on and sizzle the brainpan
with layer upon layer of connotation,

from the archetypal Paleolithic bison,
to Chairman Lenin in Andy Warhol's
screen print and inside a discarded tampon—

not to be menstrual flow but its meaning,
not to be the Russian Bolshevik Revolution
but a pop icon, not to be the trace of a hunt,

but to be the hunt for whatever trace, bones
and ciphers our ancestors left on cave walls
to help us decipher our own topographies.

Image 42

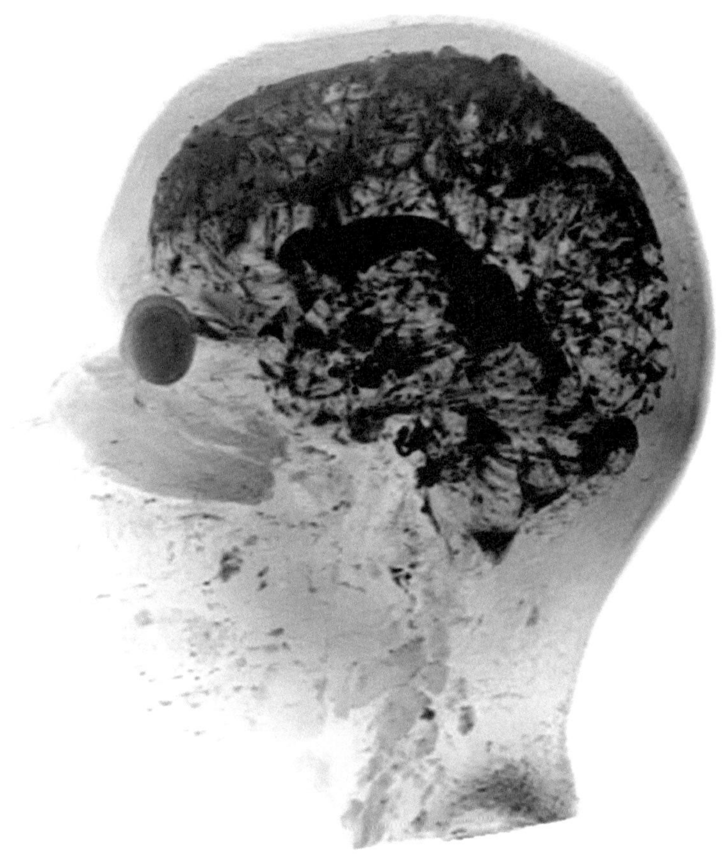

Synaesthetic Submersion

Sue Joseph

Swimming. You see swimming, instantly. And smile.
A profiled one-eyed goggle and a brain on fire, swirling in water.
Senses buzzing; dissolving; re-animating.
Swirling. With happiness. Free.
You yearn to swim.
It is winter and too cold to swim in backyard pools; too rough
and cold in the ocean; public pools, Covid-slammed-shut. You
think about not being able to swim; prevented, caged by the cold;
caged by fear of contagion in a public place. A virus that thrives
and multiplies in frosty weather, immersing the globe, swarming
and submerging continents, overflowing countries and cities and
towns and streets and roads and avenues. Flooding through front
doors into homes. Inundating families.
Smashing shut what used to be.
Smashing.
You yearn to swim; for spring warmth to heat the waters and
hunt the virus down; hound it into summer submission; starve this
feasting on the cold.
But now, the cold: icy, callous, uncaring; hard-hearted; chill;
unemotional; indifferent.
    Apt words match; not surprising coldness is virus nourishment;
nurtures its virulence.

But to swim—to glide through the water; to submerge and block
out the sounds above; a muffling, underwater. Merged senses
melt; chromatic colours flash, photon-like. It quiets and blurs—a
deafening silent clamour of tonal quicksilver molecules. It sounds
like violet. It tastes like clear cyan. It feels like red velvet. It smells
like blue. It looks like flaxen yellow.
Engulfed by water holding, enfolding you.
You suspend …
… from stress and worry; from feeling or thinking;
from copious demands and tasks; the pressure.
Relief from grief; from loss; from pain in
the calmness down here, under the water.
It roils and churns, soft mould–like, moulding,
possessing you.

Submerge.

Peace.

When breath is spent you break through the surface and gasp, an assault of shapes and sounds and smells, feelings and the taste of salt or chemical on lips; as your consciousness comes back into focus, one sense leading another:

light into images; waves into sound; air chemicals and skin and tongue receptors—you see and hear, you smell and touch and taste.

So you swim, hard. Convince yourself you are as sturdy and swift as ever; muscles speeding through water, ever-faster. Agile and lithe and limber and flowing.

You swim to stretch; to extend; to think; to remember; to feel strong.

To be strong. You are strong.

You hope. You wonder. You aspire once again.

Head Study

Dominique Hecq

Now that it's done, I pore over the work. It looks like a radiography of your head in profile. Your mouth is neither open nor closed; lips faintly stretched in a grimace; you ate your smile.

… anger makes one clench one's teeth, terror and atrocious suffering make the mouth the organ of tearing cries …

I hear Adrian Leverkühn's diabolical laughter and it does not want to fade. Recall that somewhere Julia links laughter to cries, for both are *evaporation of meaning and the only possibility of communication.* Antonin would have screamed. Both are speechless—mere spasms of the body. The inarticulacy of overflowing emotion.

I love the monocle you wear in death. You look as though you went blinded in art's headlights. How Joycean!

I gave you sanitised memories and a brain tumour named after Le Lac Majeur. If I rotate the work, you are an axolotl burdened with signs that come alive. Could have spawned snakes wreathing, Gorgon-like. But it was music I was after, Orpheus.

Chance marks thrown, scrubbed, sponged to trap the real real. Break the spell.

We turned back, together, you said, searching the scramble of wild rose, looking at the long field where we'd often walked, climbing the stile at the far end, entering the wood, and I kissed you there, holding your head as if to secure it, saying please don't regret this, and before you could reply, seeing a wide blue flower in the corner of my field of vision, your lips unfurled forgotten feeling, when a woman my mother knew, bent over me … and you exclaimed at the flower, saying why is it here in this woodland, bending over it, and in its intense colour it might have been a kiss on the soil, something to bruise the senses, as you said I've come a long way to understand this.

In this last letter to you, the carpet of your mind oozes black blood because fear makes the heart burn black.

And squirting out a sharp death-gush of blood / It strikes me with dark drizzle of murderous dew.

You slip out of sight.

Notes: In writing this piece, quotations from various sources came to mind:

The line *... anger makes one clench one's teeth, terror and atrocious suffering make the mouth the organ of tearing cries ...* is from Georges Bataille, 'La bouche', *Documents*, Paris, no. 5, 1930, p. 300.

Julia's words are from Julia Kristeva, 'Bataille, l'expérience et la pratique', *Bataille*, Paris, 1973.

And squirting out a sharp death-gush of blood / He strikes me with dark drizzle of murderous dew are Aeschylus' actual verses from *The Oresteia*, trans. R. Eagles, London, 1976.

Image 43

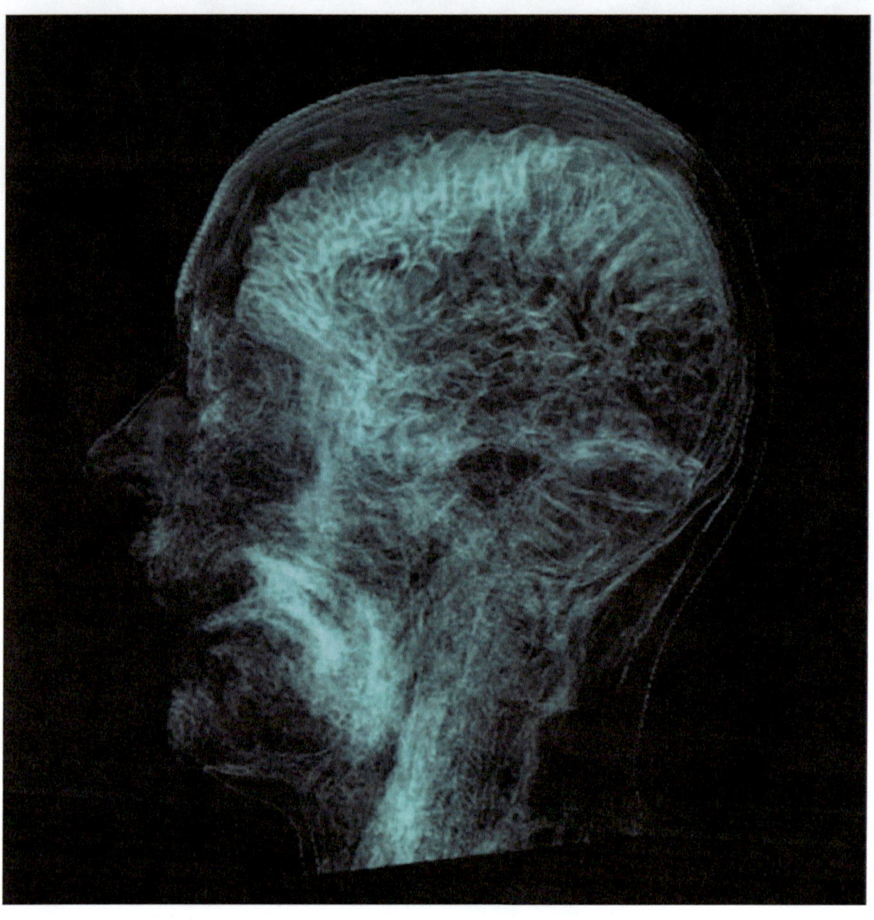

Untitled

Debra Adelaide

Whose is this cool blue brain? Mine is red. Hot, burning, throbbing red. Inside it hundreds or maybe thousands of migraines (I do not dare count) have hatched, thrived, and then departed. Like viviparous reptiles—crocodiles or rattlesnakes—these migraines are born fighting and clawing. From the moment of birth these savage creatures scratch and bite and pummel my brain with merciless ferocity until they get bored and depart.

And yet my brain bears no sign of injury. There is no bruising. There are no red marks. No sign of scarring anywhere. Scans reveal a perfectly healthy organ. Were it to be cut open, in thin layers on one of those deli meat slicers used in autopsies, every section would be revealed as pristine. No clots, no smudges, no crumbly sections, black scabs or purple explosions. When gripped by the pain inflicted by these sharp-toothed and poisonous baby monsters, I feel that my entire head will surely explode with pressure. But there is not even a trace of discolouration, nothing to disfigure the creamy pale pink of those coiled tubes that form my brain. The baby monsters come and go without leaving a single shred of flesh, fragment of shell or trail of bloodstains. I have no blood clot, no tumour. I emerge from the pain without the faintest sign of my suffering. How could my brain be immolated like this yet survive, without burns, punctures or swelling? My brain makes such a comprehensive recovery that it is almost like I have not, in fact, experienced this pain at all.

So monstrous is this red-hot suffering, and yet so lacking in evidence, that it is easy to deny the experience, to believe it will never, ever, happen again. And it seems that my brain colludes in this preposterous denial, this massive corporeal cover-up, this comprehensive fraud on a scale so mighty it should be investigated by the correct authorities. I should send in Interpol or ASIC. But so desperate is my desire never to suffer a single more migraine, that I deny it too. When the police come knocking, I slam the door. I refuse to admit the prospect of the next and the next migraine. Lying even to myself, I pretend that my brain is cool blue instead, and have done so for my entire life.

Mourning

Deb Wain

Foetally curled around my own thoughts, I pull the blankets tighter over my shoulder and wish it wasn't too warm to bury my head completely beneath the bedclothes. 'Things go from bad to worse,' Gran used to say, a cigarette hanging limply at the side of her mouth, the lit end bobbing as she spoke. I had to resist the urge to follow her around with an ashtray. From bad to worse. What kind of grandmother inoculates a child with such negativity? Grandmas are supposed to be all heated-roller soft curls, talcum powder scent, and sponge cakes for afternoon tea.

I can feel my spine tighten and protest against the curve I have balled myself into—like an Olympic diver tucked and navigating buoyant air before a minimal splash, my brilliance only clear to the lay onlooker in the slow-motion replay. I resist the urge to stretch out, avoiding the cooler parts of the bed that aren't body-warmed and sleep-heavy. I try to retreat further into the casing of linen, close out the day, keep my eyes shut, return to the peaceful oblivion of sleep where my protean subconscious will possibly make more of a mess of things and bring more nightmares.

But he has made the coffee and the smell of it creeps in, weighted with thoughtfulness. I push the covers back, stretch into the cool air of the room, and get up.

Image 44

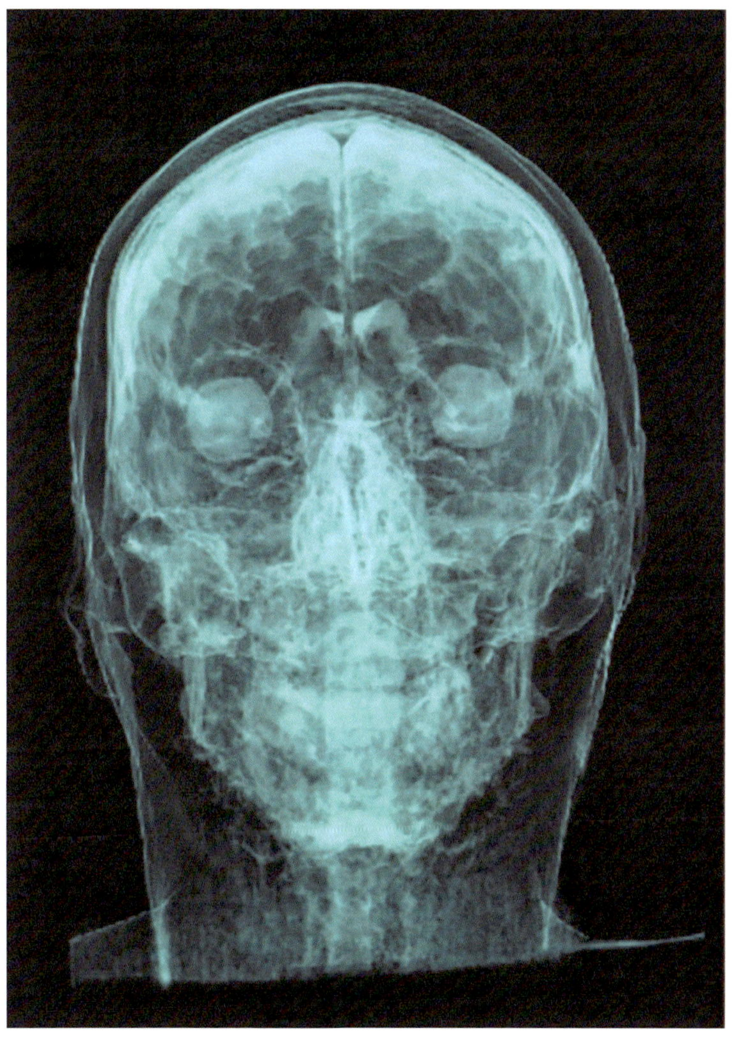

The Green Light

Sam Meekings

Something inside you glows
green
as if a bulb had been nestled in your skull

all filament and spark:
lit
the stuff of the soul

and the soul is something that swims
sleek
in green light, in the hollows of your body

something alight in your skeleton
like fireflies
your other hidden life

the one you glimpse sometimes in reflection
double-take
something inside you glows

and in our dreams this other self
slips free
and stakes through empty towns

and comes to linger in libraries
ablaze
where the pages of every book are blank.

Nature Abhors a Vacuum

Roanna Gonsalves

Nature came home from Woolies, only to find that her partner Shay had been vacuuming. Earlier that afternoon, Shay had expressed a desire for Darjeeling with a splash of milk. Nature herself preferred her tea green and her lactose untouched but off she went to get the milk. Upon her return she heard the vacuum gnashing in the bedroom. In the living room she saw that the carpet had still not bounced back from the sucking impressions left by the machine and its relentless operator.

Nature was looking forward to scrapbooking that afternoon. She had laid out her supplies in a logical sequence on the floor: pinking shears, washi tape, Japanese lace paper. Now, they were nowhere to be seen. This was not the first time that Shay had desired milk, Nature lapped off to fetch it, only to return to tumult caused by constant vacuuming. It was not even the second time or the tenth. It was the seventeen-times-seventh time and then some more. Nature suddenly realised that Shay desired her absence, just as, oh God, she realised that she desired his more. The wind sang outside, an aria, or perhaps it was a dirge. Nature felt a rise that filled her chest cavity.

She went to the fuse box and switched off the electricity. Then she walked into the bedroom just as Shay began to look confused about this sudden loss of power. Nature noticed her pinking shears on the bed. She picked them up and began to cut up the cord that tethered the vacuum cleaner to the wall. At first it was hard because she was only used to cutting delicate handmade paper with those shears. But soon, after the application of more pressure, she felt the first sweet severing of cord from cord. She began to cut and cut and cut until all around her lay jagged pieces of black, like tiny mouths that had lost their bite. She gathered them up and began to arrange them into a message on the floor. Shay, enraged, kicked the pieces around, messing up her alphabet. But he soon ran out of puff. Nature used her washi tape to secure the pieces of the useless power cord back in place. Then she walked out of the house but not before she saw Shay crumple as he read the message that filled the floor: I abhor your vacuum but I abhor you more.

Image 45

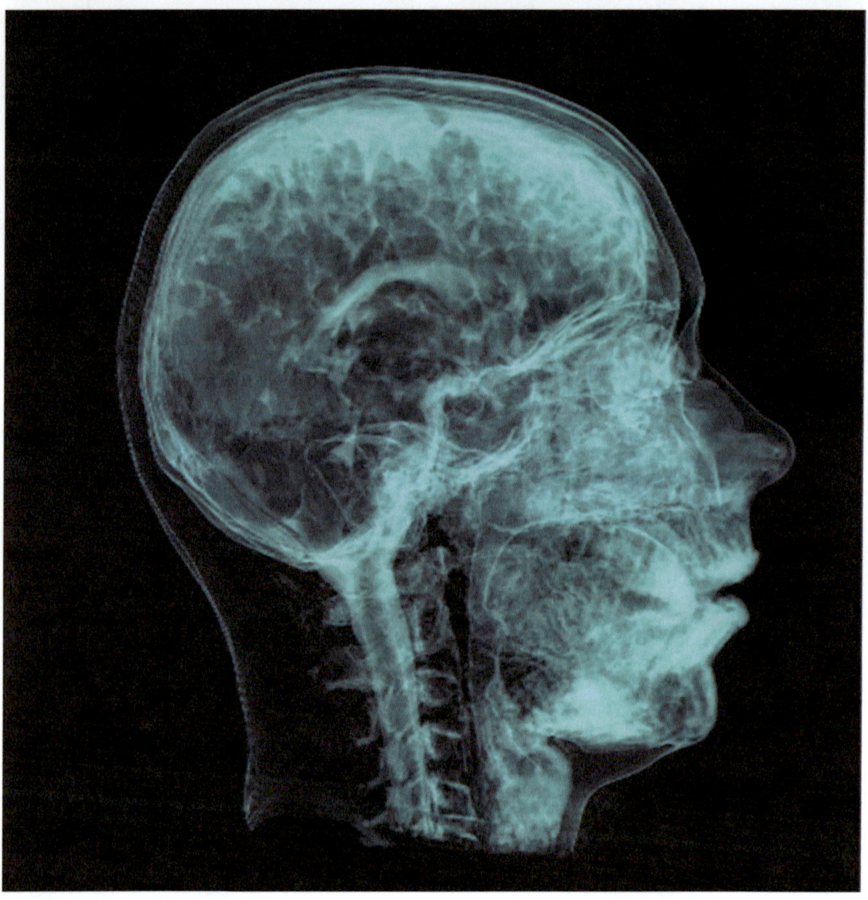

Blue Smoke Inside My Head

Michael Salcman

Today I saw a blue jay land on a backyard poplar
While I puffed away on a Parejo from Havana
Its blue smoke rising inside my head
Behind my eyes and along my spinal cord
Bristling like a tree or worn-out toilet brush
In Baltimore.

This season I'm covered in blue—
My mouth, my throat, my unhappy mood dressed
In the world's favourite colour by actual vote,
Coiling and uncoiling like a blue racer's spawn
As my brain's cyanotype fills with musical notes.

This year there was no fire just the smoke
It seemed to extinguish every hope; I know
The ancient Greeks had no word for the colour blue,
See Homer's wine-red sea and rosy-fingered dawn.

Blue Hour

Paul Hetherington

The Venetian blue hour settles with the city's lit parade. The mind's painted over as the sky's width deepens. I recollect evenings when we tucked ourselves into truncated vistas of closed rooms; climbed into the rucked sheets of window-nudging beds; reached for skin's supine entanglements, as words washed and seethed. The blue hour subsides toward extinguishment. You roll over and, again, your silhouette becomes an embrace—uncanny and protean; unreadable aspect of hauled, purpling hours. The hour vanishes and you're absent, unreasonable, unable to be reached. Your alert gestures are shadow-play. As the clotted hour brings you close, night has you breathing on my palm, as if we're practising a form of benediction, with the colour of feeling riddling chemical brains.

Image 46

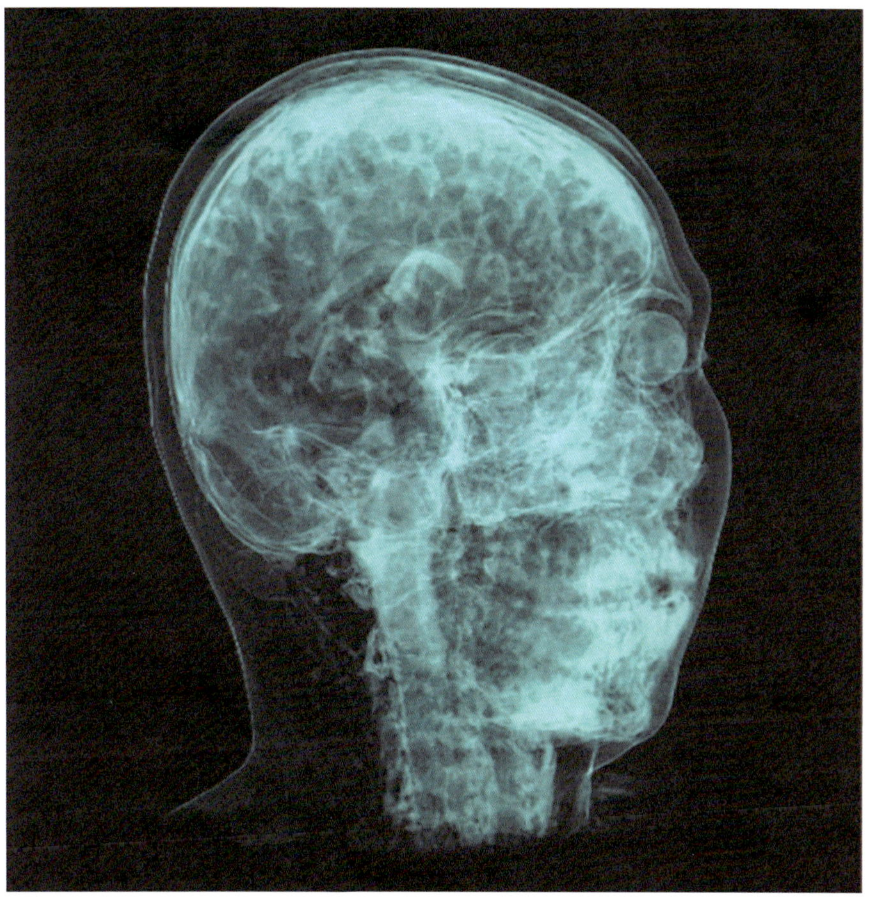

Alas, Poor Yorick

Christine Howe

Here you are, Yorick.
Dead.
Soon to be met by
the fair Ophelia;
her brother;
her boyfriend,
his mother
and his uncle.

Yorick, your eloquent skull
(full now of fine dirt)
once contained the universe.
Fissures of lightning
splintered your cerebral sky;
runnels of seawater
slipped along the shore of your jaw;
the trunk of an ash
reached up your spine
in the gathering dark of your neck.
Mare's tails and mackerel scales
wafted through your parietal lobe
heralding rain.

You contained multitudes:
fish eyes, embryos, crowding saints;
the wash of waves on a pebbled beach;
craters in a cortex moon;
phosphorescent jellyfish.
Danish mud, potato peel,
herring bones, a flapping crane,
laughter in a toothy mouth.

You, court-jester Yorick,
Shakespeare's existential joke
provoke not pity, but wonder:
within that aqua canopy
where nested tenderness?
where fluttered grief?

Logos

Spiri Tsintziras

Self within self
encased by membrane
fluid, flashing synapses
sparking ideas,
spirit,
words

Συνεργια. Πραξις.
Hands, brain,
white unlined paper
working together
defying logic

Λογος
Logic. Order.
Speech. Cause. Reason.
Consideration.
So much meaning
encased within its compact form

Meaning
welling up from a
fluid place,
takes form,
fluttering and landing on the page

Nero
Water,
wild and dirty
pushes through hard earth,
roots, worms and flesh

The words
inherited from those before me
bodies no longer here
squeeze past

Pulsing with blood
enveloped by warm flesh,
they break through
the membrane
despite myself

All I need do is capture them
before they disappear
into the afternoon light

Image 47

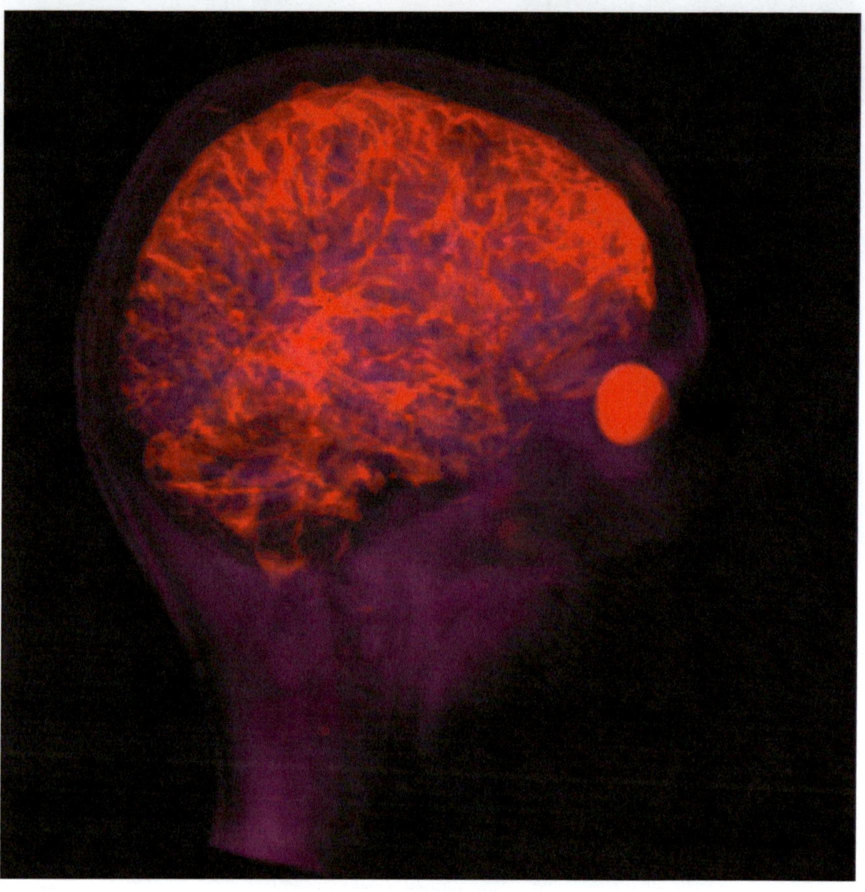

Full On Mind

Elisabeth Wentworth

Neurons like constellations
Lighting up the night sky
Body locked in stasis
Mind blowing itself to smithereens
Firefly fragments of fear and yearning
Hope, and the loss of it

So this is how we travel through time and space
No wonder there is no ease in sleep

Chronics

Amelia Walker

Years ago, I shocked myself, trying to fix the oven clock. My error was daft, too daft to relay. The thing is, I was sad. Sadness makes me tired, and tiredness saddens me more. My tired, sad self thinks crooked, does thoughtless things. That day, I was fed up with the clock's four zeroes constantly flashing, with it being always midnight. They were like square mouths, screaming where I was at:

Stuck—neither moving forward nor able to spin back and reclaim lost life racing past in lightning colours like warp speed in some old-school lo-fi sci-fi, like one of those show rides that busts gravity and simulates flight by spinning in place.

Also years ago, though far apart, a school friend phoned, distressed. She was hospitalised, being forced into ECT. Could I get her out?

The old hospital's winding corridors also reminded me of the retro space age—a vortex, being pulled along. Exposed pipes. No windows. The air was pine-o-clean and salt-damp. I found my friend shaking, shrunken under the weight of medications. Cocking her head towards the glassed nurses' station, she whisper-screamed,

I used to be a lioness, but those sharks, they've made me a goldfish.

Failing to fix the clock, I found myself on the linoleum. How long had I blacked out? The clock was still broken. I heard laughter. Mine. My body was laughing. Why? It wasn't funny. Yet it *was*—funny-odd how the sad-tiredness had shifted. It was no longer midnight, regardless of the clock.

When I told my friend's family I could help advocate for a different treatment, they had me barred from visiting. After she got out, I apologised to her for my powerlessness. She said it had been for the best. It had fixed her, she said. But soon she was hospitalised again. Then back out. Then gone. Then back. Then …

This is life, for some people. It is not my place to comment.

The sad-tiredness from before my shock returned too. Then went. And came back. And went. Not because I'd shocked myself again. Just with time, like breathing. This is life for me: my brain is my body is a clock: I breathe, I tick, I am rhythm, falling in and out. I still do daft things—frequently—but stay clear of sockets. My oven still flashes four blue zeroes. Years later, it's sometimes still always midnight.

Image 48

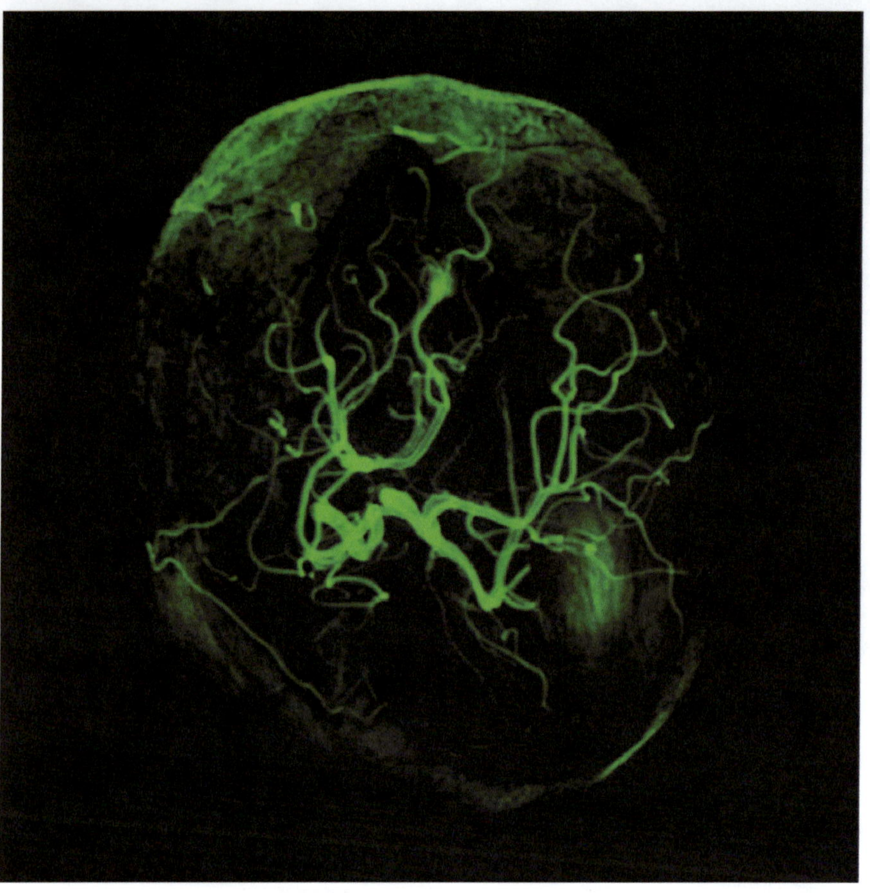

Untitled

Jessie Seymour

The brain is basically sentient jelly.
I'll leave you for a moment to think about that.

A first drop of absinthe into a pool of water spreads out like tendrils, reaching, searching, and curling. A mind's heart sends messages that thrust and take root and coax the body into acting; a pilot in a tank, surrounded by blood and ooze, watching an upside-down signal sent along from external lenses. Fluorescent arms reach, and my arms reach at the same time. Searching and seeking and hoping for something to connect with the way that the mind connects within itself and outside of itself.

I find it absolutely unsettling that every thought and feeling I've ever had was electricity in my head.

Every image I see is interpreted by the sentient jelly between my ears. I make meaning by trusting that my jelly guessed it right.

Monsters glowing in the dark. A deep sea of creatures unknown and unacknowledged, seeking nothing but to live and eat and mate, sending out soft light to attract unwitting victims into gaping, jagged jaws. A colour so unusual in the dark that no creature can bear to ignore it, even knowing that none who sought it out ever returned. The glow eases the isolation. Just for a moment. Just until the new companion is devoured, and the darkness descends for digestion, and then the light flickers back into eery long silence.

Sometimes, the sentient jelly misfires. Electric shocks meant for one part of the brain end up in another. When that happens, I forget what I came into the room for.

Or the voices in my head tell me things I know aren't true.

Or I forget I'm wearing a mask, try to take a sip of coffee and pour it onto my chest.

The colour of poison; the colour of moss. Chlorophyll that draws in sunlight which nourishes as it turns leaves darker with life. Vines push long trails through the air, seeking something strong to connect to and curl around like fingers intertwining. A long, slow growth that searches, finds, and then searches again. The stronger the vine, the stronger connections it needs. An isolated vine is a weed.

The brain is basically sentient jelly.

Please make sure that your jelly behaves itself, as its behaviour will reflect on you. If it doesn't produce the appropriate chemicals to maintain behaviour naturally, store-bought is fine.

B-Sides; Memories

Daniel Juckes

at an oxbow of a river in the shallow of a valley on a square of a map, before hills begin to sprout a-green, i bear the callow weight of laser beams. dendritic, they spar with stars and win; curve; meander; bend in ways that light should not (perhaps i am misremembering). imagine like i am somewhere in the belly of a mob, bathed virescent in delirium, and credulous: a lesser collage of this current pliable shape. the night is sylvan. sopped. blurs and outlines echoing, echoing, exiting.

there is a small man wallpapered in sweat. the bellow of another. a signal made by one guitar. the bellow of another. we climb a fence, cut wires and cables, bury secrets; are limed in sour grapes, then oaked. move from self-obsessed to spent. and still this green like lightning spreads. cut it off. cut it off. cut it on.

start anew. an open field. across the counter of a bookshop. a stage; a hat; a scrunched-up piece of paper. silvern moments. then weeks of life spent stalled by the toxic curves of algorithms: napoleon in verdigris—or even an entire self, curled circular. now, it is impossible to pay attention to details. everything, everyone, every time.

Image 49

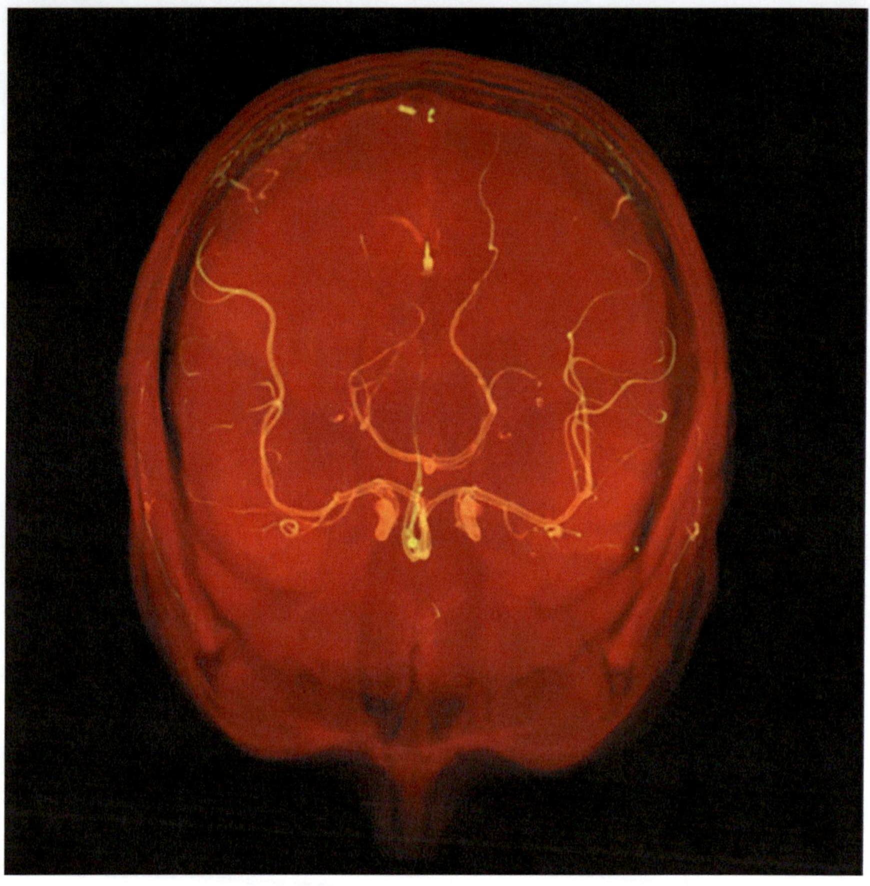

Meta-Musical Field

Frank T. Simes

Every strummed chord transmutes
the senses into an electrochemical torrent.
The spark begins, and the sense of self

and body subsumes into a haze.
A coalescing begins to unfurl,
blurring within and without.

The body's aglow, hovers
into the meta-musical field,
scintillating with charged intent.

The spark swells from the viscera,
up the spinal meridian,
and emerges from the shoulders,

bursting like a fusillade of falcons,
singing in colour and molten light,
or a battalion of angels

conjuring structures out of space,
drawn with solemn ink,
or rejoiced in insect ecstasy

with the pulse of celestial bodies
to form the arc between
the beginning of time

with time's end, and the inner
heart within the heart
becomes the outermost nodes

on the arc of the infinite
from the florid essence
of my being.

Untitled

Graeme Harper

I have begun to exchange words, unintentionally. Reading a leaflet left yesterday afternoon in my roadside mailbox, my eyes see 'flowers' but my brain registers 'fountains'. I read online of a 'rewarded cop' and ponder the horror of a 'rogue cat'. Where there should be 'weather' there appears 'wonder', and where someone has declared 'victory' I find only 'vicinity'. When I mention this in passing to my dentist, in that familiar moment when the numbness starts to take effect, he says I am likely a murdering creep, though I suspect he actually said I am a marvelous creator. The condition waxes and wanes. Sometimes all is as it appears, other times all appears as it most certainly isn't. I fear what will become of things or, more worryingly, if things will become of fear. What if my car is now a cow and my house is now a horse? What more, what if Lucy is Land and any land is Lucy? Love languishes as loosing and our future rots as fruit. I don't dare imagine what will become of kitchen appliances or the love I have for our guinea fowl (those newly minted gangrenous fools) or the position I occupy at school, where children hang on my every word and every word now threatens those children. All the adventures I bring them are now avarice, all the dogs are dragons, all the math is monstrous, all those great stories are gross stones. I ponder if clearing my mind with a brace of lizards would resolve things—though I am actually referring to a bottle of vodka. Or if some kind of consultation with a thermodynamicist would assist, by which I mean a therapist. By the time the afternoon has turned to night I am wedged into a coroner in the bed roam, my heart in my hold, my oars firmly shut, my loops folded under me, hymning hopelessly. What now? I weather. Weigh should I dough?

Image 50

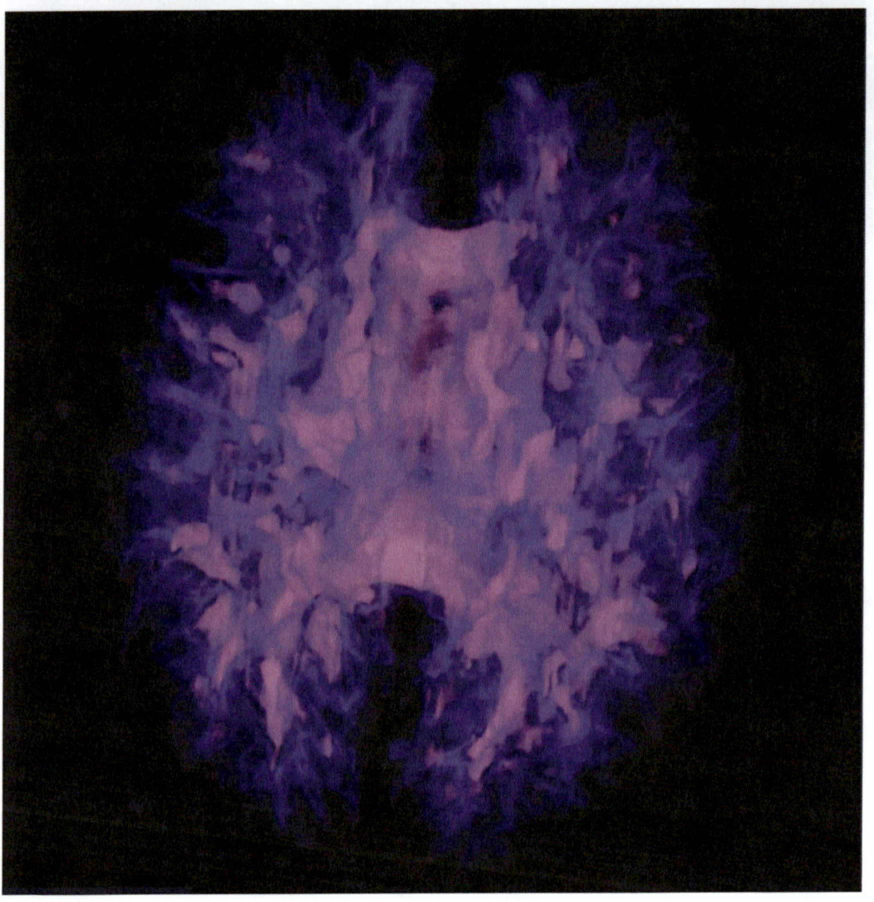

Prince and Dr John

Dan O'Carroll

I have a friend. We'll call him Dr John. I say 'have', but I haven't spoken to him in thirteen years. Before that, maybe another thirteen. One of those friends you know deep enough for long enough when you're young enough, to know that if life goes on and you don't see each other, you can always reach out if you want to and the other will take your hand. And they'll do their best.

I remember dissecting a brain with him at medical school. Differentiating the lobes. Feeling the strange, cupped heft of it in my hand. Wondering how what happened in there became what happened out here.

Although despite dropping out of medicine that year after losing my faith (Ireland was still Ireland then), some part of me thought: there must be more to it than that.

And I see this image now, and I see John. Immediately. Not Dr John, or even the consultant, Mr. John, on the other side of the surgeon's mask. I see John, before we held that brain in our hands, and I lost my faith and certainty. John, with his wide gait and National Health glasses, tender and fierce in the uncertainty of his exam-earned place at the Catholic grammar school. I see us in the front room of his parent's ex-council house in Belfast, flicking through his brother's Springsteen records. Discovering Prince and the Revolution, and the bone-deep, sap-rising funk and swagger of them. Dirty Mind. Controversy.

Purple Rain.

I see John, and I feel fourteen years old again, sitting in the back of a cheap school bus on the way to a basketball game somewhere in Wexford, holding on to my spending money so I can go and buy Parade.

And I want to sit with him somewhere quiet and not say very much. Maybe give him the odd grin and see if he returns it with a nod of the head or a caught-breath laugh of his own. Or tell him I love him and that I hope he and his wife and family are well, because we are long past the halfway point of our lives. Which I could, of course, do any day of the week on Facebook.

But reaching out means something different now than it did in the nineteen eighties.

And there is always much more to it than that.

Purple Haze

Barrie Sherwood

It only occurred to me after a few minutes
that this image was purple. It was just texture
at first—my mother's knit cardigan, an old
friend's woolly sweater set, the sweater Jack Palance
is wearing when he dies in Le Mépris. And within
that fuzzy exterior there's a skull—the gaping
bone-holes where the living thing would be
most tender.
This isn't automatic enough. I'm trying
to formulate, phrase and polish even
in a first draft. I want this thing
supposedly immediate and raw to come
neatly full circle, as if
my brain's just wired like that.
And there is it, the brain. The thing
in the image. I want to set off in
a new direction, Ramones lyrics,
something-something-tell 'em
that I got no cerebellum.
Ramones—rock and roll—the brain—purple
haze. What is there here? It's never neat enough,
the conclusion, but getting anywhere close
is only ever a matter of trust.

Image 51

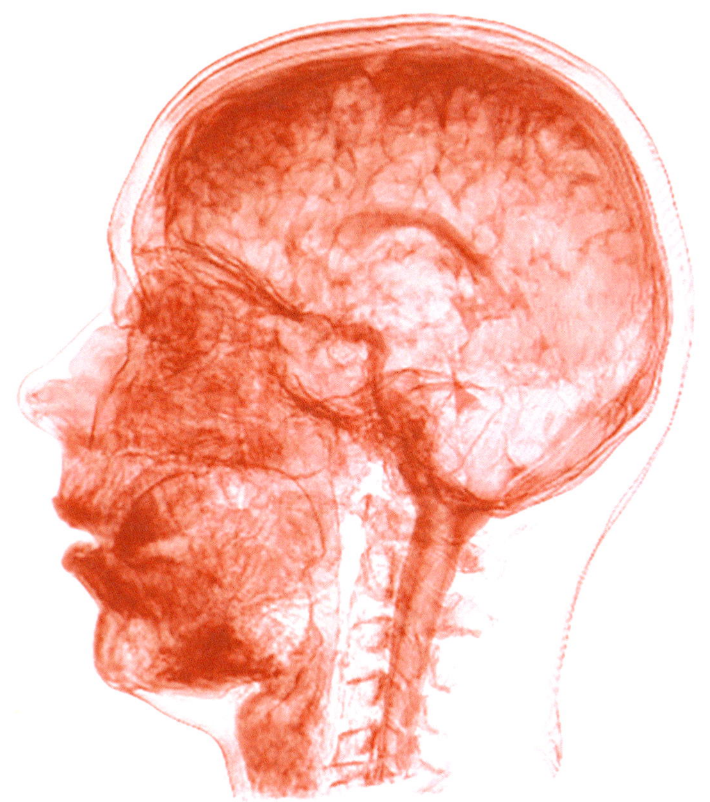

Pigments and Paints

Donna Lee Brien

I have always disliked the colour red. Especially blood and cherry hues. My entire life, I have shied away from choosing red clothes, accessories, homewares, stationery, even flowers.

I don't know why. I know red symbolises all that is energetic, dynamic and exciting—yet to me red is loud, and harsh, and jarring. Red is angry; all hot, flaming danger. The colour of wounds. Stop signs are red. So are lobsters after they have been boiled alive.

On the other hand, I am extremely fond of pink (which I know is actually light red), all pinks from Barbie bubblegum to purpled eucalyptus and dusty tea rose.

My husband W. and I have renovated five houses. Well, W. did most of the work and I decorated the results. My paint palette has always consisted of only three colours. 'Blade', a pale cool green for living and sleeping areas, 'William Byrd', a delicate eggshell blue for the kitchen, bathrooms and laundry, and 'Silver Thaw', a clear mid-grey for exteriors. We paint everything in a room with the same hue, walls, ceilings, bookcases—low-sheen acrylic on the walls and high gloss, oil-based enamel for the skirting boards, woodwork and doors. Three colours plus white for curtains and blinds, accented with pops of watermelon, cherry blossom or subdued tea rose pinks.

We started following this colour program two decades ago, and I still revel in how these shades glow from within, and how paintings seem to pulse against them. At once tender and serene, they are also hopeful, the colours of spring and new growth, of the soft furze covering gum branches and the reflection of a flawless sky at the creek's edge.

Sometimes I imagine repainting everything a bright flat white. But then, I see our cat purringly rubbing his dusty head against the doorway and the old dog stretched out asleep in the afternoon sun, feet dancing against a wall, chasing rabbits in her dreams. I remember that it doesn't matter if our boots leave mud scrapes on the skirting, or those thin little wisps of smoke waft up to the ceiling when we add more logs to the fire. Soft and gentle can be quite tough and forgiving.

Red Brain Fog

Gay Lynch

'Why is the dye red?' he says, in bed. Pokes at the exam. 'Unusual for a CT scan.' Fingers the right side. Lists encephalon, cerebellum, cervical spine bones, occipital cortex, spinal cord. Labels spill from his right hemisphere. Impatience from his left.

Child-me views chin, eyes, nose, mouth, rosy silhouette. Ruddy-headed puppet or skeleton, wobbling on its sprockety stem. Painted mask, hominoid head, Martian physog pluming red dust within; evidence of mass oxidation. Radiation.

Medico names frontal cortex, oesophagus, sinuses. Seeks simple clarity; my mess interests him less. I see teeth. Stop! Something ruptured? No, no aneurism. No bullet or cranial bleed. I hex him with my fingers. Red signals alarm.

Red amplifies, demands, dominates. In Landscape with Red Spots, No. 2, Kandinsky heard red as violin. In Tension in Red he sharpens a scalpel. Ratchets up volume in Heavy Red.

After my pastel childhood flashes by, mercurial red beckons, lights me up. Followed by full-blooded adolescence. Red dress, rags, ribbon, rouge, shoes. Capricious blood contuses beneath my skin, rushes from my cervix, tenses in my gut, constrains youthful whimsy.

Neurologists speculate via Covid autopsies whether thick blood clots, rather than protect vessels, push hard against them, leak through them, into surrounding brain tissue, violently breech boundaries. Causing oxygen to plummet.

Imagine the process as a gory but beautiful image, the slow seep, the breaching of walls, the rubicund explosion. Neurotransmitters inflame, implode, zap, surge. Scramble chemical-signalling molecules, dopamine, norepinephrine, serotonin. Red does not behave well.

Brains should fight back, better arm their microglia. Murderous
armies always over-reach, Covid hallucinations, toxic shock, death
by delirium, one case in eleven. Red roars.

> Think rusty, cinnabar reek of menstruation.
> Think voluminous vivid blood of birth.
> Think vermillion wildfires devouring country.
> Think women's rage; overlooked, unexamined.

> Think darkening stains, Leo rising over Mars.
> Think paint, hematite, red ochre, pomegranate.
> Think, cherry velvet, scarlet, Borgias, their blooded foils.
> Think chilli, crimson, rubescent.
> Think flush of poppy, opio dreams, demise.

Which lobe lights up for pain and touch? Red words are social. Foot
tickle terror, symphony, sadness, grief, orgasm. Art blushes in bed
with neuroscience. Red dye, why? Red card it. Let it bleed out.

Image 52

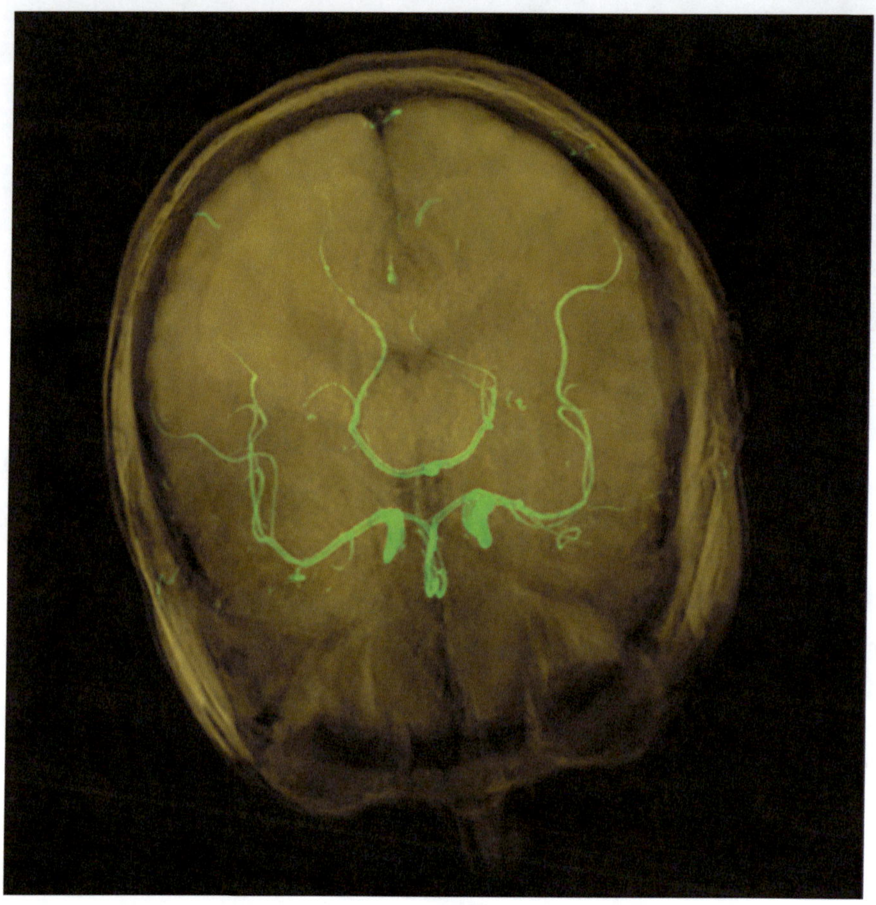

Blacking Out

Lynda Hawryluk

Swirling tendril thoughts dance like embers into a deepening
night sky
Becoming long-dead stars, twinkling twice, and disappearing
Somewhere into the dark beyond
I turn my head sideways then back again
Epley manoeuvring my head until the vertigo abates
Nystagmus flutters through my vision
Then settles again behind beyond-tired eyes
Leaving only uncertainty in its wake

Like little internal earthquakes, these shudders and shakes leave
me trembling
A body performing unsteady double-step dance moves
Without any background music or end
This shuffling footfall is heavy, like wearing wet turnout gear to
a dance party
The cacophony of noise from within the unquiet mind
Brings back the rush of thermonuclear heat from a bushfire
Black days to remember and try to forget in equal measure
And a fugue state you can't wait to return from

These brushfires in my brain can't be contained
By contoured fire breaks carved into the earth
This backcountry is conceded, and remains so
Despite the best intentions of the strike teams
Boundaries, borders, and fence lines disappear behind the backburn
While the wispy lines of a crowning potential
Sparks up then fades out in an instant
Just like fire would

The Seasons of Ambivalence

Jacqueline Ross

You are the gloom of winter and the glare of summer. If you were spring and autumn, there would be breath and space. Spring and autumn make no demands—they are seasons that give back.

But you are all want and need.

In summer you spark. Creativity thrums through you, inspiration flashing neon in your eyes. How seductive is the shape of that light, the generosity of curves and circles that promise forever but can only last one season. The words and music are all glare and reflection. Because neon shines too brightly, and although it promises to be real, cannot be sustained. Like summer, it flares but then flickers, and is gone.

You are never autumn, tumbling instead into the bitter rut of winter. Autumn could be your transition. A time when your eyes see amber, russet, gold—a kaleidoscope of colour and possibility to store away for sustenance before the instant fall of winter's dark. In autumn you could let those fat words languish. Left alone they might find a way to illuminate another season.

Now you are winter and creativity has fled. There is not even a wink of light. Your eyes turn inky black in the smothering fog, and there is nothing but surrender. When you are winter, words and music have disappeared, and you cannot imagine a time that they were ever yours.

But eventually the season turns. Now you face an impossible task, turning into a neon summer once again, without pause for spring. And this is your greatest loss. Because in spring stories abound and the world hums with music, for this is the season of beginnings. In spring, your imagination would roam, free from the demands of summer brilliance. Your eyes would see budding stories and fresh tunes that sing of the future—and how clear that vision would be.

Because in spring, want and need are gone.

There is only love.

Image 53

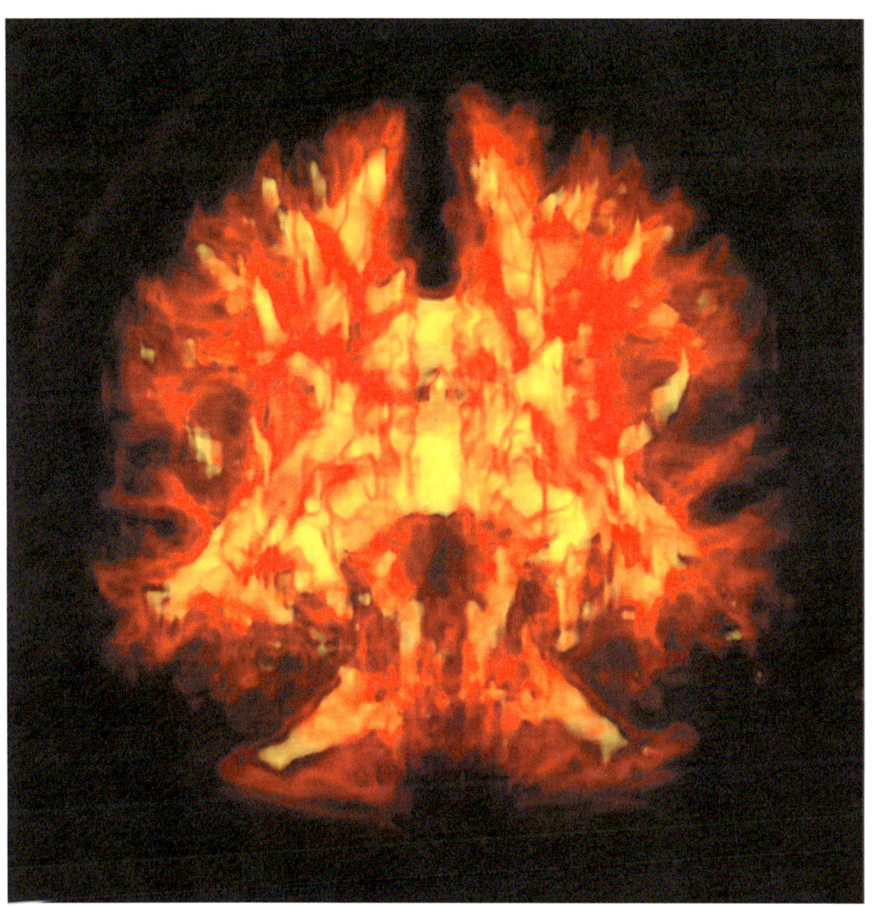

Covid Dreaming

Shady Cosgrove

Your message, the playlist: you're breaking up with me. I saw a band tonight for the first time in over a year. Shoulder-to-shoulder—strangers bumping into each other, my hand brushes a woman's waist. A colleague's up there, standing in front of the stage: something's changed since we were in the office, the slope of his shoulders, maybe. Lights cast yellow-orange as the saxophone radiates, the intoxicated fury of bodies near each other. We know what it means now, to be pack animals. We are waking up. The girls in the restroom, toilet door open. One asking the other: 'Are your friends here? Can I call them?' The smell of vomit as the drunk one's walk-carried out, black denim skirt caught on her waist, butt-cheek exposed. It makes me think of date rape, which makes me think of that client and the suicide attempt. But I'm on the dancefloor and the beat moves through me, and there's a voice that belongs to a singer who's wearing a pale slip that hugs her beautiful, sturdy thighs. She holds the microphone up on that stage like it's a triumph and I want her to keep singing as long as I'm alive, but the show ends and the lights come up—remorse—and that song by Talking Heads comes on. You know the one. You've sent it to me, you posted it on your wife's Facebook page when she found our messages.

The Forest

Sarah Giles

It's Good Friday. Lou and I are continuing a tradition launched the year before when, realising our fridge was bare and all the shops closed, we drove across town to have dinner with her parents, appearing on the doorstep with nothing to offer but wanting.

The painting hanging in the lounge room of Lou's childhood home is called 'The Forest', by an artist named Jenny Reddin—a mixed media piece spread across an enormous canvas, oils dripping in multiple directions, manipulating gravity's effects, an intricate weave of abstract shapes.

Lou and her mum are prepping the steaks we'll eat for dinner, with smoked mussels and roasted potatoes. I'm transfixed by 'The Forest'. Dark stems reaching from the centre of an orange cloud, cords of paint shoot upward. A dark core at the centre of the canvas, like a root, stares back at me, the forest growing from her, splitting through brain and bone, opening its branches completely. Dripping from her mind in strings of yellow and orange and thick stalks of shadow that burst like hands above the surface of still water, scrambling to pull her under.

Behind me, Lou pours out more wine and asks if I want a glass. When I don't answer she comes with one filled and puts it in my hand.

It's a still night. Lou sleeps beside me, sedated by the wine. The trees outside usually rustle and scrape against the window. It's eerily quiet. I rub my hand across my leg, trying to figure out the difference between my hand touching my thigh or my thigh being touched by a hand. When the trees talk, they block the sound of the clock ticking outside the bedroom door. On quiet nights, I used to listen to music or a podcast, but my therapist won't let me do that anymore. Lou prefers it this way, too. The clock is loud, every stroke laps at my insides, strange, like going down in a lift. I'm lying on my back but I'm not comfortable. I can't lie on my side since I had heard the story about a man who came in the night and stole another man's kidneys, leaving him in a bath full of ice to die, before selling his kidneys on eBay.

Image 54

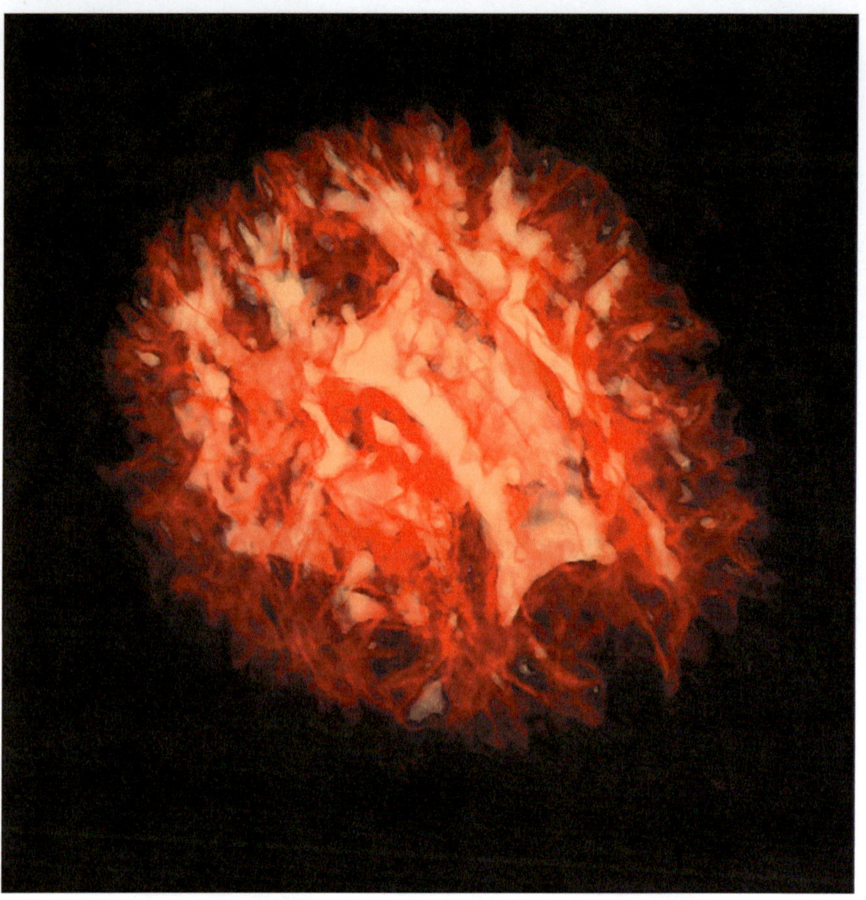

Pomegranate

Paul Hetherington

Red splashes of sunlight enter the brain—that ripe
pomegranate with its spills of seed; a scarf in Morocco
that was stained with blood. You cradled her head
until she sat up to say, 'Leave me alone.' The sun was
a lolly on a washed-out cloth; the vendor hoisted fruit
on an intricate tray. You were suddenly flushed and
had to sit down, thoughts running like animals in a
long alleyway. Someone had promised to meet you
but they wouldn't be there—you knew it suddenly,
as this injured woman returned your care, saying
'he's coddled by passion', as if love were an egg—and
grimaced in saying it. The Moroccan translator waved
you off, sunset was paint splotched on a wide board
and your plane pointed at it like the tip of a brush.

Intergenerational Trauma in Five Parts

Helen Thomas

1945

The nightmares ravaged him. Flashbacks and macabre dreamscapes melded into an unbearable spectre. The baby's cry sounded like an alarm. He woke in terror, soaked in cold sweat. Stranger-wife in the spare room again. Body tensed. Brain on fire. He stood over the cot, paralysed, unable to touch. Her cries became louder. Red contorted face, limbs flailing. He retreated and stumbled his way to the garage. Gun in his hand, bullets already loaded in readiness. Hard, cold steel. This was best for everyone. He turned it towards himself and noted once more how steady his hand was as he prepared to take a life. Oblivion.

1970

Front door slammed. He would be on the way to the pub to douse his rage. Silence billowed. She stayed where she was, cold lino under bare legs, and tried to still her body. A throbbing ache in her jaw began to reveal itself. She was suddenly aware of the boy's quiet presence, watching her. If she kept her eyes closed it would be ok. He was a good boy. He knew to stay away until later. She let herself unhook from her body and float. Oblivion.

1995

Shame twisted and writhed like an eel beneath his rib cage, joining the fear that always lurked. His daughter's fifth birthday. A spark of guilt flicked away. This was a day of celebration! At least he wasn't loud and violent like his old man. Flame. Spoon. Liquid bubbling. His heart leapt in anticipation. Thrumming heartbeat, trembling fingers. Needle in. Clothed in safety, peace and love. Sweet, warm relief. Oblivion.

2020

Locked up. Again. Doing head miles. So many of the other girls slept to trick time. But, for her, sleep was tumultuous. Her dreams were crowded, filled with casts of unknown people. She knew it was the new meds. Another attempt to make her 'compliant'. The taut hypervigilance she maintained during the day stretched through the night. Until last night. A lone man entered her dream. Nameless and faceless. Young and strong. Without words, he wrapped her in a tight, full embrace; enveloping her in safety, peace and love. It crossed the filmy barrier between subconscious and conscious. Calm. Oblivion.

Image 55

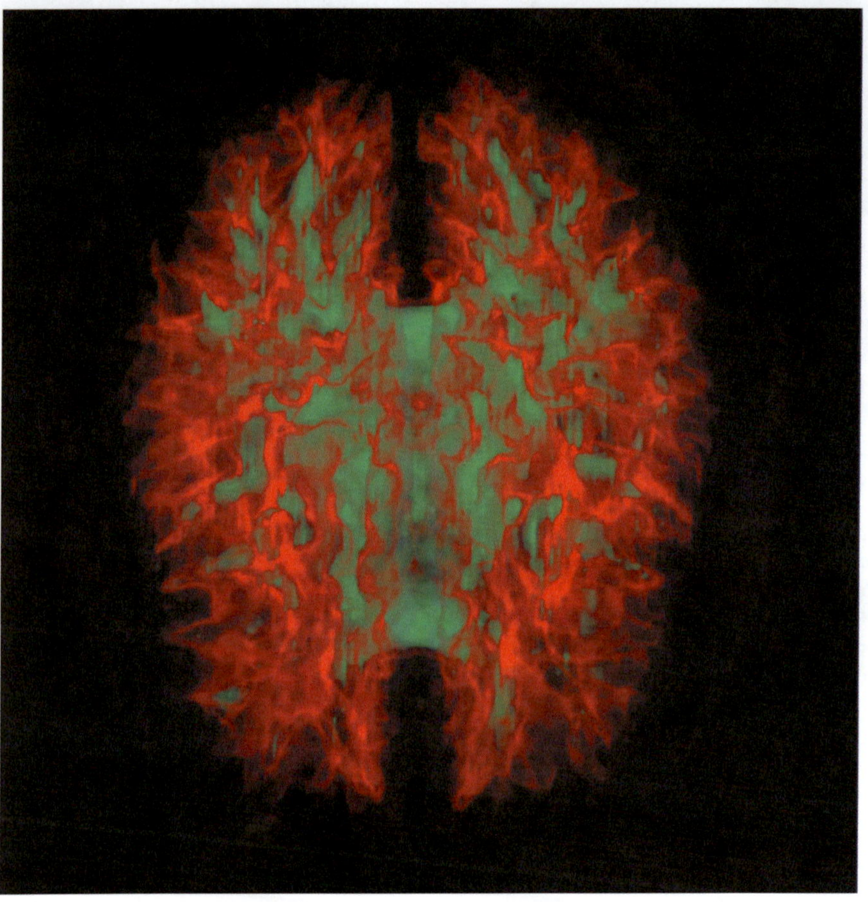

Endings

Catherine McKinnon

At fourteen, Mia and Violette would still write teen-girl love letters to each other, despite Mia sleeping at Vi's place most Saturday nights. On Sunday mornings they'd clean the pub Vi's parents managed, then rattle around in the pub's blue-tiled kitchen cooking breakfast for the live-ins: old men with nowhere to go. It didn't seem like work. They were curious about the world and everything in it. On weeknights, Mia and her brother Jack would sprint along pot-holed roads that weaved through their suburb as he trained her for athletic competitions. This was her life and she loved it.

When Mia and Vi started going to church dances, Jack and his girlfriend Beth were their reliable guardians, dropping them off and picking them up. Often Mia and Vi would nick off from the dance and hitch into town to play pool or meet boys. They were experimenting with their independence. One Friday night when they were hitching, a man in a hearse picked them up. No coffin in the back, yet he wore white gloves and a black suit, as if on his way to a funeral. He dropped them at the party, offered to pick them up the next Friday and take them wherever they needed to go. Mia said yes, thrilled by the strangeness of it all. When they stepped away from the hearse, Vi let rip. They had their first big fight. Eventually Mia talked Vi round. The hearse man picked them up for the next few Friday nights, until Vi, patient but persistent, convinced Mia that hearse man was dangerous and most likely grooming them.

But hearse man marked a division. Niggling arguments about right and wrong, good and evil, tore through the solid ground of their friendship. Mia started staying out late, partying. Vi became a dedicated student. Then Jack left home, broke up with Beth and started going out with Vi. Mia would make plans to meet up with the pair, but Vi would call at the last minute and cancel. Mia knew Vi was making a polite withdrawal. She was losing two friends, not one, as her brother was monosyllabic whenever she'd ring him.

Eventually the pair stopped seeing her altogether. Not one big rift, instead lots of small irreparable ones. Mia's attempts to mend made things worse. Finally, she understood, love is fragile but its death must be respected.

Brain Coral

Shady Cosgrove

My wet-suit skin constricts until I tip back, off the boat. That splash of water and I'm mobile. I adjust my mask—whiff of brine, rubber—and this context turns me miraculous: I breathe underwater, both heavy and weightless in the echoed silence. Reefs stretch below. Fish and crustaceans dart through red-pink spines. Sponges and sea turtles current-drift. And below: that coral ecosystem—one tiny exo-skeleton at a time, growing on top of ancestor fossils. But there are reef worlds, deeper than this, existing in near-complete darkness. Species that live in trenches, beneath acidic waters and bleaching, might just survive.

Perhaps our brains are reefs. Perhaps our survival, too, depends on dropping deeper—breathing into presence, below waves, into quiet.

Image 56

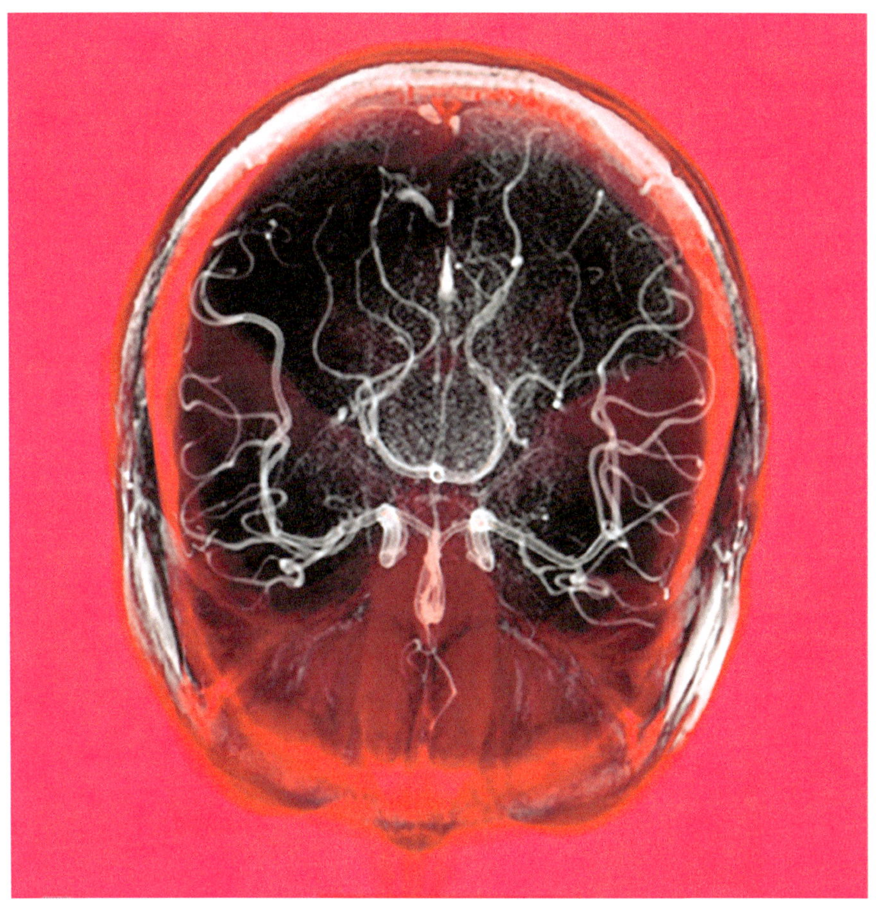

Every Gesture Like Thought

Stephanie Green

In my mind's eye against the bright static of the sea
you're leaning with the fishing rods against the jetty rail,
long beams riven by salt, wind cradling your hair.
Out to sea, the longed-for horizon under a shadowed sky,
your forearm folding, hand to mouth, as you talk.
Cigarette tucked between third and fourth fingers,
a tiny amber warning flaring and fading with the light,
the smoke on your breath a pale filigree of repeated pulses
spiralling into air against a rose canvas, like thought.
Sometimes when I watch, like this, I see your words,
though I can't hear you now, charged connections
moving through space, drawn together under your arc.
Sometimes I think you were a kind of octopus.
By day you sent out elaborate tentacles,
stirring, latching on, gathering in what you saw.
At night you were surreptitious, haunting rock pools,
a hunter, a victim, alert to a troubled world.
For you, there was never a solution to the struggle.
In that sense, you were the realist, and I was too loose,
shifting between the caves and cornices of the ocean.
Placid if left undisturbed, clasping your limbs together,
you were ready to lash out, sensing in myriad directions,
trawling through ruffled seaweed waters in search of prey.
More than once, in those island days, when we hoped for so much,
I wished you could see beyond the violet breakers,
discern dark matter between sequin grit left by stars.
But all we'll ever really have is this one moment, a feeling,
as if something important happened neither of us really noticed,
and afterwards knowing we would never come back to this place
again.

Bloodheat

Rose Lucas

pounds in cranium's
dark spaces

a sudden roar of temperature   stirring
a primordial wash of impulse

this viscous seedbed of what
drives   something

out   into the incipient
receptivity of   somewhere else

medium of turbulence   curlicue of
synapse that leads on

to synapse   building threads of distinct
and overlapping patterns

this beautiful cross-section   of what sees
or makes   what might be

considered meaningful
the brevity of this temporal moment

of fire   it flares waves of vermillion heat
sparking the world

Image 57

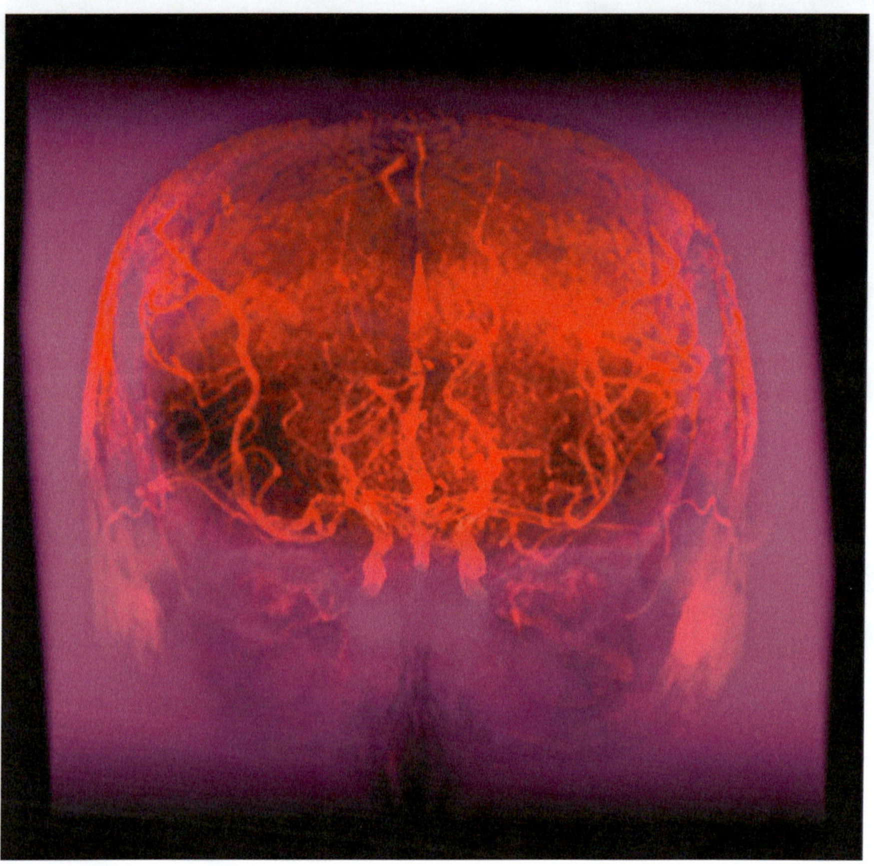

Raising a Subject

Autumn Royal

It's time to dress your body in this unrevised
final draft. My mind is full of hollows and Valarie
Solanas' voice—*I'm a writer not an actress.*
One must become perverse when adapting
to this genre. I've flattened myself to fit through
scripted doorways and babbled away my dimensions.
This series leaves no suspense.
We're dealing with pre-existing material
and I've forgotten who speaks next. I need a prompt—

Gotcha

Nicolas Brasch

Jimmy reached for his whip halfway down the straight. He was in front but could hear the hooves behind, getting closer, louder. He needed this win, more than the others did. He flourished the whip but did not strike his horse; there was still time for that. He'd ridden this horse before and knew that it shied when hit. The whip had to be the last resort.

At the hundred-metre mark, he could hear Ollie yelling behind him. Ollie always yelled when it got close and willing. He reckoned his horses reacted, that they knew he was yelling at them. Jimmy wasn't so sure but Ollie's record spoke for itself.

Hands and heels, hands and heels, Jimmy urged his horse towards the line.

'Gotcha,' he heard from Ollie, now just a neck away.

Jimmy thought he could hold on for the win. Here was the post.

'Gotcha Jimmy,' from Ollie, almost alongside.

Jimmy panicked. He needn't have. He would have been home. Sure, only by a nose, but a nose is as good as a length, is as good as a mile.

Jimmy gave his horse one sharp whack on the flank and his horse veered to the right. It gave Ollie's horse one almighty shove, and Ollie, high in the stirrups, lost balance, teetered, tottered and eventually fell to the ground.

Jimmy turned his head as his horse kept galloping. He saw Ollie hitting the turf, and three, four, five, six horses thundering over him. Six times four—that's twenty-four hooves.

They raced Ollie to hospital but they might as well not have bothered.

Jimmy didn't go to the funeral. No one blamed him—these things happened—but he blamed himself. What if? What if? What if?

He gathered the courage to go to the wake. He was at the bar, queuing for a drink.

He felt a pair of hands grabbing him from behind. A friendly gesture, nothing in malice.

'Gotcha,' a voice said. Nothing in malice.

Jimmy crumbled to the floor.

Image 58

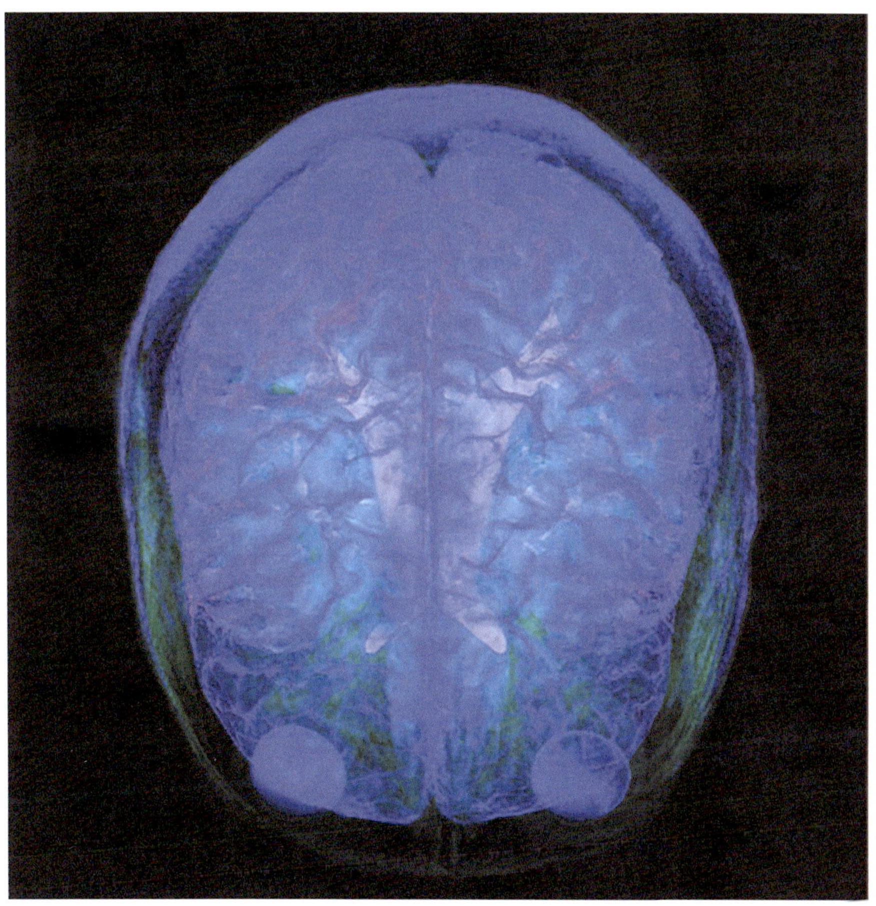

Mind's Eye

Julian Novitz

The eyes. It's difficult for me to reconcile the image of the brain on its own with consciousness. Aristotle was similar, insisting that the heart was the centre of the self, its noble chambers containing our capacity for motion, sensation, and intelligence. The brain, by contrast, is an unassuming organ: wrinkled, faintly absurd, forever underwhelming. Perhaps that's why we find such pleasure and horror in exposing it. Zombies chewing apart the heads of their victims; innumerable autopsy scenes; Mordred splitting Arthur's 'brain-pan' at the climax of Le Morte d'Arthur. There's a transgressive thrill in revealing these small, neat coils of anticlimactic grey matter.

But the eyes—present in this picture, two translucent jelly orbs, hovering above the frontal lobe—transform the brain into something uncanny. A school friend told me that the eyes were part of the brain when I was five or six, and I remember recoiling, horrified but also strangely delighted by the idea that my brain wasn't hidden and mysterious, but grossly exposed, open to the touch. With the eyes attached, the image of the brain becomes more human and more monstrous, something achingly incomplete. At around the same age, I was transfixed by an old *Dr Who* serial where the creature of the week was a brain in a globe with distended artificial eye stalks. It looked grotesque to me, but also strangely mournful; the fake eyes without a mouth or face, the brain floating in liquid behind them. One scene stands out, where a mad scientist is transferring the living brain into a new body, and their hulking, deformed lab assistant drops it. I remember the deliciously wet splattering sound, and the visceral cry of sympathetic pain from the actor playing the scientist, the sense of affront to the dignity of the organ. Sometime later, a schoolteacher took to reading Roald Dahl's *Tales of the Unexpected* to our class. One story featured a woman whose husband, after an accident, is reduced to a brain and an eyeball preserved in a vat. She proceeds to torment her helpless husband with all the things he had denied her in their married life: music, television, smoking. The last line of the story has the eyeball dilating with fury as she blows cigarette smoke across the glass, and that image has stayed with me ever since. The last flicker of emotion possible when everything else is stripped away.

The Entombment

Dominique Hecq

In the sky-blubbering sea stands entombed a dead alive elephant with sawn tusks under a dome of azure ice. The elephant looks through me with pecked at lapis lazuli eyes. Its accusatory stare reaches not only beyond the sea but also beyond the horizon that bleeds into violet stars strewn on the crust of the earth. This could be a still from a Disney cartoon. A photograph from Fantasia after the Apocalypse. A hologram portending impending doom. I want to coax out the blue. But it would take days to knead and press and squeeze a dough of powdered lapis, wax, resin and linseed oil. Besides, the water is frozen and I have no wood ash. I'm Queen Boadicea dunked in woad cobalt oxide wailing for a child I never had. I'm a stone Buddha facing Ganesh. I'm Kubla Kahn turning Midnight Blue. I'm a petrified bird of paradise shooting through the Anthropocene. The elephant charges. Waves crash. I'm the Mount Lebanon Blue butterfly smashed to smithereens. I'm dancing matter that does not matter. I'm ultramarine. Utter darkness. I'm a mind unminding itself. Entombing itself. I'm Ash in this sunless sea sinking in tumult to a lifeless ocean. I'm molecules of oxygen and hydrogen. I'm particles of dust in frozen H_2O. In this inky pleasure dome with caves of ice. I'm nameless.

Notes: The title is sourced from Coleridge's 'Kubla Khan' as remembered through free association.

Image 59

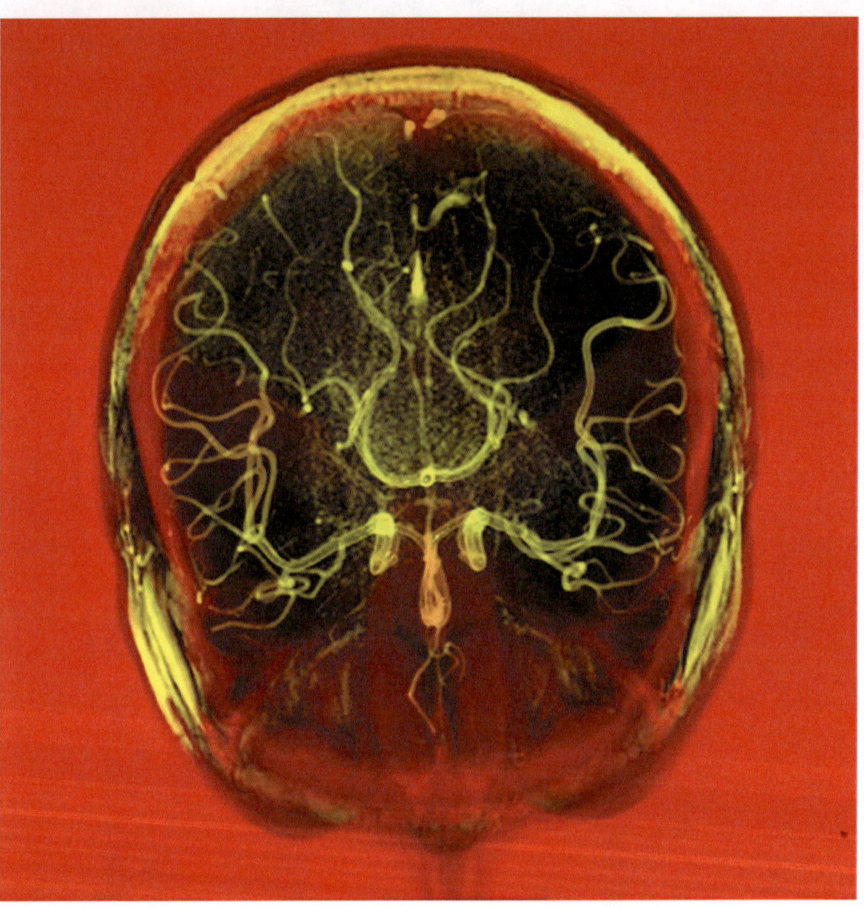

Clueless

Dominic Symes

Mick Jagger has been seen (in person) by more people than anyone on the planet, did you know? he's lived the least private life of anyone who has ever lived. they say each photograph keeps a part of you: each time your photograph is taken, your image is captured as is, forever. And sometimes that's for the best—when you can say I don't look like that, this isn't me—the version of you that isn't you can be deleted. my generation is likely the first that has been so aware of their own image, perhaps, with the exception of a Victorian portraiture painter, like a character in an Austen novel: staring at themselves in the mirror for hours on end, alone, beneath the heavy drapes in the boudoir ignoring the suitors standing outside in the parlour who've come just to see them. it smarts like an impression burnt into the silver copper of my most prurient self, truly, I feel the loss of innocence, missing the palpable excitement of high school students in the 90s when someone brought a video camera into the hall (picture here a scene from clueless) where they just all freak out, pull faces, hug each other, generally clueless about what this will look like played back in thirty years. I think this all while knowingly pouting at myself in the reflection of the glass door as the stones play on in the background, a little drunk, wearing a ruffled shirt (I guess a bit like Mr Darcy?) seeing myself like Jagger, though no one else will ever see me this way because we never leave the house. I know what this sounds like, but imagine having your photo taken with the most advanced technology, only you can't say cheese, not blink, pout, ask for another one on your good side, or decide if you want to delete it or not because it doesn't look enough like you—it's you for all to see.

Mandragora/The Hand of Glory

Tom Evershed

Genesis 30:14–17

Something wrong was growing in her sister's garden. From the window, in the gleam of the moon, Leah saw it sprouting by the lemon tree, its pale heart clutched in dark foliage.

It was something that could not be there.

Jake still slumbered, broad back bare, in his and Rachael's bed. Leah felt no guilt. The man had been hers before her sister took him. Only Leah had borne his child.

Hauling tight her dressing gown, she opened the bedroom door and trod barefoot down the passage. She skulked past the room where Roo lay sleeping, resisting the temptation to look in on him.

Fatherhood had come too soon for Jake. By keeping the baby, Leah had known what she was ending. For six months, their relationship had hung, gibbeted, at a crossroads of possibilities; then Jake had moved in with Rachael. Leah had dragged her swelling body through the days and nights like a corpse.

She could have been angry at them. Instead she kept them close. Jake could be around for Roo, and Leah could be around Jake.

As the years had passed, Leah's heart still stuttered when she was near him. Electricity danced on her skin. She had waited so long for a moment such as this, with Rachael away on business. When her hand had reached out for Jake it seemed to bear a light only she could see; then he had seen it too.

She went out to the garden, clicking shut the door behind. She could smell rain.

By the lemon tree grew the rosette of a stemless plant. Its leaves were dark and crinkled. At its centre the flowers were moonlight blue, furled tight like skulls.

Only that morning, walking in the fields, Roo had found some twisted roots. He had wanted to plant them in Jake and Rachael's garden. They had dug in the ground by the lemon tree and buried them deep.

Leah stepped closer, feet on cool grass, biting her lip. She nearly called out to Jake, but it had to be a dream.

She scooped her hands beneath foliage, around the plant's base, and pulled. At first there was nothing; then a loosening, the crackle of green filaments torn apart. She pulled harder, feet braced, knuckles pressing into the soil. Up it came in a burst of earth: purple-faced, eyes screwed shut, screaming.

Image 60

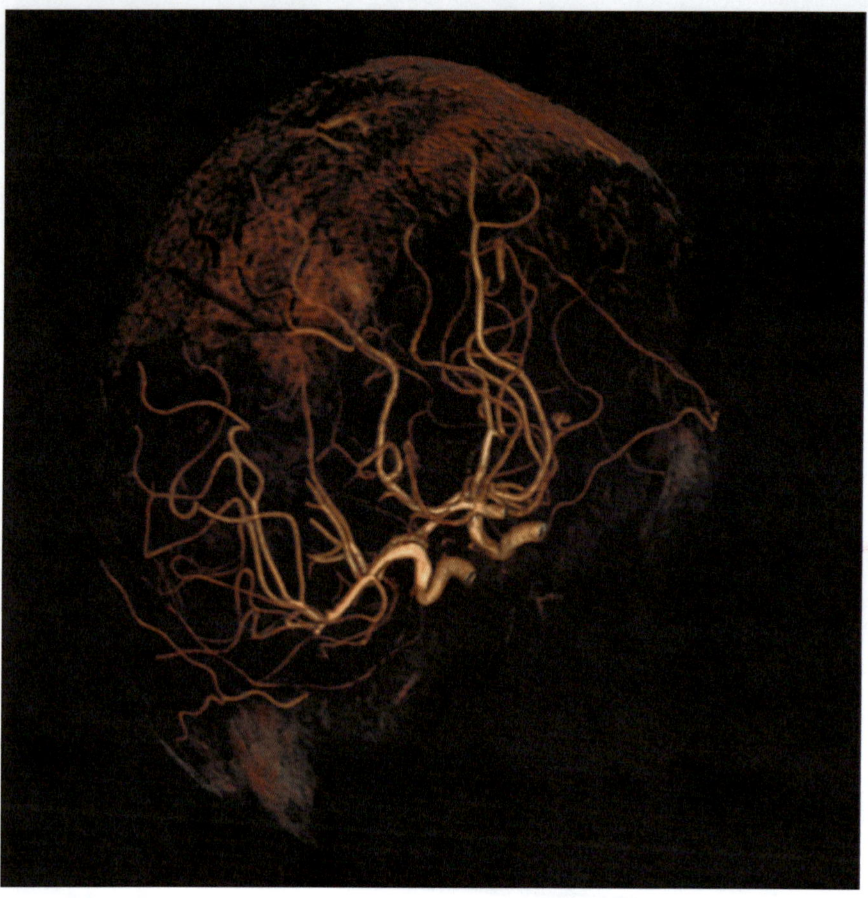

Crossed Wires

Julia Prendergast

Our wires are crossed—a copper-lit crossing of wires—but never
mind, it's just a game—a family version of *Guess Who?*
Extended family (dead, alive, present, othered), they're all here in
the game, represented by their photo and first name.
The guessing begins.

A: *Am I well off?*
B: *No.*
Flip—flip—flip. Down go some of the options (about two-thirds).

B: *Am I blood-related?*
A: *No.*
Flip—flip—flip (the board is culled by more than half again).

A: *Have I been to a strip club (to your knowledge)?*
That's such a random question, I say. *I mean how would you know?*
Shush. You're not playing, they say.
B: *Dad, have you been to a strip club?*
No, he says.
B: *He's doing the lying face,* she says, and flips him.

B: *Do I give-off 'mental health problem' vibes?*
That's so subjective, I say. *And so wrongtown …*
Go away, they say. *You're not in the game.*
But I am in the game—indeed I am—I see my photo.
B: (repeats): *Mental health problems—Yes or no?*
If you ask questions like that the game won't work, I say—*not unless
you DEFINITELY know what the other person thinks.*
You're being annoying, they say.
A: *Am I annoying?* They laugh, in unison, as if they are one—
psychically aligned.
Flip—flip—flip.

On it goes:
Have I done hard drugs?

Do you like me?
Have I had more than eight sexual partners?
Do I bat for both teams (or would I like to)?
Am I pretty—at least six out ten?
Do I have fucked-up habits?
We all do, I say.
They look at each other. Ignore me.
Am I a reformed smoker?
Do I have a criminal record?
Do I have substance-abuse problems?
Would I punch you? Wait—let me say that again—would you be
surprised if you saw me on the news for a violent crime?
Everyone has a tipping point, I say.
You're wrecking the game, they say.
It's not a yes or no question though, I say.
It's a G-A-M-E, they say.
I say: *Are you suggesting that some people are not capable of violence,*
under any possible circumstances?
Go back to your study, they say.
You'll get a false positive, I say, *if your wires are crossed.*
They roll their eyes. *PLEASE fuck off,* they say.

My Two Sons, for Winifred

Rebekah Clarkson

Today I know I am never going to breathe again
and here's you, still
tugging at my dress, twirling your fingers in mine,
twisting the gold
around and around and around.
And here's you, too
still playing in my bloodstream, fistfuls of nutrients,
oxygen for then, antibodies for later.
My bones will forever bend for you, my darling
my skin stretch parchment-thin
leaving translucent trails, perfect, as they were,
for your brother's matchbox cars.
I broke over you and I will die broken.
My two sons,
sitting quietly at the base of my skull.
Nothing left to do or say, now.
All I want and all I wanted, was.

Coda

Tom Evershed

The dogs had perished days before, swallowed by a crevasse. His sledge was lost too, yet the creature had fallen clear. He had cursed his fate and continued north.

The air howled. The ice creaked. Snow crunched under his boots. His gut-gripping hunger had passed but the polar wind had blasted for two days, paring the parchment flesh from his cheeks. The glare was relentless and his eyes bloated in their sockets like carbuncles.

All this was of little consequence. He had been tracking a distant speck and it was coming closer.

Since leaping from the ship where his creator had died, the creature had lost track of time. Mostly, the land cycled monochrome with the days, from a white that pierced to a black that was absolute, then back again. Every shade of gloaming lay between, with the sky the same nothing as the land.

Sometimes, though, the stars came out and sprayed the night in faerie dust. On occasion, in the day, the sky would be blue, or transformed in festivals of pink or orange. Then, the creature's desolate eyes grew wetter than usual.

He trudged on and the approaching dot was larger. He could better discern its shape and he sighed with the groaning of the restless ice. His hair hung in black daggers. In a mantra, he recited other names for icicles: water-ickles and ice-candles; conkabells and aquabobs.

In places the ice towered in white stacks with hearts of iridescent blue and green. Light swam in them like spirits trapped in shards of turquoise, or the universe in a bottle. They sang like the feathers of a fabulous bird, the flit of a dragonfly, the dash of a fish in a river; yet cold and hard, as though all those things were dead and turned to glass.

The creature watched it all. He spoke to the wastes and the wind. 'Better to reign in Hell than serve in Heaven.' He looked around, taking in the bleakness with a smile. 'The mind is its own place …'

One night, the black sky had been radiant with eels of green and purple. Their curves weaved through the ether, the heavens pirouetting over the ice. The creature had turned in circles, raising up his hands and laughing.

The approaching shape grew closer still. It was large, white and shaggy. At a certain distance, it began to lope.

The Wind in My Open Mouth

Julia Prendergast

The wind in my open mouth reminds me of you.

You were killed on your motorbike. But I'm not thinking about
that.

I'm thinking of our kissing like a novel that you can't-put-down.
The dry leaves beneath us like love ghosts, clearing their throats.
Your urgent fingers flexed, both of us gasping, breaking the kiss,
crying out like small children, lost and bewildered under the
ancient trees—
—leaves adrift, wafting in the half-light like papery stars.

I want to rewind time, stay in the cave by the roiling sea rather
than crawling up the embankment.

Who cares if the others come along and see us in the cave?

They could watch for all I care, now.

They say you were killed instantaneously. As if instants can't be
forever-long.

It was a scorching day. I wonder if you were wearing bike pants
or if your beautiful thighs were massacred.

The wind scoops dry leaves in whirlpools of broken light.
Everywhere, pages turning.

Author Biographies

Debra Adelaide is the author or editor of 18 books, including fiction, non-fiction, edited collections and reference works. Her 2018 novel, *The Household Guide to Dying*, was published to acclaim in Australia and around the world, and was short- and long-listed for several literary awards, including the former international Orange Prize, now the Women's Prize, for fiction. Other fiction includes *Letter to George Clooney* (2013), which was shortlisted for the Nita B. Kibble Award, *The Women's Pages* (2015), and *Zebra* (2019), winner of the short story category in the Queensland Literary Awards. Her most recent books are *The Innocent Reader: reflections on reading & writing* (2019) and *Creative Writing Practice: reflections on form & process* (ed with Sarah Attfield, 2021). Debra Adelaide taught creative writing for 20 years and is now an Adjunct Associate Professor at the University of Technology Sydney. She lives and writes on Bidjigal country in Sydney's inner west.

Patrick Allington is a writer and editor who lives on Kaurna land (Adelaide, South Australia). His novels are *Rise & Shine* (Scribe, shortlisted for the Adelaide Festival Awards for Literature) and *Figurehead* (Black Inc., longlisted for the Miles Franklin Literary Award). His shorter non-fiction, fiction and book criticism have been widely published. Patrick works at the University of South Australia and is an Adjunct Senior Lecturer in Creative and Performing Arts at Flinders University.

Kay Are is a writer, artist and researcher with interests in multimodal poetry; in experimentation in writing processes, translation and pedagogy in the expanded field; and in posthumanist, feminist and materialist approaches to all the above. Collaborations and discussion welcome: kay.l.are@outlook.com. See https://beautiful-nuisance.net/.

Cassandra Atherton is an award-winning prose poet and international expert on prose poetry. She was a Visiting Scholar in English at Harvard University, a Visiting Fellow at Sophia University, Japan, and is currently Professor of Writing and Literature at Deakin University. Cassandra co-authored *Prose Poetry: An Introduction* and co-edited the *Anthology of Australian Prose Poetry*, her most recent book of prose poetry is *Leftovers*. She is a Commissioning Editor for *Westerly* magazine and Associate Editor at MadHat Press (USA).

Nicolas Brasch is the author of more than 400 books (mainly for children and young adults) for many leading international publishers. Several of his books have won Australian and international awards. He also teaches professional and creative writing at Swinburne University; presents workshops and seminars on writing and storytelling; is the founder of Writing 101, a platform of online writing courses; and currently undertaking a PhD in creative writing.

Donna Lee Brien, BEd (Deakin), GCHEd (UNE), MA (Prelim) (USyd), MA (Writing)(Research) (UTS), PhD (QUT), is Emeritus Professor, Central Queensland University, Australia, and teaches at the Australian Catholic University. Donna has authored over 20 books and monographs and over 300 refereed published journal articles, book chapters, scholarly conference papers and creative works. Her latest books are *Paradox, Image and Identity: The Shadow Side of Nursing* (2020) and *SpeculativeBiography: Opportunities, Experiments and Provocations* (2022) both for Routledge, UK. Donna is currently studying for her second doctorate at the Australian Catholic University, writing a history of Bondi Beach.

Rebekah Clarkson is the author of *Barking Dogs* (Affirm Press), a short story cycle set in Mount Barker, South Australia where the author lives. Her stories have been recognised in major awards in Australia and overseas, including the ABR Elizabeth Jolley Short Story Prize, Fish Publishing Short Story Prize, and Glimmer Train's Fiction Open. Her short stories have appeared in publications including *Griffith Review*, *Best Australian Stories* and *Something Special, Something Rare: Outstanding Short Stories* by Australian Women (Black Inc.). She has taught fiction writing at a number of Australian Universities and at the University of Texas at Austin. Rebekah is a Board Member of the Society for the Study of the Short Story.

Katharine Coles' ninth collection of poems, *Ghost Apples*, was released in 2023 by Red Hen Press; her book of essays, *The Stranger I Become: on Walking, Looking, and Writing*, was published by Turtle Point Press in June 2021. From 2018–19, Katharine was Poet-in-Residence at the Natural History Museum of Utah and the Salt Lake Public Library for the Poets House FIELD WORK program. She has received awards from the US National Endowment for the Arts, National Endowment for the Humanities, and National Science Foundation, as well as the Guggenheim Foundation. She is a Distinguished Professor at the University of Utah.

Shady Cosgrove is the author of *What the Ground Can't Hold* (Picador) and *She Played Elvis* (Allen and Unwin). Her short works have appeared in *Best Australian Stories*, *Overland*, *Antipodes*, *Cordite*, *Southerly*, *Eunoia*, *takahe*, and various Spineless Wonders anthologies. She teaches creative writing and editing at the University of Wollongong.

Willo Drummond is a Sydney poet, early career researcher, sessional lecturer and supervisor in creative writing. Her debut collection *Moon Wrasse* was published by Puncher & Wattmann in 2023. Willo has been the recipient of a Career

Development Grant (poetry) from the Australia Council for the Arts, runner-up in the Tom Collins Poetry Prize and shortlisted for the Val Vallis Award. She holds a PhD in creative writing from Macquarie University, and her interdisciplinary research draws upon theories of distributed cognition to illuminate the materiality of literary influence, creative writing cognition and practice.

Quinn Eades is a Senior Lecturer in Creative Writing at The University of Melbourne. A writer, researcher, editor and poet, his book *Rallying* was awarded the 2018 Mary Gilmore Award for best first book of poetry. He is the author of *all the beginnings: a queer autobiography of the body* and the Co-Editor *of Going Postal: More than 'Yes' or 'No',* and *Offshoot: Contemporary Life Writing Methodologies and Practice.* Quinn's creative research is grounded in experimental and hybrid writing practices and works across/through trans, queer, and feminist theories of the body, poetry and life writing.

Tom Evershed is a British writer working with the disquiet. He lives in Melbourne with his wife, Kate, and works at Swinburne University of Technology.

Katrina Finlayson is an independent researcher and a creative writer, who lives on Kaurna country and writes mostly creative nonfiction. She holds a creative writing doctorate from Flinders University, and her PhD research used the psychoanalytical theory of the Uncanny as a launch point to explore ideas about the anxiety of being a stranger and its use in creative writing. Katrina's personal and critical essays have been published in *Meanjin, TEXT Journal,* and *Axon: Creative Explorations.* Her writing explores ideas about strangeness, place and displacement, home and travel, and the nature and significance of memory.

Sarah Giles (she/her) is a writer and PhD candidate at Swinburne University. She is researching the possibilities of the contemporary short story cycle for exploring women's experiences of isolation, trauma, mental illness, and relational agency. Sarah's creative work is informed by the life and art of Joy Hester (1920–1960). Her writing has been published by *Recent Work Press, TEXT Journal, The Victorian Writer* and *Lip Magazine* among others. Sarah currently works as the Marketing and Communications Coordinator at Writers Victoria and the Jewish Museum of Australia.

Roanna Gonsalves is the award-winning author of the acclaimed collection of short fiction *The Permanent Resident* (UWAP) published in India as *Sunita De Souza Goes To Sydney* (Speaking Tiger). Her writing has been compared to the work of Alice Munro and Jhumpa Lahiri. Her four-part radio series *On the Tip of a Billion Tongues,* commissioned and broadcast by ABC RN's *Earshot* program, is an acerbic portrayal of contemporary India through its multilingual writers. She works as a Lecturer in Creative Writing at UNSW Sydney.

Stephanie Green has recently published short fiction, poetry and travel essays in *Meniscus, Burrow, StylusLit, TEXT Journal, Axon* and *Live Encounters*. Her work also appears in recent anthologies, including *Fire and Rain* (*Pratik*/APWT 2023) and the *Anthology of Australian Prose Poetry* (MUP 2020). Stephanie released a collection of prose poems, *Breathing in Stormy Seasons*, with RWP in 2019. Her latest collection, *Seams of Repair*, will be published with Calanthe Press in November 2023. Stephanie lives and writes on the lands of the Yugembeh/Kombumerri peoples and is currently an Adjunct Senior Lecturer with Griffith University.

Graeme Harper's latest novel is *Releasing the Animals* (Parlor, 2023). Editor-in-Chief of *New Writing: The International Journal for the Practice and Theory of Creative Writing* (Routledge), he is a Professor of Creative Writing and Dean in Michigan, USA.

Dr Lynda Hawryluk is a Senior Lecturer in Creative Writing and Education at Southern Cross University where she is the Course Coordinator of the Associate Degree of Creative Writing. An experienced writing workshop facilitator, Lynda has presented workshops in Australia and Canada. She is a past President / Chair of the Australasian Association of Writing Programs and on the Board of Directors of the Byron Writers Festival. Lynda has been published in a variety of academic and creative publications on Gothic coastlines, Islomania and work on landscape poetry.

Dominique Hecq lives on unceded Wurundjeri land. Her creative works include a novel, five collections of short stories, and fifteen books of poetry. *Smacked & Other Stories of Addiction* (Spineless Wonders, 2022) is her most recent fiction publication. Her latest poetry pamphlets are *After Cage* (2nd ed., Liquid Amber Press, 2022), *Songlines* (Hedgehog, 2023) and *Endgame with No Ending* (SurVision, 2023), winner of the 2022 James Tate Prize for Poetry. Among other honours, Hecq is a recipient of the International Best Poets Prize administered by the International Poetry Translation and Research Centre in conjunction with the International Academy of Arts and Letters.

Eileen Herbert-Goodall worked as a Sessional Academic (in creative writing and literature) for many years. She presently works as an Academic Editor as well as an editor of fiction. Eileen has written fiction and non-fiction for a wide range of publications and journals. Her short stories have been recognised in international awards, including the Fish Publishing Short Story Prize, Inktears International Short Story Contest, the Raven Short Story Contest, and Glimmer Train's Short Story Award. She is the author of the 2017 novella *The Sherbrooke Brothers* (Moonshine Cove Publishing, USA). Eileen holds a Doctorate of Creative Arts.

Paul Hetherington is a distinguished Australian poet and scholar who has published seventeen full-length books of poetry and prose poetry—including the co-authored *Fugitive Letters* (2020)—and a verse novel. He has won or been nominated for over forty national and international awards and competitions. He is Emeritus Professor of Writing at the University of Canberra and joint founding editor of the journal *Axon: Creative Explorations*. He founded the International Prose Poetry Group and is co-author of *Prose Poetry: An Introduction* (Princeton University Press, 2020) and Co-Editor of *Anthology of Australian Prose Poetry* (MUP, 2020).

Christine Howe is a writer and academic who teaches at the University of Wollongong. Her first novel, *Song in the Dark*, was published by Penguin, and her poetry and other short works have appeared in journals such as the *Griffith Review, Cordite, Island,* and in various *Spineless Wonders* anthologies.

Luke Johnson was born and raised in Young, NSW. He is the author of the short story collection *Ferocious Animals* (RWP 2021), and a senior lecturer in creative writing at the University of Wollongong.

Sue Joseph has been a journalist for more than forty years. Sue began working as an academic, teaching print journalism at the University of Technology Sydney in 1997. As a Senior Lecturer, she taught in journalism and creative writing, particularly creative non-fiction writing. Now as Associate Professor, she holds an Adjunct position at Avondale University, is a Senior Research Fellow at the University of South Australia and a doctoral supervisor at the University of Sydney and Central Queensland University. She is currently Joint Editor of *Ethical Space: The International Journal of Communication Ethics* and Special Issues Editor of *TEXT Journal*.

Daniel Juckes is a writer from Perth, Western Australia. He is a Lecturer in Creative Writing at UWA, Associate Editor at *Westerly Magazine*, and holds a PhD in Creative Writing from Curtin University. His creative and critical work has been published in journals such as *Axon, Life Writing, M/C Journal, TEXT Journal*, and *Westerly*, and he was highly commended in the 2021 Fogarty Literary Award.

Nigel Krauth is Professor of Creative Writing at Griffith University. He has published novels, stories, essays, articles and reviews. His research investigates creative writing processes and the teaching of creative writing. He was the founding Co-Editor of *TEXT: Journal of writing and writing courses* for more than 25 years. In 2022 he published *The Creative Writer's Mind* (MLM).

Jeri Kroll is Emeritus Professor of English and Creative Writing at Flinders University and an Adjunct Professor Creative Arts at Central Queensland

University. *Vanishing Point* (verse novel) was shortlisted for the 2015 Queensland Literary Awards. A George Washington University stage adaptation was a winner in the 47th Kennedy Center American College Theatre Festival. Recent critical books are *Creative Writing: Drafting, Revising and Editing* (2020), '*Old and New, Tried and Untried': Creativity and Research in the 21st Century University* (2016) and *Research Methods in Creative Writing* (2013). She recently submitted her Doctor of Creative Arts thesis at the University of Wollongong.

Nathan Langston is an artist based in Seattle, Washington, USA. He works as a software designer, has run a ballet company, toured with bands, and recently founded Psychopomp Projects, an interdisciplinary events company working in dance, music, literature, architecture, and experimental forms. His major work, published in 2021, is called *TELEPHONE*, an intersemiotic game of ekphrasis, which incorporated original, connected works by almost 1,000 artists from 473 cities in 72 countries. The planning stages for the next game, many magnitudes larger, are currently underway and expected to launch in 2024.

Joshua Lobb is the author of *The Flight of Birds* (Sydney University Press) and one of the authors of the collection of collaborative essays, *100 Atmospheres: Studies in Scale and Wonder* (Open Humanities Press). His stories have appeared in *Animal Studies Journal*, *Best Australian Stories*, *Bridport Prize Anthology*, *Griffith Review*, *Plumwood Mountain*, *Southerly*, and *TEXT Journal*. He teaches creative writing at the University of Wollongong.

Rose Lucas is a poet living and working in Naarm and an academic at Victoria University. Her most recent publications are *2020 Shelter in Place*, a collaborative project with visual artist Sharon Monagle, *This Shuttered Eye* (Liquid Amber Press, 2021) and *Increments of the Everyday* (Puncher and Wattmann, 2022). She is Foundation Editor at Liquid Amber Poetry Press.

Gay Lynch writes and researches essays, novels, academic papers, book reviews, and short stories, on unceded Boonwurrung land and adjunct to Flinders University. Recent works include *Unsettled* (2019), an historical novel, 'On Work,' in *Meanjin* (2021), 'On Dance' *TEXT Journal* (2021) and 'On Smoking' *TEXT Journal* (October 2022). Essays and stories can be found in Black Inc's *Growing up in Country Australia* (2022), *Best Australian Stories*, *Island*, *Meanjin*, *Meniscus*, *Pratek*, *TEXT Journal*, *Verity La* and *Westerly*. Lynch is engaged with national and international short story organisations.

Catherine McKinnon is the author of *Storyland* (2017) and *The Nearly Happy Family* (2008). Catherine lectures in creative writing at the University of Wollongong and is Co-Convenor of UOW's Centre for Critical Creative Practice (C3P). *Storyland* was shortlisted for 2018 Miles Franklin Literary Award, Barbara Jefferis Award, and the Voss Literary Prize, and in 2020 a play adaption was commissioned by Merrigong Theatre. Catherine's plays have been produced nationally and her short stories, reviews and essays have appeared in *Transnational Literature, TEXT Journal, RealTime, Narrative, Sydney Morning Herald, Meanjin* and *Griffith Review*. She is currently completing her next novel for Fourth Estate.

Alan McMonagle lives in Galway, Ireland. In 2015, he signed a two-book deal with Picador, and in March 2017, Ithaca, his debut novel was published and longlisted for the Desmond Elliott Award for first novels and shortlisted for an Irish Book Award. He has published two collections of short stories (*Psychotic Episodes* and *Liar Liar*). He also writes for radio and his plays, *Oscar Night, People Walking On Water*, and *Shirley Temple Killer Queen* have been produced and broadcast as part of Ireland National Radio's Drama on One season. His second novel, *Laura Cassidy's Walk Of Fame*, appeared in 2020.

Sam Meekings is a British poet and novelist. He is the author of *Under Fishbone Clouds* (called 'a poetic evocation of the country and its people' by *The New York Times), The Book of Crows*, and *The Afterlives of Dr Gachet*. He has spent the last ten years teaching writing in Asia and the Middle East, and currently works as an Associate Professor of Creative Writing at Northwestern University in Qatar. His website is www.sammeekings.com.

Sudesh Mishra was born in Suva, Fiji, and is Professor in Literature at the University of the South Pacific. He has previously worked at universities in Australia (Flinders University, Deakin University) and Britain (University of Stirling). He has been the recipient of an Australian Research Council Postdoctoral Fellowship, the Harri Jones Memorial Prize for Poetry, an Asialink Residency in India, the Ratu Sir Kamisese Mara Fellowship (Otago University) and an Erskine Canterbury Fellowship (Canterbury University). He is the author of five books of poems, including *Tandava* (Meanjin Press, 1992), *Diaspora and the Difficult Art of Dying* (Otago University Press, 2002) and *The Lives of Coat Hangers* (Otago UP, 2016). He has completed a draft of his sixth volume.

Julian Novitz is a Senior Lecturer in Writing and Literature at Swinburne University of Technology, Melbourne. He is the author of two novels and a collection of short stories (PRH, New Zealand) and his fiction and criticism have appeared in a wide range of journals, magazines and anthologies.

Dan O'Carroll's bio not supplied.

Antonia Pont writes poetry, essays and theoretical work on unceded Wurundjeri country. She works at Deakin University as Associate Professor in Writing, Literature and Culture, teaching and supervising students at under- and post-graduate levels. She is widely published across theoretical, critical and creative platforms. Relevant works include: *A Philosophy of Practising with Deleuze's*

Difference and Repetition (EUP, 2021) and *Practising with Deleuze* (co-authored, EUP, 2017), *You Will Not Know in Advance What You'll Feel* (Rabbit Poets Series, 2019), along with publications in *Literary Hub*, *The Lifted Brow*, *Antithesis*, *Colloquy*, *Meanjin*, *Axon*, *Cordite*, *TEXT Journal* and others.

Julia Prendergast lives in Melbourne, Australia, on unceded Wurundjeri land. Her novel, *The Earth Does Not Get Fat* (2018) was longlisted for the Indie Book Awards (debut fiction). Her short story collection, *Bloodrust and Other Stories*, was published in 2022. Julia is a practice-led researcher—an enthusiastic supporter of transdisciplinary, collaborative research practices, with a particular interest in neuro|psychoanalytic approaches to writing and creativity. Julia is President|Chair of the Australasian Association of Writing Programs (AAWP), the peak academic body representing the discipline of Creative Writing (Australasia). She is Associate Professor and Discipline Leader (Creative Writing and Publishing) at Swinburne University, Melbourne.

Nicola Redhouse is the author of *Unlike the Heart: A Memoir of Brain and Mind* (UQP). Her writing, which appears in places including *The Monthly*, *The Australian*, *The Age*, and *Best Australian Stories*, turns frequently on the tensions between psyche and soma. She is currently writing a novel and completing a PhD by PRS (Creative Writing) at RMIT.

Deedle Rodriguez-Tomlinson was born and raised in the Philippines. Her work has appeared in *The Incompleteness Book* and *The Incompleteness Book II* by the Australasian Association of Writing Programs (AAWP) about life during and after COVID-19 lockdown. Her poems, reflecting her peripatetic life, appear in the online travel publication *Wonderlust Travel*, *Live Encounter*, the literary issue of *Silliman University Journal*, as well as *Tomas*, the University of Santo Tomas literary journal. Her first published short story, 'The Babaylan' (*Mom Egg Review*) was nominated for the PEN/Robert J. Dau Prize for Emerging Writers. She is Project Manager for New York Writers Workshop and currently lives in Brooklyn.

Jacqueline Ross is the author of several novels including *Blackwater*, published by Affirm Press in 2023. She has written non-fiction books, feature articles for newspapers, and short stories for literary journals. She has a PhD in Creative Writing and a BA in Professional Writing and Editing. Jacqueline teaches writing at Swinburne University.

Autumn Royal creates drama, poetry, and criticism on unceded Wurundjeri land. Autumn is an arts worker and the Interviews Editor at *Cordite Poetry Review*. Her poetry collections include *She Woke and Rose*, *Liquidation* and *The Drama Student*, which was shortlisted for the 2023 Queensland Premier's Judith Wright Calanthe Award.

Michael Salcman was Chairman of Neurosurgery at the University of Maryland and President of the Contemporary Museum. His poems appear in *Arts & Letters*, *Barrow Street*, *Café Review*, *Harvard Review*, *Hopkins Review*, *Hudson Review*, and *New Letters*. Books include *The Clock Made of Confetti*, *The Enemy of Good is Better*, and *Poetry in Medicine*, his popular anthology of classic and contemporary poems on doctors, patients, illness & healing. *A Prague Spring, Before & After*, won the 2015 Sinclair Poetry Prize, and *Shades & Graces: New Poems*, was the inaugural winner of The Daniel Hoffman Legacy Book Prize (Spuyten Duyvil, 2020). *Necessary Speech: New & Selected Poems* was published by Spuyten Duyvil in 2022.

Dr Jessica Seymour is an Australian researcher and lecturer at Fukuoka University, Japan. Her research interests include children's and young adult literature, Tolkien studies, popular culture, and literary adaptation. She has contributed chapters to several essay collections, which range in topic from fan studies, to online/transmedia writing, to TV series like *Doctor Who* and *Supernatural*, to ecocriticism in the works of JRR Tolkien.

Dr Ravi Shankar is a Pushcart prize-winning poet, translator and professor who has published 15 books, including **W.W.** Norton's *Language for a New Century: Contemporary Poetry from the Middle East, Asia & Beyond* and *The Many Uses of Mint*. He has appeared in print, radio and TV in *The New York Times*, NPR, BBC and the PBS Newshour. He has won awards to the Corporation of Yaddo and the MacDowell Colony, fellowships from the Rhode Island Counsel on the Arts, and recently finished his PhD from the University of Sydney. His memoir *Correctional* was published in 2022.

Barrie Sherwood is Assistant Professor in English at NTU, Singapore. He has written a collection of short fiction and three novels, including *The Macanese Pro-Wrestler's Cookbook*, published in November 2021.

Frank T. Simes is a platinum-record and Grammy-awarded musician, songwriter, composer, and producer. He was also *The Who's* musical director for the world tours of *Quadrophenia, The Who Hits 50! Tommy*, and the 2012 Olympics performance. Frank was Don Henley's guitarist and co-writer and recorded and toured with Mick Jagger and Stevie Nicks. He has composed over 1,500 pieces of music for Paramount TV and other productions, written music for commercials, and created scores and cues for TV and film. Frank's current projects include a music album entitled *Skyrocket* and authoring a book about music and science entitled *The Big Strum Theory*.

Shane Strange's writing has appeared in various print and online journals in Australia and internationally. He is the author of two chapbooks and a collection of poetry, *All Suspicions Have Been Confirmed*. He is Artistic Director of Queensland Poetry and publisher at Recent Work Press.

Dominic Symes lives and writes in Naarm (Melbourne). His poetry and criticism have appeared in *Overland*, *Cordite*, *Australian Book Review*, and *Australian Poetry Journal*. He has been the editor for reviews at *TEXT Journal* and is a sessional staff member at Swinburne University.

Maria Takolander is a Finnish-Australian poet, fiction writer, and independent scholar. She is the author of four books of poetry, the most recent of which, *Trigger Warning* (UQP 2021), won a Victorian Premier's Literary Award. Maria was also the inaugural winner of the *Australian Book Review* Elizabeth Jolley Short Story Competition and is the author of *The Double (and Other Stories)* (Text 2013), which was short-listed for a Melbourne Prize for Literature. Her widely published scholarly work covers two areas: magical realist literature, and theorising creativity. Her website is mariatakolander.com.

Helen Thomas is a practising psychologist and emerging author. Her extensive work within the criminal justice system and child protection space has led to a deep interest in complex trauma. Helen is in the process of writing a work of fiction exploring complex trauma and the impact on survivors' life trajectories and relationships. She has previously participated in the Writers Victoria 'Cells for Writers' program, writing from a cell at the Old Melbourne Gaol.

Tim Tomlinson is the author of the chapbook *Yolanda: An Oral History in Verse*, the poetry collection, *Requiem for the Tree Fort I Set on Fire*, and the short story collection, *This Is Not Happening to You*. Recent work appears in *Bangalore Literary Review*, *Live Encounters*, *Tin Can Literary Review*, and the anthology, *Best Asian Short Stories 2023*. A new collection, *Listening to Fish: Meditations from the Wet World*, will appear on Nirala books later this year. Tim is the director of New York Writers Workshop and co-author of its popular text, The Portable MFA in Creative Writing. He teaches writing in NYU's Global Liberal Studies.

Spiri Tsintziras is the author of memoirs *My Ikaria* and *Afternoons in Ithaka*. She is the co-author of the award-winning title *Parlour Games for Modern Families*, which has been published internationally. Her life writing and short non-fiction have been published in anthologies, newspapers and magazines. She teaches professional writing at Swinburne University and blogs about food, family and connection at www.tribaltomato.com.

Julienne van Loon is Associate Professor in Creative Writing at the University of Melbourne. Her most recent books are *The Thinking Woman* (2019) and the co-edited collection *A to Z of Creative Writing Methods* (2023). She is Managing Editor at *TEXT Journal* and a series editor for the Bloomsbury Academic Research in Creative Writing series.

Deb Wain holds a PhD in Creative Writing. Her research interests include women, food and culture, which she has investigated through writing short stories. Her work, which has been published in *Colloquy*, *Meniscus*, *Journal of Post-Colonial Cultures and Societies*, *Verity La*, and *Tincture* is often inspired by the Australian communities in which she has lived. She is a Sessional Academic in Creative Writing, a copyeditor, and writing coach.

Amelia Walker has published collections of poetry, the most recent being *alogopoiesis* (Life Before Man / Gazebo Books 2023). She has also published educational resource books, academic writing, and reviews. Amelia holds a PhD in creative writing and lectures at the University of South Australia, on Kaurna Yerta (Kaurna Country). Her research resides at the nexus of the critically-creative as a mode of knowledge-making that enables innovative responses to fast-changing challenges of our times.

Jen Webb is Distinguished Professor of Creative Practice at the University of Canberra. Recent books include *Researching Creative Writing* (Frontinus, 2015), *Art and Human Rights: Contemporary Asian Contexts* (Manchester UP, 2016), and the poetry collections *Moving Targets* (Recent Work Press, 2018) and *Flight Mode* (with Shé Hawke; RWP, 2020). She is Co-Editor of the literary journal *Meniscus* and the scholarly journal *Axon: Creative Explorations*, the Mandarin/ English collection 窗口:当代澳大利亚诗歌—英汉对照选集 | *Open Windows: Contemporary Australian Poetry*; and, with Kavita Nandan, *Writing the Pacific*.

Elisabeth Wentworth is a Melbourne poet and playwright. Her poems have been published in the collection *When Anzac Day Comes Around* and under Les Murray's editorship in *Quadrant*. Her play, *The Transformation of Wilfred Cross,* starred the late Bud Tingwell in its debut performance. She has also been an actor and scriptwriter in various ensemble theatre productions.

www.ingramcontent.com/pod-product-compliance
Lightning Source LLC
Chambersburg PA
CBRC090958100726
47911CB00011B/186